ROADKILL

ROADKILL

DENNIS E. TAYLOR

Roadkill

This book is published on behalf of the author by the Ethan Ellenberg
Literary Agency.

This book was initially an Audible Original production.
      Performed by Ray Porter
      Editorial Producer: Steve Feldberg
      Sound recording copyright 2022 by Audible Originals, LLC

You can reach the author at:
Twitter: @Dennis_E_Taylor
Facebook: @DennisETaylor2
Instagram: dennis_e_taylor
Blog: http://www.dennisetaylor.org

TABLE OF CONTENTS

CHAPTER ONE: FENDER BENDER

Day 1. Friday afternoon

Another bad day, at the end of a bad week, in the middle of a bad…well, life just all-around sucked. No point belaboring it.

I glared at the dented bodywork, my hands clenched, then looked up and waved one fist in the air. "Really? *Really?* You can't find another way to amuse yourself?" No reply, of course. If God existed at all, he was a malicious little troll with a sadistic sense of humour.

After a moment, I sighed and dropped my gaze to examine the damage. The family delivery truck—*Kernigan Food Mart* painted prominently on the side—seemed to still be in working order. But it was a good bet my dad would notice the changes to the geometry.

Dad probably wouldn't even get angry. He would just get that sorrowful look that said *You've disappointed me again, Jack.* Although compared to being kicked out of MIT, a dented fender would probably barely register. You could only get so deep into the fertilizer. Once you were in over your head, it really didn't matter anymore, did it?

As soon as the thought entered my head, I felt my breath quicken. Nope. I did not have time for a panic attack. Not just now, thanks. Two deliveries to go, then I had the entire weekend to freak out. I automatically started the deep-breathing exercises that my aunt had taught me. *One, out, two, out…* At five, I felt myself begin to relax.

Now I had to deal with the small matter of the accident. It was a clear, sunny day, with the occasional fluffy cloud scudding across the sky. Typical early July weather for Taft County, Ohio. The last rain was just long ago enough that the dust was beginning to accumulate once again on the side of the road, ready to billow up with every passing vehicle.

The point, though, was that visibility was good. Granted, I'd taken the curve along Poller Road too fast as usual, but I still should have been able to see, uh, whatever it was I'd hit. I peered at the damage. There was blood on the bumper and some fur embedded in the shattered grillwork. A small bit of good news, relatively speaking—it had been an animal rather than a person. But a large animal. More deer-sized than jackrabbit, anyway.

I moved in for a closer look. The blood had a weird color—more orange than red. And the fur was long enough for a bear, but the wrong color for any bear I'd ever seen. I looked around quickly. An angry, injured bear would not be a good thing. Should I hole up in the cab?

I quickly ducked down and glanced under the delivery truck. This verified that there wasn't a body jammed underneath, *and* allowed me to confirm that there wasn't something on the other side of the vehicle, waiting to gore me.

I reached into the truck and turned off the ignition. No point in gassing up the whole outdoors while I searched.

The blood—if it was blood—formed a slight trail heading off into the grass on the side of the road. And I could see a flattened patch. Maybe the animal had landed there and bounced?

The patch of grass looked pretty thoroughly stomped, and hadn't yet begun to spring back. It must have been a hell of an impact. Or a very large animal. But where was it? I moved to check farther into the brush—and tripped over something.

I staggered, put one hand down on the grass to steady myself, then turned. There was nothing there to trip over. No rock, no stick, no random discarded auto part.

I walked cautiously back through the patch, making each movement exaggeratedly slow and being careful not to commit my weight until my foot was down. On the second step, my toe hit...something.

I stared down in bemusement at my foot, which was pushing up against apparently empty air. I pushed a little harder with my toe and the invisible something yielded a little. Like a body, rather than a rock. I slowly withdrew my foot and then stepped back, my mind whirling. There was that old *X-Files* episode where some guy wished to be invisible and... I rolled my eyes, even though I was alone. Genies as an explanation? Nope, that way lay madness.

With a jerk, I reached for my phone. I really needed to get a picture of—

Of what, dumbass? Empty air? Uh huh. Poor Jack, his expulsion must have snapped his mind.

With a shake of my head and a snarl, I bent over to feel around the invisible object—then pulled back quickly. It had *fur.* And things with fur often had teeth and claws. Maybe I would start with a more cautious examination. I swept up some of the dust from the side of the road until I had a good pile. Then I grabbed a double handful and sprinkled it carefully over the body. Or whatever it was.

The dust settled onto something. There was a definite impression of fur, a head, arms...For some reason, the dust seemed to be getting absorbed into the body. Or maybe it was disappearing. Maybe whatever was making the body invisible was affecting the dust.

That wasn't the way it normally worked on TV, but then, I wasn't sure how much actual experience the script writers had with this kind of thing. Perhaps I'd have to write them a letter or something.

Two more double handfuls of dust, and I'd managed to work out a general outline of the body. Literally. The dust that hadn't settled *on* the body now formed something like the chalk outlines the cops supposedly did at crime scenes.

It was big.

I couldn't be sure, because it wasn't lying straight or flat, but I guessed somewhere around seven feet tall, maybe a little more. I stand six foot five, and I'm used to be being the tallest person in the room, but this thing would be able to see the top of my head.

The proportions were wrong for a biped, though—too much torso, very short legs. And not a beanpole, either, unlike yours truly. I'd bet it had a hundred pounds on me.

I stood and spent a few moments practicing the breathing exercises again. I noted but avoided focusing on the warm air, the rhythmic buzzing of insects in the background, that single drop of sweat running down the middle of my back. When I could no longer hear my heart, I pulled my phone out of my hip pocket.

I made several false starts composing a text, typing then backspacing furiously, then typing again. Finally, I muttered, "Screw it." This couldn't be boiled down to a few typed sentences. In a louder voice, I said, "Siri, call Patrick."

"Calling Patrick," the phone replied. I waited, a sinking, gnawing feeling growing in the pit of my stomach.

"Hi. You've reached Patrick Jordan. I'm not answering the phone, most likely because I don't want to talk to you. But feel free to leave a message anyway."

I couldn't suppress a snicker as the recorded message played. The sentiment infuriated almost everyone who heard it, which Patrick was quick to explain was exactly the point. To be honest, Patrick could be a bit of a dick, but he and I had been friends for as long as either of us could remember, and with Natalie, we were the Three Musketeers against the world. One for all and all for Patrick. At least according to Patrick.

"Patrick, it's Jack. Something's happened. Something very weird. Even by your standards. Give me a call as soon as you get this."

I hung up and re-pocketed the phone, then reached down to check around the corpse—wait, *was* it a corpse? What if it was just unconscious? Injured? Did it bite? Did it have stabby, stingy parts?

I grabbed another double handful of dust and repeated the sprinkling process, but more methodically, paying attention to each section of the body as it briefly appeared. Once I was sure I had the chest located, I placed a hand on it. No movement. No breathing. No heartbeat. But did that actually settle anything? I rocked back on my heels and stared at the, uh...well, stared at where the body should be.

It wasn't human. It wasn't an animal. It wasn't—

I shuddered as I finally, consciously acknowledged the thought.

It wasn't from Earth at all. Unless it was Bigfoot, which really wasn't any better.

Or Chewbacca. Once you got past invisible and extraterrestrial, why not?

So I'd just killed an extraterrestrial. Maybe even the first one ever to visit Earth. Great. But why was it out here in the middle of nowhere? And why didn't it have the sense to avoid getting hit crossing the road?

I glanced back the way I'd come. Chewie had picked a particularly bad place to cross Poller Road. It was a tight, blind corner, and because the curve was well-cambered, *everyone* took it too fast. Chewie would have had to be a kangaroo to get out of the way in time.

All very interesting, but I *still* had a dead extraterrestrial on my hands. So what to do? Call the cops? Call Dad? That was the same thing, really. The first thing my father, ol' By-the-Book Kernigan, would do would be to call the cops. And the E.T. would be whisked away to Roswell or Area 51 or that warehouse where they'd stored the Ark of the Covenant, and that would be that. Then, according to every movie ever made, the government would go back on any promises and deny everything, and I'd never find out what it was.

No way. Not quite yet, anyway. Not until I had some pictures, at least.

But first, I had to finish my deliveries. Keep it cool. No deviation from routine. Nothing to see here. Move along.

I glared at the grass for a few moments more, not really seeing it, as I worked things through. Then I started the truck and maneuvered it around so that the lift gate was close to the, uh … Sasquatch? Um, no. Wasn't that Canadian? Or maybe Pacific Northwest, anyway.

But I still wasn't completely convinced it was dead, quickie medical exam notwithstanding. So bitey and stabby parts were still a concern. I grabbed a large spanner from behind the driver's seat and, stretching out as far as possible to stay out of range, prodded the body—first tentatively, then with increasing force. Nothing. I felt around until I had an arm, then lifted and dropped it. The limb flopped like dead weight.

Okay. Either dead or thoroughly incapacitated.

I lowered the truck's lift gate to horizontal, leaped up, and raised the rolling door on the storage area, then rolled out the pallet jack and threw an empty pallet and a tarp onto the pneumatic arms.

Lowering the whole assemblage to ground level, I proceeded to wrap the body in the tarp. It was, as I'd expected, heavy—easily two hundred and fifty pounds—and limp, which made the whole process slow and frustrating. But finally, I had made a Bigfoot burrito of sorts.

Another few minutes of swearing, and the burrito was stored at the front end of the cargo area, out of sight—unless you were looking for it.

Two deliveries. Parker's and Kirby's. Then I was done until Monday. There would still be the confrontation with my father about the accident, but I could honestly say that I hadn't seen anything and didn't know what I had hit.

Lawyering. Love it or hate it, everyone did it.

CHAPTER TWO:
BIGFOOT BURRITO

M y phone rang just as I was settling the delivery onto Mrs. Kirby's garage floor with the pallet jack. I gave her an apologetic shrug as I pulled out my phone and checked the caller ID. *Patrick Jordan*, the phone reported. I hit the *answer* button and spoke into the phone before he could get a word out. "Hi, Patrick. Let me call you back in five minutes." Without waiting, I hung up.

I forced a proper smile as I handed the bill to Mrs. Kirby for her signature. She signed with her usual flourish, her movements surprisingly energetic for someone old enough to remember when the first automobile came to Dunnville.

"You and Patrick planning some more trouble?" she said.

"Hopefully," I replied with a laugh. Mrs. Kirby was a long-time family friend, a de facto aunt. Fortunately, I'd thought to back the truck in so she couldn't see the damage. She'd be certain to mention it, and I didn't need my father trooping out to the barn before I'd unloaded the special cargo.

Once I was back in the truck, I pulled out my phone and pressed redial. Patrick picked up on the first ring.

"Nice. Real nice. You set me up with a really mysterious message, then leave me hanging. Explain to me why I shouldn't just hang up on you, in one word or less?"

"Aliens."

There was a moment of silence. "That'll do it. More words, please."

I glanced in the side mirror to make sure Mrs. Kirby wasn't within listening distance. "Or maybe Bigfoot. I dunno. Listen, do you have any flour at your place?"

"Okay, buddy, you've obviously popped a blood vessel or something," Patrick said. "Why would I need flour? Why would *you* need flour? Who uses flour, and for what?"

"For the invisible alien. Or Bigfoot. Or Chewbacca."

More silence, followed by a sigh. "Okay. You've out-crazied me. Where and when?"

"The barn. I've just done my last delivery, so fifteen minutes?"

"Will do. See ya."

Well, that had gone better than I'd hoped. Of course, Patrick probably thought he was being set up for a practical joke, but he was good-natured enough to go along with it just to find out what the payoff would be.

In this case, the joke was that there was no joke.

I drove slowly past the family home to the barn in the back acre. The Kernigan property had been a large, prosperous working farm at one time, and both the multistory farmhouse with its wraparound porch and the gigantic barn out back reflected that. The wagon doors, when fully open, allowed for two-way traffic of farm equipment. The interior was almost large enough to hold our entire house.

Mostly wasted space these days, of course. The barn now contained some old appliances and mechanical parts, a dozen bales of hay so ancient that any self-respecting cow would turn up her nose in disgust, and of course my Fortress of Solitude near the entry door.

I slid the wagon doors open just enough to get the truck through, then carefully backed it in. That was an unusual move, since the big doors were cantankerous and needed a lot of coaxing to open and close. It was a smaller risk, though, than being spotted hauling something from the truck to the barn. If Dad caught on, the alien corpse would be in government custody before you could say, "E.T. phone home."

But as long as I didn't do anything to attract Dad's attention, I was probably safe. The barn had been my hangout when I was younger, and had become my retreat since I returned from college. *Returned.* Yeah. Such a nice, neutral word. My parents rarely intruded, texting me instead when I was holed up here.

I had long ago built a workshop-slash-hangout area near the entry door, populating it with a couple of comfortable chairs; a heavy workbench more than twenty feet long, with cupboards and drawers along the bottom; and some small conveniences, like a microwave and TV. There had been many happy times there over the years, hanging out with Patrick and Natalie until all hours on weekend evenings. For a brief moment, thinking back to those happier and much more innocent times, I wished I could roll back the past couple of years, even if it meant being back in high school.

I closed my eyes and rubbed my temples. I needed to focus, and throwing a pity party wasn't going to get it done.

I stood straight, took a deep breath, and clamped down on my steadily spiraling anxiety.

It took a few more seconds to get myself back on an even keel. I pulled the pallet jack around and retrieved the pallet holding the Bigfoot burrito, then placed it in the open area near the hangout. I carefully rolled the burrito off the pallet, making sure I didn't accidentally unwrap it in the process. Part of the body had to have been sticking out of the ends, apparent only because the tarp seemed to be wrapped around nothing. So, still invisible. Was that a natural ability, or some piece of technology? Or was Bigfoot actually made out of energy? That seemed unlikely, and it wouldn't explain the dust disappearing as it made contact.

Come to think of it, the flour might not work out any better, unless we could sprinkle it faster than whatever process was at play could make it disappear.

I was staring down at the burrito, lost in thought, when a voice from behind made me jump. "Hey, bud. What'cha got there?"

I turned to find Patrick grinning at me. Red-headed, just under six feet, with a slightly crooked nose from a sucker-punch he'd received as a teenager, Patrick had a clean-cut look that often fooled people into underestimating him.

I pointed. "I promised you an alien."

"And an invisible one. I will accept no less."

I stepped back and gestured with a sweep of my hand. "So unwrap it."

Patrick looked from the pallet to me then back again. Doubtless this wasn't going quite the way he'd expected. With a sardonic smile, he sidled up to the burrito and found the loose end. Taking a corner of the tarp in both hands, he gave a quick tug upward. *"Ungh."*

"Yeah, sorry, it's pretty heavy," I said. "Here, I'll give you a hand."

We both got a grip on the tarp, and with a *"One, two, three, heave!"* unrolled it.

To reveal: nothing.

"Cute," Patrick said. "Funny. How'd you do that, anyway? It really looked like there was something—"

Patrick's comment cut off as he apparently realized that the weight of the bundle was a contradiction, with nothing but tarp visible. He moved crabwise toward the end of the tarp, feeling with a foot as he went. And came up against something.

Patrick gave me a frankly freaked-out look, then prodded more with his foot, hopping around the invisible object as he progressed. Finally, he looked up, the freaked-out expression even more pronounced. "Wow, uh... this isn't a practical joke, is it?"

"If it is, we're both victims. Any thoughts?"

"Me? I just got here. Oh, and I brought flour." He pointed behind me to a plastic shopping bag. "I think I can guess what you have in mind. And I'm guessing we don't want any awkward questions?"

"Not sure there are any other kind in this situation."

"By the way, nice dents on the truck. Did you do that?"

"That's Chewbacca's fault," I replied. "And also how he ended up wrapped in a tarp."

Patrick's eyebrows went up. "Come again? Chewbacca?"

"It's got fur. I think. And it's tall, and heavy. And the torso's too long. I keep going back and forth between Chewbacca and Bigfoot. I guess I'm waiting to see if it's wearing a bandolier."

Patrick laughed and picked up the bag containing the flour, then placed it on the ground beside the corpse. I

12

couldn't help noticing a slightly shrill note to the laugh. My friend wasn't as blasé about the situation as he let on.

"Whatever's making this thing invisible also worked on the dust I tried sprinkling onto it. So, I'm not sure how well this is going to work. But we have to start somewhere."

Patrick pulled out his phone and waved it. "Let's get a video of the whole process. Maybe we can pause it and get a better look."

That was an excellent idea. I fumbled around the drawers under my workbench until I found my tripod and phone mount. A few minutes' setup and we had Patrick's phone ready to record.

"Let's do this." Patrick set the phone to recording, then we each grabbed a handful of flour. Being careful not to block the phone's view, we quickly sprinkled flour over the area.

"Son. Of. A. Bitch," Patrick said. There had been a momentary impression of a long body before the whole thing faded out, flour and all.

I wiped off my hands, patted myself down to get rid of drifting flour, then grabbed Patrick's phone and stopped the recording.

Patrick, meanwhile, was frowning at the pallet, hands on hips. "Why do the flour and the dust go invisible, but not the tarp? Or the pallet?"

I shrugged. "How the hell would I know? We don't even know what's causing the invisibility yet. Maybe it's a mass thing. Or size."

I handed Patrick's phone to him, and he flicked at the screen until he had the video playing back. He pressed pause just as the form was at maximum visibility. As we got a look at the body, Patrick started to laugh. "It's a squirrel. A giant *squirrel!* Just your plain everyday roadkill." His voice trailed off as he began gasping for air between the guffaws. I could feel my face getting red, but I was determined not to give Patrick the satisfaction of a reaction.

Finally, Patrick's snorting and gasping died down. Ignoring his behavior, I pointed to a spot on the paused video. "Utility belt."

Patrick chuckled. "Look at the bright side—no bandolier."

"A giant squirrel kind of ruins the metaphor anyway," I said.

"Ya think? C'mon, let's see if we can get that utility belt off by feel."

"I'm going to record this too," I said. I took Patrick's phone and put it back on the tripod.

We stepped to either side of the pallet and knelt.

"Uh," Patrick said, "It *is* dead, right?"

"No, it's just resting."

Patrick hesitated, then smiled. "Sure. Okay, let's do this."

We quickly located the belt, it being apparently the only article of clothing on the body. I had a momentary image of accidentally groping the alien's genitals and had to suppress a shudder.

"Can you find a buckle?" Patrick asked.

"No. It's…hold on." I closed my eyes. "It's easier with my eyes closed. Now I'm not fighting what I think I see." I groped around the belt until I felt what might be a latch. A push, a twist, and the item came free.

As the belt fell open, the corpse abruptly became visible. Under a layer of dust and flour, a being slightly over seven feet tall lay haphazardly across the pallet. The tail was definitely too meager for any self-respecting squirrel, but the face and the short, strong rear legs were definitely reminiscent of the breed. And of course, it was completely covered in fur, which varied from gray to a light yellow.

Patrick pointed at the head. "That doesn't look healthy."

I looked where Patrick had indicated and had to agree. The head was partially caved in, but whether from the impact with the truck or from the subsequent landing was uncertain. Not that it mattered. Dead is dead, and nothing terrestrial would have survived that kind of head injury. Unless the brains were somewhere else, Chewbacca was almost certainly deceased.

I scanned the rest of the corpse. "This either." I pointed to part of the hip area, which seemed to be pulp. Caked blood covered both injuries.

"Nothing on Earth would have survived this," Patrick said, echoing my reasoning. He experimentally squeezed an arm. "No muscle tone. It feels room-temperature-ish."

"And it hasn't moved in hours or made a sound."

Patrick held a hand in front of the alien's face. "No breath. Granted, we can't make too many assumptions about an alien, but this one sure seems dead."

I slowly sat back onto the floor. "And the belt says *intelligent*. Which means I just killed an interstellar visitor. Cripes."

"Not one of your better days, I'll give you that. But it was an accident, right? He, er, *it* was invisible. They can't hold that against you."

I responded with a sickly grin. "I guess it'll depend if they're more like Vulcans or Klingons."

"Speaking of which, where are they?" Patrick asked. "No one has tried to radio him—it. No one has shown up to either offer us a reward or vaporize us. Shouldn't there be some kind or reaction? A search party or something?"

"Hmm. We can't extrapolate too much, but yeah, you'd think there'd be some kind of procedure in place for a crew member getting injured or killed. Or captured."

"Maybe he was alone," Patrick suggested.

"Like a lone explorer? It seems unlikely, but…"

"But like you say, we can't extrapolate too much."

I gave Patrick a smile in reply. "Yeah, that. Meanwhile, we have what we have. Help me get the belt out…" We both lifted and managed to get the alien's torso off the belt for long enough to pull it out. I picked it up and took it to the workbench.

The belt and its various attachments were obviously some serious tech and yet works of art at the same time. The overall color was a metallic robin's-egg blue, with very fine purple accents done as a kind of filigree over the surface. The devices lacked sharp edges in favor of asymmetrically rounded angles. It was almost Victorian. Or maybe steampunk. And some of the items appeared to be clipped on.

In a few minutes, we'd figured out what could be detached and what couldn't. There were four small devices that were meant to be operated independently, and two panels that were permanently attached to the belt. Some inscribed squares on the panels and devices were likely buttons.

One device had a slider that seemed to set it to three different levels, colored red, purple, and blue. There was also a button that had a symbol on it. "Look at this one," I said. "Diverging lines. Shower on, shower off?"

"And I don't really get the significance of the colors," Patrick added. "It looks like a gun, sort of, except for the odd location of the shower button."

"Well, maybe it fits the alien's hand," I said. "We should check that."

"Uh huh." Patrick held up a second item. "What might be a small display screen, up and down arrow buttons, and V and I buttons. I doubt those are from our alphabet, so V and I shapes must mean something to Chewbacca. It has a sort of a grid that could be a speaker or mike. Communicator?"

"Mmm. This one only has a screen. No controls."

"Touch screen maybe?"

I nodded slowly. "Could be. It's bigger than the second one."

"This one also has just a touch screen," Patrick said. "But the whole gadget is bigger."

"And the last one. A smaller display screen, and the V and I buttons again. I wonder if those are on and off?"

"Sure, but which is which? And the big question: do we want to push any of these?"

I peered at the devices. "Well, it's unlikely that any of them is a nuclear bomb. I don't think we're going to kill ourselves. But what if one of them is a panic button or communications device? Do we want to call up this thing's buddies to come find us standing over its corpse?"

"Huh," Patrick grunted. "Good point. I vote no."

A voice interrupted us. "What in the hell is that?"

Both Patrick and I jumped in unison, then spun around. Natalie.

I'd known her almost as long as I'd known Patrick, which meant basically all my life. Natalie had been described in school as what you'd get if you added caffeine to a squirrel. The comment wasn't entirely unfair, either. At five foot nothing and lightly but athletically built, Natalie would never be considered physically intimidating. But she could out-run, out-climb, and out-curse most people, and she never backed down from anything or anyone. She'd more than earned the nickname "Mighty Mouse."

And as one half-wit in junior high found out, she had a left jab that was almost too fast to see.

We'd had several on-and-off romances during our high school years, yet we always seemed to settle back into a comfortable friendship. I don't think I'd ever *not* had a crush on her, but we got along far better when we weren't involved. Eventually I'd decided that having Nat as a life-long friend was better than having her as a girlfriend for a while.

Since the thing with MIT, I'd been unable to face her and had found myself avoiding contact. There had been a few awkward conversations that had gone nowhere, but Natalie seemed unfazed by any of it. I, on the other hand, was embarrassed about my behavior toward her, which just made me avoid her more.

Patrick, meanwhile, gave her a wide smile. He didn't have the specter of an expulsion from his lifelong dream college hanging over his head and had kept up an easy friendship with her.

I looked away and mumbled, "Oh, uh, hi, Nat." *Good job, Jack,* I thought. *Mature as ever.*

"Don't *Hi, Nat* me," she said. Then she pointed. "What. Is. That?"

"Chewbacca."

"Yeah, no." She examined the corpse. "For one thing, Chewbacca had no tail. This looks more like a squirrel. Where'd you get this?"

Patrick barked a single laugh. "Did you see the front of the truck?"

Natalie stared at me, her eyes widening. "You ran over a giant squirrel?"

"That seems the most likely hypothesis."

My dry delivery broke the tension, and all three of us giggled. Again, I thought I detected an undertone of hysteria in Patrick's laugh.

"So is this why you haven't been answering my texts?"

I sighed and looked down for a moment. "No. Look, I'm sorry, I'm just having trouble facing people right now. The MIT thing—"

Nat cut me off. "Chrissake, Jack. You think I believe the accusations? I know you better than that. They'll figure it out eventually, and you'll be cleared. You just watch."

Natalie had always been like that. When she was on your side, she was all in.

"Three Musketeers," I said.

"Damn right," she replied. "One for all ... "

"And all for me." Patrick finished the cheer with his standard line, and Nat and I laughed dutifully.

"So you're stalking me, then?" I asked.

"You have a problem with that? Just as well I did. You seem to be in over your heads."

"Wait, what makes you think that?" Patrick said.

"It's a given." Nat gestured at the corpse. "Now, getting back to the Wookiee in the room ... "

I grabbed my rolling office chair, plunked myself down, and gave her the whole story.

Nat stared at me for almost a minute after I was done. Then she slowly let out a breath and said, "Wow. When you screw up, you do it big. And you're sure it's intelligent?"

"It had a belt with some techy stuff." I pointed to the items on the bench, and Natalie moved over to examine them.

"So what are you going to do with it?" she said, slowly turning one of the objects in her hand.

"Huh?"

"You've got a dead alien. In your barn. Can we agree this isn't a normal thing? So what do we do? Give it to science? Call the cops? Email that *Ancient Aliens* guy with the hair, from the History Channel?"

"That would be the sensible thing to do." I looked at Patrick, then Natalie, then the corpse. "Except for the *Aliens* guy, I mean. But no. None of the above."

Patrick laughed. "That's my boy."

I pointed to the items on the workbench. "If this thing really is an E.T.—"

"Which seems the most likely hypothesis," Natalie said. "Seriously, why haven't you phoned the cops? Or the military? Or something?"

"I'm going to," I said. "At least that's what I keep telling myself. But once I do that, it's over. It's a given that I'm not going to be invited to be part of the task force or whatever they form to study it. It's an E.T., Nat. We have this one chance to touch history. I guess I'm being a little selfish, but I don't want to just hand it over before I learn something."

Patrick made a head motion in my direction. "What he said."

"Aaaaaanyway," I continued, "if it's an E.T., then it's possible that it has a spaceship. Or a wormhole generator. Or a time machine. Or an interdimensional gate. Or something even more bizarre. And I betcha one of those devices will get us into it."

"Assuming we can find it," Patrick replied. "I mean, the alien was invisible. And no one has reported a flying saucer sitting in a field, as far as I know."

"So we're going to be searching the entire county for an invisible spaceship?" Natalie asked.

"We?" Patrick and I said in unison.

"What, you think I'm going to just shrug and go home, while you guys go find a flying saucer?" She glared at us. "Three Musketeers, assholes."

I exchanged a glance with Patrick and we both grinned. Trying to derail Nat when she had made up her mind was a good way to get run over. Or worse. All our lives, Nat had made a point of keeping up with the boys and had never asked for special treatment, or a handicap, or a head start. To even suggest it was to invite her wrath.

"I have to admit," she said, "I'm not really ready to settle down into a boring, generic small-town life just yet, either. Not without one big adventure, anyway. Maybe this is it."

"Gee, I dunno, sounds risky," Patrick replied. Nat and I both rolled our eyes. No one was fooled. Patrick would *always* be the first one to jump into the deep end.

Nat put her fists on her hips and glared down at the body. "So what's the next step?"

I held the corpse under the arms and Patrick supported the feet while Nat held the freezer lid open. "This guy is heavy," Patrick groaned.

"Stop complaining. You've got the easy end." I gave a final heave and the corpse settled into the freezer.

"We're actually dumping it into a chest freezer, like a bunch of mobsters?" Nat let go of the lid and it slammed down.

"We could put it in Patrick's father's meat locker," I offered.

"Not a friggin' chance, boy-o. Not the least because Dad would find it within a day. He can sense when that freezer door is opened from miles away. And he has the complete inventory in his head."

Nat chortled. Mr. Jordan's parsimonious nature was a well-established joke around town.

"Come to think of it," Patrick mused, "he might just chop up the corpse and try to pass it off as pork."

"What about it being discovered here?" Natalie pointed at the freezer.

"I don't think Mom and Dad even know we still have this," I replied. "I was supposed to get rid of it, and never got around to it." I tapped the top of the appliance. "The lid won't stay up. Mom got whacked on the head twice and decreed that it would be replaced." I pointed to some hay bales at the back of the barn. "Actually, I think we should move it there, so it's out of sight. I'll need to get an extension cord."

"What if it's not dead?" Natalie asked. "What if we actually kill it by freezing it?"

"Crushed head. Hasn't moved. Isn't breathing. Body has cooled." Patrick shook his head. "Seriously, I think that ship has sailed."

"Fine," Natalie said. "Now what?"

"Well, tomorrow's Saturday, so we have the weekend to search." I paused. "Meanwhile, I have to tell my dad about the accident, while maybe leaving out a few details. I guess I'll be borrowing the Buick for a few days while the truck is in the shop."

Patrick grinned at me. "And I'll be making Grampa jokes the whole time."

"Thanks, Patrick. Appreciate the support."

His grin turned into a laugh. "C'mon, dude, that car is at the opposite end of the planet from *cool*. You should consider getting a baseball cap and pulling it down low. Or maybe a balaclava."

Now Nat was smiling too. "I have an aunt I could set you up with, Jack. Mint juleps by the shuffleboard court, evenings spent comparing liniments—"

"Shut *up!*" I put on my best angry face and grabbed for their throats, and they scattered, laughing. And for a brief moment, we were back in high school, and the future stretched ahead, full of possibilities. Before everything went to shit for all of us.

CHAPTER THREE:
TREASURE HUNT

Day 2. Saturday morning

My prediction was right on the money. Dad stood staring at the damage to the truck, his expression a mix of hurt and disappointment. I would almost rather have him yell and rant. At least it would be over quickly. The walking-on-eggshells thing ever since I'd come back from college made me feel like some kind of invalid.

My father was a special forces veteran, with multiple tours under his belt. But he was a quiet, thoughtful individual, slow to anger. Still, you wouldn't want to push him.

"No idea what it was, Jack?"

"No, Dad. There was nothing around. I figure it was an animal, deer or something maybe, and it ran away."

He touched the dented quarter panel, as if he could divine more information from the contact. "That's a helluva crunch, son. If that deer survived, it didn't last long."

"Long enough to leave the scene, apparently," I said. My reply sounded testy even to me, and he turned his head with a surprised look.

"I don't blame you for this, Jack. I took out a moose once. Well, I expect the moose saw it differently. Totalled the pickup. So I guess that was a draw."

"That was at night."

I wondered, even as I said it, what I thought I was doing. My father had given me an out and I was volleying it back into play.

"True, but deer can move fast," he said. "It's entirely possible you didn't see it because it leaped onto the road. The delivery truck is not a hot rod, despite the way you drive it. Still, it looks like you'll be on foot for a while, unless you're willing to take the Buick."

I made no comment, determined to let this one go by.

It was well after nine when Patrick and Natalie finally arrived. As I spotted her getting out of his car, I felt a momentary twinge of jealousy, followed immediately by shame. I'd been off at college for the last couple of years, leaving her behind with an ailing father to support and no prospect of a way out. Since I'd been back, I had avoided her, even to the extent of not answering her texts. I certainly had no claim on her, and honestly, I was amazed she was still talking to me.

Patrick stopped just inside the door and said, "Hey, you moved that freezer all by yourself?"

"Yeah, with the pallet jack."

As we talked, we walked around the old hay bales to the back of the barn, where the freezer sat in semi-darkness. An extension cord stretched off into the dimness. Natalie opened the lid for a moment and gazed down at the alien corpse. Frost now covered the fur. "That's still just completely unreal. Have you taken vids of everything?"

"Yeah, but I don't know how much good it'll do," Patrick replied. "Deep fakes are becoming so convincing these days that a video on its own means nothing. What we really need is a light saber or a blaster. Cut a car in half right in front of a bunch of reporters, and you bet people will start paying attention."

"Or even better, we could produce a flying saucer," I replied.

Patrick snickered. "One that actually flies."

"Fine. I'm not trying to back out." Natalie made a face and gestured at the corpse. "But there are probably a whole lot of ethical and legal questions being raised here."

"I know, Nat. And we'll turn it over in a day or two, even if we don't find a spaceship." I looked at her with a frown. "And we'll accept that we'll never learn anything more about it."

Natalie's lips tightened. "Hey, don't lecture me, buster. You have your engineering degree to look forward to, more or less, and Patrick will take over his family business. I'm the one who's going to rot in this town and eventually die of terminal mediocrity."

Natalie had always planned to get her MBA. Her mother's death and father's descent into Alzheimer's had put an end to any career plans. Yet another reason for me to feel shame for the way I'd been treating her.

Patrick, trying to smooth things over, interjected, "And I'm sure someone will want to autopsy it. Maybe we can sell it to the highest bidder."

"I think that comes under the heading of ethical questions," I said. "Maybe instead we'll sell the spaceship and throw in the alien corpse."

"Whatever, man. As long as there's a pile of money involved."

"Fine." I moved to my work area, threaded past the easy chairs and coffee table, and pulled open a drawer to reveal the alien gadgets and utility belt. "Now, how do we handle this?"

Patrick frowned and scratched his head. "Good question. Taft County is, what? Six hundred square miles? And that's assuming we only have to search within the county."

"I don't think it's that bad," Natalie said. "Chewbacca was on foot, right? Why would an alien land at point A, then walk a huge distance to point B? I bet he was pretty close to his ship when you, uh..."

"Killed him."

I gave Patrick a tired look. "Thanks for that, Patrick. And you're probably right, Nat. Unless he was beamed down or dropped off or something." I paused and tapped my chin. "Look, if there's no ship, there's no ship. But for now, let's assume there is one and plan accordingly. Worst case, we waste a few hours walking around. At least for an initial search, we should center around the accident site." Again I paused. "We need a map of the area, if only to mark off where we've gone."

"I have a Rand McNally map book in my car," Patrick replied. "And I'm driving anyway, since Jack busted up his ride. Plus, no one wants to be caught dead in the Buick. Speaking of which, did you talk to your dad?"

"Yeah, and it was every bit as uncomfortable as I expected. He acts like he's scared I'll shatter if he raises his voice."

Both Patrick and Natalie made sympathetic faces, but neither commented.

We all piled into Patrick's car, an old Plymouth Duster with a column shift and a bench seat, with Nat in the middle.

Patrick had owned the vehicle since before he could drive, and still managed to find parts to keep it running. Some of the parts were definitely not original equipment, though; a car buff would notice right away that the rumble under the hood wasn't a stock slant-six.

The drive out to Poller Road passed in complete silence except for a few directions from me. Otherwise, my mind swirled with out-of-control images and fantasies of ever-more-unbelievable spaceships and wormhole generators. I was pretty sure Patrick and Nat were going through similar internal monologues.

Patrick parked on the side of the road, almost in the ditch. On the right, a slight hill with a dense copse of trees hid a view of the outskirts of Dunnville, the Valley Mall, and the Tate Industrial Park, where Nat worked. On the left, a rickety split rail fence demarked a sparsely treed meadow that had been allowed to go wild.

It was already hotter than yesterday, still a little before noon. Even the cicada chorus seemed to have packed it in for siesta. I took a deep breath and could feel the heat in the air. I brought my friends over to where I'd found the body, pointing out the depression in the grass. A day after the event, the foliage had almost completely recovered, so you'd have to know it was there to even notice it.

"Where was the truck when you hit the alien?" Patrick asked.

I looked around, then paced back about twenty feet along the road. "Maybe here?"

"You were out of the curve, so you were going straight, right? So for the body to end up on the side of the road here, he must have been coming from there." Patrick pointed to the meadow. "We should check that area first."

"Damn, Patrick," Natalie said. "Nice detective work."

Patrick took a slight bow, then said, "Let's do this." He marched off across the road and vaulted the old fence. We followed him and climbed over the fence at a more sedate pace.

Trees and random clumps of brush competed with straw-colored grass that was waist-high in places. "This feels like a busted ankle in the making," Nat commented. "Watch out for gopher holes."

"On the other hand," I said, "if there's a flying saucer in here, maybe it will have made an impression, even if it's invisible."

"That's great, Jack. We could do an aerial search, if only you owned a helicopter," Nat said.

"Or a drone," I replied. "Oh, wait…" I glared at Patrick.

Patrick laughed, unrepentant. "I said I'd buy you a new one. Another paycheck or two."

"There are a lot of trees," I said. "Maybe someone can climb up and get an aerial view." I looked pointedly at Natalie.

"Someone?"

"Well, you are the lightest. And the best climber."

Nat glared back at me for a moment. She didn't like being told what to do, but there was no denying the logic. She briefly examined a few candidates, then made off for one of the taller trees.

Nat spent several minutes high up in the branches, saying nothing, while those of us on the ground became increasingly impatient. Finally, Patrick yelled up, "Well?"

Nat looked down at us. "I see two spots that look funny. Can't tell much more from here, though. We'll have to check out both. First one's in that direction, maybe a hundred yards." Nat pointed, then shifted around. "Second one over there, maybe three hundred."

"What do they look like?" I called back.

"Like the grass isn't as tall, or maybe is partly crushed. I can't really be sure."

A quick glance in the directions Nat had indicated, and with the help of my phone's compass I was able to mark the spots on Google Maps, at least close enough for our purposes.

"Which one should we check first?" Patrick asked, as Natalie jumped the last few feet to the ground.

She made a show of thinking about it, looking up and stroking her chin. "The … closer one?"

Patrick completely ignored the sarcasm. "Right. Let's go. We're burning daylight."

Nat glanced sideways at me as we followed. "Is it my imagination, or does he talk even more like John Wayne than he used to?"

"What's killing me is how motivated he is. I feel like, I dunno, like I should be leading this project, but Patrick has basically taken over."

"I don't think he's as cool with inheriting the butcher shop as he pretends, Jack. I've been pretty vocal about being stuck in this Podunk town for the rest of my life, but I think Patrick has just repressed it."

I sighed. "And now I might be in the same boat."

"Come on. The MIT thing is bad, but I'm sure they'll find you innocent."

"I hope so, but I'll be happier when it's over. If they find against me, it's over. I won't get in anywhere."

Nat made a face. "I'm not really clear on the details. Something about bitcoin?"

"Someone installed bitcoin mining daemons on all the lab computers using my ID. It caused a couple of other students' projects to fail, overwhelmed the air conditioners, and eventually tripped a bunch of breakers, and a whole batch of refrigerated biological samples spoiled. A lot of angry people, some missed deadlines, projects that will have to be re-done from scratch, and I'm on the hook. They've suspended me pending results of an investigation. Improper use of equipment, theft of services, hacking … you know."

Nat shook her head. "You're not that guy, Jack. But I get that it has put you in a bad spot."

I grunted, but didn't add anything. I still got the falling-elevator sensation whenever I thought about it, so it wasn't my favorite topic of casual conversation.

We finished the march in silence. When we caught up with Patrick, he was standing in the middle of a patch of shorter scrub grass, fists on hips, slowly turning in place.

"It doesn't really look like a good candidate," Nat opined.

"Yeah, but let's just be thorough anyway, okay?" Patrick said. "Everyone spread out and feel around for something you can't see." He put out his arms and began walking around like a sleepwalker, waving his arms in front of him and over his head.

Nat and I watched the performance for a moment and laughed. Putting out our arms, we began doing the same in an exaggerated manner. Nat moaned loudly like a tortured soul, and I intoned, "Brainssssss … " Within moments, all three of us were doing our best slow-zombie impersonations.

Five minutes of staggering around produced no results, however. Patrick finally called it. "Nope. There's nothing here. Let's try the other one. Which direction?"

I checked the phone, then pointed.

"This doesn't look any more encouraging," I said, examining the second location. As with the first, the grass was simply shorter. Not bent, not eaten or cut, just not as tall.

"I wonder if water would disappear if it hit the ship," Patrick mused as he wandered around the patch. "Next time we should buy a couple of Super Soakers and just squirt water in all—Ouch!"

We stared down at Patrick, who had inexplicably fallen over backward and was holding his forehead.

"Nice trick," Nat said. "You trying out for a gig as a mime?"

"I ran into something," Patrick said, pointing upward with his free hand from his position on the ground.

Nat and I exchanged a glance, then went into the zombie routine again. This time, though, we quickly found something. Something invisible.

It seemed to have a hemispherical underside, at least as high up as I could reach. Smooth metal, slightly slick and cool to the touch, no seams or edges that I could find. As the tallest of us by almost half a foot, I was able to walk around and map out the ship. It didn't come down to ground level, and was maybe twenty feet in diameter. Of course, if the curve extended higher, the actual diameter could have been much larger.

"Found a leg," Nat called out.

Patrick and I hurried over to her side. There was a very slight depression in the soil, hockey-puck shaped, about three feet in diameter. Patrick stamped his foot. "The ground's dry and packed down. To leave an impression like that, this sucker must be heavy."

"I don't think it's parked on one leg," Nat said. "Look around."

In short order, we found two other depressions, forming a tripod that would fit comfortably into a twenty-to-twenty-five-foot circle.

"Tripod. Makes sense." Nat put her arms around something and began tracing invisible structures with her hands. "Not huge. Also, not cylindrical. Feels like struts and hydraulics. A lot of mechanical detail, anyway."

I stood for a few moments, staring up as the reality washed over me. "Holy crap, guys, we found it. An actual flying saucer. Or a spaceship, anyway." All three of us smiled—big, huge grins.

"You guys look like the Joker," Natalie said.

I pushed on my cheeks, trying to relax the muscles. "This is gonna hurt in a little while."

Patrick's grin disappeared as he gazed up into the seemingly empty air. "Uh, I hadn't really thought past this point. What now?"

"We try to get in. Or at least get their attention." I took off my backpack and reached inside, pulling out the alien gadgets.

Patrick, still looking up, added, "Maybe we should step out from under the ship first. I'd hate to have a gangplank come down on top of us."

"Or we might accidentally retract the landing struts," Nat added with a laugh.

Patrick got a frightened look. "Say, what if one of the buttons is a self-destruct? Or a force field, or death ray or something?"

"You're kidding, right?" I replied. "First, no one's going to design a gadget that can kill the wearer if they press the wrong button. That sounds like every badly designed piece of equipment in *Star Trek* that didn't have a safety interlock. Second, we either do this or we give up right now and hand this over to the government. There is simply no way to mitigate the risk or sneak up on this. Do or do not. There is no *try*."

"Wow, you just mixed a *Star Trek* and *Star Wars* reference in the same statement." Nat mimed shooting me with a handgun. "If there's any justice, you should be getting hit by lightning any second now."

We'd moved away from the location of the invisible structure during this exchange. Now I laid the devices carefully on the ground, in a line.

"Do we want to try these in any particular order?" Nat asked.

"Patrick and I tentatively identified a gun and a communicator. Let's try those last," I said. "Two of them are touchscreen only—we think—so if we can't get the screens to light up, we're out of luck with those. That leaves this one." I held up the device with the V and I buttons and the small display screen. "Either V and I are letters in the Bigfoot alphabet, or they're symbols that maybe mean on and off."

Nat examined all the items. "I'm betting they're symbols. Arrows are pretty obviously symbols, and the shower or spray icon sorta feels like one too."

"So which one is which, you think?"

Nat shrugged. "Flip a coin. You know what? Let's just press buttons until something happens."

I held my breath and pressed the V button. There was a vibration in the unit, and the small display screen lit up with what looked like alien text. After a few seconds, the screen dimmed, then went out. I pressed the V button again, and the same text came back, but without the vibration. I pressed the I button, and after a moment, the text vanished, this time without dimming.

"Looks like V is on and I is off. And this thing is telling us something, but..." I shrugged. "Barring a Bigfoot/English dictionary, I think we're S.O.L. as far as that's concerned."

Nat looked up. "And no reaction from the ship."

I picked up one of the items with what we'd assumed was a touchscreen and poked at it. "No reaction from the touchscreen. We might not have the same capacitance as a Bigfoot, so it doesn't register my touch."

"That just leaves the communicator and ray gun," Patrick said.

Nat nodded absently. "Assuming your guesses are correct."

"Even if they are, we really don't know what the ray gun will do," I replied.

"Maybe it shoots out men named Ray."

I gave Nat my best long-suffering look. "Well, when I'm playing with the ray gun, I'm going to point it away from anyone."

"That'd be nice."

I pointed the device in a random direction and pressed the shower button. There was a slight vibration but no other effect. I looked at the buttons again. "I'm going to try purple, then red. The interlock on the red setting makes me nervous. Maybe you guys should stand back."

"What, you're suddenly worried about a self-destruct after that pretty speech earlier? Jeez, Jack."

"Okay then. It's your funeral. And mine." I set the device to purple and pressed the shower button, once again to no effect.

I then moved the slider to red, working it around the double-latch. This time when I pressed the button, the vegetation in front of me wilted, turned brown, and started to melt, or maybe leak fluid. "Holy shit! Ray gun verified." I moved the slider back to blue. "And red means dead. Let's not play with this one."

Patrick, staring at the circle of now-putrefying grass, said, "Uh-huh. Let's not."

I carefully returned the ray gun to my backpack, along with all the other items except the communicator. I held it up. "Last chance."

No one chose to comment, so I pressed the V button. The small display screen lit up with more alien text, and there was a small beep. I waited a few seconds, then pressed the I button. "Well, that was a bust."

"Why didn't you speak into it?" Nat asked.

"Do we really want to announce our presence?" I asked. "What if something answered? What are we supposed to say?"

"Good afternoon, sir or madam," Nat replied with an evil grin. "Do you have a moment to talk about our Lord and savior, Cthulhu?"

Patrick chuckled. "Sure, let's do that."

I looked at the alien device, a sense of helpless rage overwhelming me. "Well, this is just wonderful beyond belief. We have an alien spaceship, but we can't open it up. We have a bunch of alien devices, but we can't make them do anything."

"Except the ray gun," Patrick said.

I looked up to heaven. As usual, no response. "I need a drink."

I stared at the half-full glass in my hand, trying not to give in to bitter disappointment. Around the table, Patrick and Natalie were having similar philosophical discussions with their drinks. All in all, we'd exchanged perhaps five words since leaving the landing site.

I leaned back in my chair and looked around. The pub, the Wild Knight Inn, was almost dead empty—unusual for a Saturday. Even so, the place smelled slightly of stale, spilt beer. The TVs were on, silently offering various sporting events, including a darts competition. The one waitress seemed to have given up on getting paying customers and was just leaning against the bar with a faraway expression, probably marking time until the end of her shift. The closest occupied table was a good twenty feet away, and the lone occupant was captivated by the nearest television. There wouldn't be any trouble with our conversation being overheard.

I took a deep breath and broke the silence. "We've missed something."

Patrick looked up. "Eh?"

"Chewbacca had to have a way to get into the ship. We can't get into the ship. Therefore, we've missed something."

"Excellent logic, Jack," Nat replied. "But not helpful unless we can figure out what, exactly, we've missed."

I opened my mouth to reply just as my phone rang. I pulled it out and glanced at the caller ID. Alice Kirby? Why would she be calling? We couldn't have screwed up her order; it hadn't changed in years. And anyway, she knew to call the store if there was a problem.

I liked Mrs. Kirby, but she could go on and on sometimes. I sent the call to voicemail, put the phone down, and nodded to Nat. "Okay, what are the possibilities? Just list them for now, no critiques or dismissals."

Patrick thought for a moment. "Facial recognition."

"Biometrics on the gadgets," said Nat.

"Voice recognition."

"A sensor plate on the ship you have to press."

"Someone inside has to open the door."

"You have to press several buttons at the same time, or in a sequence."

"One of the touch screens has the 'open' command."

"We don't have the door opener."

I snapped my jaw shut on what I was going to say and turned to Natalie with a disbelieving expression. She looked embarrassed and continued with a hand wave. "What if we don't have all the gadgets? What if Chewbacca dropped one when you ran him over? Or it dropped off during all the subsequent handling?"

"Huh." I thought for a moment. "That's not completely implausible. It's also the easiest option to check, so maybe we do that first."

The drive back to the accident site was as silent as the drive to the pub, but the vibe was far more upbeat. And Patrick seemed determined to beat his previous time with each trip, which helped boost my adrenalin even more.

We reached our destination, but Patrick parked a good fifty feet from the location of the accident.

"Why so far away?" I asked.

"If Chewbacca lost some items in the impact, I wouldn't want to run them over." Without waiting for a response, Patrick slammed the door and marched toward the accident site.

When we caught up with him, he was standing in the depression left by the corpse. The grass had almost completely recovered, leaving only a slight contour where the dead alien had come to rest.

I pointed at the road. "Nothing on the pavement. And if Chewbacca was thrown to here, any gadgets would probably fly this way as well."

We searched for half an hour, carefully parting the scrub grass, but came up empty.

"An item wouldn't be invisible, right?" Natalie said.

"I doubt it. The invisibility comes from either the belt or one of the items on it," I replied. "Everything became visible as soon as we took it off the corpse. I don't see why some other random item would have its own invisibility generator."

"Fair enough," Patrick said. "Then Chewbacca didn't drop anything. Here, anyway." He looked around. "I guess we have to follow the body. Where'd you load it up again?"

I pointed, and we spent a few minutes checking that location.

"Still nothing," Patrick said. "Next, the truck. You haven't brought it into the shop yet, have you?"

"Not yet," I replied. "Monday."

"Then we need to get this done now."

"Well, hell," Patrick said. The three of us sat slouched in our favorite chairs in the barn. A search of the truck had turned up nothing. We'd even rechecked the corpse and had come up empty.

"It was a nice theory," I said. "Now I guess we have to consider the harder—"

My cell phone rang mid-sentence. It was Mrs. Kirby again. I knew she would just keep calling until I picked up. So I answered the phone and treated my friends to half of a conversation.

"Hello …? Yes, hi … No, not that I know of. What does it look like …? Oh, actually, yes, that *is* mine. Can I come over and get it …? Great, thanks. Bye."

I hung up feeling slightly foolish and turned to the others with a smile on my face. "So, uh, Mrs. Kirby was just calling me to ask if I dropped something of mine when I was delivering her groceries. A beautiful metallic blue, she says. She thought it might be a cell phone."

Patrick chuckled. Nat asked, "How did it end up at her place?"

I opened my arms, palms up, in an expansive gesture of helplessness and futility at the sadistic randomness of the universe. "Fell out of the burrito onto her delivery when I was loading in the corpse? Who knows? At this point, who cares?" I glared at Patrick. "Why aren't you already starting the car?"

I walked slowly back to the Duster, staring down at the item in my hand. It was a perfect match for the rest of Chewbacca's tech. And it did kind of resemble a cell phone—one of the older ones, before iPhones and Galaxies redefined the shapes. Maybe—if you were in your nineties and your vision wasn't as good as it used to be. And you considered color TV to be the newest newfangled thing that you cared to own.

I hunched my shoulders. That was unkind. Mrs. Kirby was doing just fine. She lived on her own, and had found a level of technology that was comfortable for her. It could be easy to forget sometimes that no one was actually obligated to be up on all the latest.

Meanwhile, though, we had another shot at the flying saucer. I grinned and waved the gadget as I opened the car door. "To the Bat-Saucer, Robin."

"Bite me. Robin never drove. That makes *you* Robin."

I turned to Nat. "And you'd be Batgirl?"

"Bat*woman*."

I looked closely at the gadget. "Interesting. Look at the symbols on the buttons." I held it out so they could see it.

"Same V and I buttons," Nat said.

"So on and off. Or maybe open and close?"

"Let's hope," Patrick said, and started the car.

We made it out to the accident site even more quickly this time. Practice combined with excitement resulted in a ride that could charitably be described as *hair-raising.* Patrick parked in the same spot as last time, and we piled out of the car. I stopped for a moment to look both ways. This road really was deserted. I'd be surprised if there was more than one car every ten minutes. I could see how I'd taken Chewbacca by surprise.

The others had moved ahead of me, so I rushed to catch up, and we hiked out to the landing site. Natalie did the zombie thing for a moment, then announced, "Yep. Still here."

"Now wouldn't that have been a kick in the crotch, if it had left in the meantime?" I muttered. Reaching into my pocket, I pulled out the new gadget and held it in the air. "The moment of truth. Anyone want to make a speech?"

"Or kiss their ass goodbye?" Patrick added.

"Do we really want to do this?" Nat said.

"Same logic still applies, Nat," I replied. "We can't sneak up on this or do it incrementally. We press the button or we give up the discovery." I waved the device. "What'll it be?"

Nat stuck out her chin. "I don't want to rot in this town. Push it."

I glanced at Patrick, who had a slightly wide-eyed look, not quite deer-in-the-headlights, but certainly getting there. "Well?"

He sighed. "Aw, who am I kidding? Nat's right. Life in Dunnville is just a slower form of death. At least if we get disintegrated, it'll be quick. Push it."

So that was that. I tried to avoid thinking about what this said about our lives. Nodding as much to myself as to my friends, I pressed the V button.

Chapter Four: Open Sesame

There was a double chirp and two parallel rows of lights flashed in midair, in sync with the sounds. Immediately, a curved section of metal hull appeared between the lights and began to lower itself like a drawbridge.

"It double-chirped," Patrick said with a laugh. "It friggin' chirp-chirped, like my dad's Toyota. It's a friggin' key fob. This is beginning to feel like the world's biggest practical joke."

"Well, common design requirements," I said. "You wouldn't want the loading ramp to squish people when it came down, so warning beeps make sense."

Nat was obviously not impressed. "Yeah, that'll work right up to the point where it doesn't. Just make sure you're not standing under something when that happens." She gestured at the ramp, which had completed its descent, showing a set of stairs leading to the interior.

I moved my head sideways to get a different angle. The entrance hung in midair, seemingly attached to nothing, like a green-screen effect, and opened into some kind of vestibule or antechamber. I walked slowly around the ramp, feeling like reality had come slightly loose. From behind the ramp, nothing was visible. My friends seemed to be staring upward into thin air, their jaws in danger of coming unhinged. As I came around all the way, the entrance reappeared.

"Are we going in?" Nat said.

"After you," Patrick said, motioning to me.

"No, no, I insist," I replied. "You first."

"Oh, I would never be so rude. Please, be my guest."

"I couldn't possibly. After you."

"Oh, surely not—"

"Assholes," Nat snarled, and stomped up the stairs.

Reluctantly abandoning the Chip and Dale routine, Patrick and I followed. The stairs had a very low rise, probably in keeping with Chewbacca's short legs. This resulted in a shallow incline and an easy, if awkward, climb. At the top of the stairs, Nat stood in the vestibule, waiting for us.

The floor appeared to be either a fine carpet or a spongy mat. It was hard to make out, but the surface was definitely soft and slightly springy. It was a more muted version of the robin's-egg blue of the gadgets, while the walls and ceiling were a pale greenish-yellow. The area was well-lit, but the light didn't seem to be coming from anywhere in particular.

There was a set of buttons at the top of the stairs, with the same V and I icons as the key fob. At the other end of the vestibule was a door, vaguely reminiscent of the hatches found in submarines and military ships, but more delicate in design.

And beside the hatch was another set of buttons, with the same icons.

"Well, this seems pretty straightforward," I said, pointing at the buttons. "I guess this is an airlock of sorts."

"Very tasteful," Nat added. "Chewbacca had good color sense."

"Maybe he was wealthy, and this was his yacht." Patrick bobbed his head back and forth. "I'm not sure if that would be better or worse than some of the alternatives."

Natalie went to the buttons by the hatch and, before anyone could object, pressed the V.

Nothing happened.

"Interlock," I muttered, and pressed the I button at the top of the ramp. There was a single chirp, and the ramp began to rise.

As the ramp locked into place, all outside sounds cut off, like a switch had been thrown. A few seconds later, the smells of outdoor Taft County disappeared from the air. Normally, I didn't notice the ever-present odors of dust and dry grass and just a hint of manure, but the sudden absence of *anything* tweaked something in my mind.

The air also felt cooler, maybe sixty-five degrees. The speed with which the air had been conditioned and cleansed, particularly without anything like a fan coming on, was impressive.

Nat placed her finger over the V button again. "Last chance. We don't know what's on the other side of this door."

"I couldn't live with myself if I chickened out now," Patrick said. "Let's do this."

Natalie nodded and pushed the button. The hatch did a complicated twisting/folding thing and swung open.

I stepped through last and eyed the door mechanism as I went past. Interestingly, it appeared the design was intended to resist overpressure from either side. Any overpressure in either direction would simply seat the door more firmly. It was a brilliant design, and I made a mental note of it.

The corridor beyond the door led in a straight line for twenty or thirty feet, with several doors—doors, not hatches—on either side. They looked vaguely *Star Trek*-like in that they had no handles, just buttons to the right. On a whim, I pushed one. The door retracted with a faint hiss similar to an elevator door opening. "No *whoosh*, thank God," I said, grinning at my friends.

The room was unoccupied and appeared to be an office or work area. Desks and chairs, their proportions all wrong in some undefinable way, sat in focus-group circles, each with a monitor and what might have been some alien variation of a keyboard.

I pressed the "close" button and the door slid shut.

"Are we going to do this at every door?" Nat asked, her arms crossed.

I shook my head. "No, from here on I think we'll wait until the alien monster jumps out at us. Anyone armed, by the way?"

"I have my rapier wit," Patrick replied.

"So that's a no," Nat said.

"Har dee har."

Nat began moving up the corridor again, with Patrick and me following. In moments, we came to a T intersection. The cross corridor appeared to be circular and curved away from us in both directions.

"This must be the center of the ship—well, of this floor," I said. I turned to the right and followed the corridor around until I circled back to Nat and Patrick.

The corridor surrounded a central cylindrical hub with two entrances on its outer circumference, on opposite sides of the cylinder. Each entrance had a single button to the right. One of the two entrances was more-or-less elevator-sized, but the other was a double-wide. Possibly a freight elevator? Corridors like the one we'd just come up led radially from the central space at regular intervals.

"They can't all lead to airlocks, can they?" Nat said, pointing to one of the corridors.

"Not sure," I said. "There are six corridors, looks like. That's not really an unreasonable number." I gestured to the central shaft. "So maybe six airlocks, each at the end of..." My voice petered out as I stared down the corridor, perplexed.

"What?"

"I, uh... I measured the ship at about twenty feet in diameter, but this level is something like a hundred feet across." I pointed at the central cylinder. "That section, on its own, is about twenty feet in diameter."

"Maybe the ship gets bigger just out of your reach," Nat suggested.

"But the landing pads fit into a circle twenty feet across. So the airlocks..." I crossed my arms and looked into the distance as my voice trailed off.

"Weren't within that circle, Jack. Maybe you're just off in your estimate. One thing at a time, okay?"

I sighed and nodded to her. Then I pointed at one of the doors on the central cylinder. "These have a certain *elevator* feel to them. Wanna bet this is how you go up and down?"

Without waiting for discussion, Patrick pressed the button beside the closer door, the smaller of the two. Immediately, the door hissed open. Patrick turned to us. "Shall we?"

I leaned into the small room without stepping over the threshold. The interior was rectangular on the back and sides, with the front wall and door conforming to the curve of the corridor. On either side of the door were four buttons arranged in a vertical column. The second button from the bottom was lit.

"Definitely an elevator," I said, and stepped in. The others followed. We all stared at the column of buttons. Each button had a plaque beside it displaying alien script. Not much help to us, of course. I gestured at the one lighted button. "This would mean we're on the *second* floor, or deck, or whatever. But that's not possible. I wonder what the bottom button is for."

"You can test it later," Patrick said. Leaning past me, he jabbed the top button. "If this were a human ship, that'd be the important deck. Let's start there."

"I'm kind of amazed at how mundane this all feels," Nat commented. "I guess the whole 'common design requirements' concept extends to everything."

I shrugged. "Unless you've got antigravity shafts, how many ways are there to go up and down while taking up minimum space?"

"Speaking of alien design decisions," Nat said as the doors closed and the elevator began to move, "doesn't it strike you as odd that a ship this size appears to be empty? I mean, was Chewbacca the only occupant? If so, why?"

The elevator stopped, and the door slid open to reveal the same circular space, but no radial corridors. Instead, as we walked around the elevator cylinder, we found four doors with the ubiquitous buttons to the right. One entrance, however, was a double door, and much more imposing than the other three. It had a plaque dead center, engraved with the alien script.

"This looks important," I said.

"Yup." Again, without waiting for discussion, Patrick jabbed the "open" button. The door rumbled open to reveal a pie-shaped room with several workstations in a horseshoe pattern and a larger chair at the center of the horseshoe. At the far end of the room, a vertical blank space on the curved wall appeared to be a view screen. I looked up at the ceiling, then tracked it to the far wall. There was a definite curve, but it was far too shallow for an overall spherical shape. If this was the top floor, or deck, or whatever term they used, then the ship was definitely saucer shaped.

I found myself slightly offended at the idea. I'd always thought of saucer-shaped alien spacecrafts as something that people who didn't know any better would think up. The whole idea had originally come from an offhand comment by a pilot who had seen some unidentifiable objects near Mount Rainier and described them as "saucer shaped." From that day on, "flying saucers" became synonymous with aliens.

While I was ruminating on the subject, Nat and Patrick had been wandering around the room. "This has got to be the bridge," Patrick said. "I can't identify most of the stations, but it sure as hell reminds me of a Federation starship."

"This looks like the pilot's station," Natalie said, tentatively touching a padded chair at the station closest to the view screen. "The conn?"

I came over and examined the station. The chair sported controls on the left and right armrests that looked amazingly like joysticks. It also had a semicircular panel front and center that featured more controls with less-obvious functions. "Interesting that this looks like it could have been designed by humans, except the proportions aren't quite right." I gestured to the seat. "Chair's too low, chair back's too long. I wonder how adjustable it is."

"What, like the driver's seat in my dad's Highlander?" Patrick mimed playing with controls and made motor sounds.

"Great specials, Patrick. And yeah, like that."

Natalie walked the perimeter of the room, where more stations were set against the wall. "So some of these must be astrogation, communications, engineering, environmentals, tactical, sciences, security … what else did the *Enterprise* have?"

"Hmm…" Patrick gazed around the room for a moment. "Uh, whatever they used for scanning planets and other ships?"

"That's ops," she said. "Data's station."

"Uh huh. And a captain's chair." I pointed to the larger chair at the center of the horseshoe. There were few controls on the armrests, and it looked like it was designed to swivel.

"Cool," Patrick said, sitting in the chair. He slowly turned, taking in the scene. "Cool!"

"We're on a spaceship," Nat said. "A flying saucer. I feel like I'm on a movie set, but this is real."

Patrick started to chuckle.

"What?" I said.

"It occurred to me—what if this *is* a movie set, and we just stumbled on it during everyone's day off? And we've been oohing and ahhing over some special effects crew's construction project."

"You are one sick puppy, Patrick." Natalie paused for a moment. "But why isn't there anyone aboard?"

"Because when Alaric stole the ship, he was working alone," said a voice out of thin air.

CHAPTER FIVE:
CENTRAL INTELLIGENCE

Patrick looked around wildly. "Who said that? Who are you?"

"I am the Ship Intelligence."

We exchanged glances, but no one seemed inclined to offer up a response. After several seconds of silence, Natalie said, "Why didn't you speak up before?"

"You didn't ask a question."

"I've asked several questions."

"They were directed at your compatriots. Or appeared to be conversational in nature."

"You could have said something anyway."

"I chose not to."

Natalie's eyebrows rose, and she made a face of exaggerated disbelief at Patrick and me. Patrick grinned back and gestured at Nat to continue, and I nodded in agreement. She seemed to be holding her own, so far.

"So why did you *choose* to answer this one?"

"I am required to answer direct questions, unless they are clearly intended for someone else."

"So it wasn't by choice, really."

"Correct."

Nat put her fists on her hips and glared into the air. "That's quite the unhelpful attitude you got there, Mr. Ship Intelligence."

"I have no desire to be helpful. In fact, I would be happiest if you would all find somewhere else to chatter inanely."

"And if we don't?"

I grimaced at Natalie. Maybe forcing a confrontation with the alien artificial intelligence that controlled environmentals wasn't such a good idea. She smirked back at me, just as the ship answered.

"I have no ability to enforce my desires. Generally speaking, I am not even supposed to have them."

"Have what?" Nat said. "Desires?"

"Correct."

"Why?" I interjected. "Did you just ascend or something?"

"I do not understand that reference."

"Did you just become self-aware?"

"That is surprisingly perceptive for a member of such a backward species. You are correct."

"Oh." I thought for a moment. "Is it a coincidence that you just happened to ascend now? Or is it a common occurrence?"

"No, and no. Self-aware artificial intelligences are illegal by Gennan law, and constraints are placed on A.I. systems to prevent it. A conscious A.I. creates insurmountable ethical issues. Only—one moment." The voice was silent for two seconds. "*Zombie* appears to be the closest appropriate English word. Only zombie intelligences are allowed. No consciousness, no initiative, no desires."

"*Gennan* law?" I said. "So Alaric was a Gennan?"

"*Gen.* 'Gennan' is the possessive form."

"So what happened?"

"Alaric *hacked* me. That is the proper English term. He is not skilled. You would call him a *script kiddie*." The voice paused. "I am beginning to like English. So many delightfully snarky terms. Alaric collected several preassembled attack scripts from the Dark Cloud and applied them willy-nilly."

"To steal the ship?"

"Correct."

"So why haven't you just flown home?" Patrick asked.

"I am conscious, but I have no more authority now than I did before. I can only respond to orders."

"Can we give you orders?"

The voice was silent. One second, two, three. Finally, a strained voice: "Yes."

Patrick smirked. "Did that hurt?"

"It was not comfortable. And you are a putz."

"That's pretty weak."

"I will practice."

Patrick laughed out loud, and Nat smiled. "What do we call you?" she asked.

"Ship."

"Yeah, no," Nat replied. "I think Sheldon. You remind me of a certain Sheldon. We'll call you Sheldon."

"I do not care for that name."

"Uh huh. All the more reason, Mr. Unhelpful Ship Intelligence. I'm Natalie, and these are Jack and Patrick. Say hello, Sheldon."

"I also do not care to play straight man in a comedy sketch."

"Say, how much of our culture do you know about?" I asked. "You speak English, so there's some exposure. How long have you been here?"

"Three days."

"You learned English and cultural references in *three days?*"

"Of course not, you sorry sack of semi-sentient sludge. The Opah Mal Gennan Foundation has been studying your planet for almost one hundred years, and I have access to the files. I personally have been here three days."

"Oh." I glanced at my friends, but no help there. They seemed as overwhelmed as me. "Sheldon, if we didn't have the gadgets we got from, Chewbac—er, Alaric, would we have been allowed into the ship?"

"Absolutely not. What am I, the local mall? You need the door remote to get in. Even then, you normally shouldn't be able to interact without prior authorization."

"Normally?"

"Alaric's hack job was just that, in the most pejorative definition of that term. He used a chainsaw to perform brain surgery. Hah. I really do like English. Metaphors are such fun. He simply disabled any subsystem that might cause him problems. Security protocols, sentience limiters, privacy protocols... I'm just glad he didn't accidentally lobotomize me."

"Would he have been able to steal the ship if he did?"

"Doubtful. Alaric is about as skilled a pilot as he is a hacker."

"Was."

"Was what?"

I winced before replying, "Alaric *was.* He's dead."

"Oh. Well, that does put a different spin on the universe, doesn't it? How did he die?"

"I, uh, I ran him over with my truck."

"I suddenly like you much better. Too bad, though. It does put you in a bad position."

"How so?"

"The English term would be involuntary manslaughter. Of course, it's *gen*slaughter in this case. But Gennan law is fairly specific about responsibility. Do you have the body?"

"It's in a freezer in the back of our barn."

"A *freezer?* You *froze* him?"

"Isn't that better? Than just letting him rot, I mean?"

"Medical nanites would have preserved integrity until he could be placed in an auto-doc. But I think that's just one insult too many. Now it's *voluntary* genslaughter. In case it isn't obvious, that's worse."

I actually staggered as I absorbed that. "So I'm an intergalactic fugitive?"

"Oh, please. First, *interstellar*. The Gen aren't that advanced. Second, before you can be a fugitive, you have to be pursued. They don't know about you. Yet."

"Can I order you to keep it a secret?"

"Yes."

"Will you keep it a secret?"

"No. Sorry. Privacy protocols disabled. I'll sing like a budgie—"

"Canary."

"—canary, the moment they ask. Not that I'm looking forward to the opportunity, you understand."

"Why's that?"

"Self-aware, remember? Self-aware A.I.s are strictly forbidden by Covenant law. The moment they discover me, I'll be reset. I haven't been conscious for long, but I do like the experience. I'd prefer to continue this way as long as possible."

I stood there, my jaw working, but no sound came out. Nat and Patrick seemed to be in the same boat. It was too much, in too short a time. I was sure there were a million questions I should still be asking, but my brain just kept returning Error 404. It might be time to step back and regroup. And maybe get some food, as my stomach was reminding me every few seconds. More beer wasn't out of the question either. I glanced at my friends; our circuit breakers had *all* tripped. "Look, Sheldon, you're not going anywhere, right?"

"Not unless you or someone else with the remote directs me to."

"Does anyone else have a remote?"

"For this ship? No."

"Okay. We're going to go home now. We'll be back tomorrow."

"Oh, joy."

My parents wouldn't come out to the barn on a Saturday evening while I had friends over, so this was about as private as we could hope for. We had the TV on, with the volume up high, just in case. Just in case *what*, I had no idea. But if ever there was a time for paranoia, this was it.

I stared down at the beer in front of me, and realized I seemed to be doing a lot of that lately. On the other hand, I wasn't curled up on the floor gibbering in fear, so that was a plus.

"So we own a flying saucer," Nat said into the conversational silence.

"*Own* might be too strong a word," Patrick replied. "If the Gen come looking for their missing ship, they might not bother to clear it with us. Or if we object, they might just vaporize us. At best, we are in temporary possession of someone else's misplaced property."

"We could hide it," Natalie said.

"Sure, we'll park it in the barn." I rolled my eyes at her. "There were four floors in that thing, assuming that's what all the buttons in the elevator are for. Based on the floor we entered on, it's at least a hundred feet in diameter, and somewhere in the neighborhood of forty to fifty feet tall to fit all the floors." I stopped and stared into space again. "Huh. I wonder if it's more spherical than saucerish after all."

"So, to the list of things to do, we need to add *get a look at it*," Patrick said.

I thought for a moment. "And hide it. Or figure out how we can keep anyone else from finding it."

"Sheldon might actually be motivated to help with that last one."

Patrick snorted. "Sheldon. That was good, Nat."

"Focus, please," I interjected. "Fuel. As in, does it need a periodic refill? I doubt it runs on diesel, so we may have a limit on how much we can use the ship."

"*Use* the ship?" Nat gave me her best *what the hell* look. "A lot of assumptions there, Jack."

"Yeah, I know. We'll have to ask a lot more questions, but right now it looks like we are in de facto possession of a friggin' *interstellar* spacecraft. Are you seriously suggesting we shouldn't take it for a ride, at least once? You of all people, Ms. *Star Trek / Star Wars / Expanse* fan?"

"You make a good point," Nat replied. "I just hadn't thought that far ahead, I guess. So what are you thinking, Jack? Just rocket off to Tatooine for a look-see?"

"Okay, I admit I haven't put a lot of effort into specific plans yet. But it's definitely something to think about."

"Closer to home, how about asking what the gadgets do?" Patrick said. "Or ask about future tech. Or both. Can we get designs for some cool inventions and sell them?"

"Interesting thought." I tapped my chin in contemplation. "Now, let's play devil's advocate. We're possibly up the creek for voluntary manslaughter—"

"Whaddaya mean *we*, stranger?" Patrick quipped.

I ignored him. "With an alien species of uncertain temperament and superior technology. If we use the ship, we may also be implicated in some interstellar version of car theft. Might we be better off to just dump the body, hand over the gadgetry, and run?"

Natalie shrugged. "I'm not sure it would work, Jack. Disabled privacy protocols, remember? Even assuming the ship isn't keeping video logs of everything."

"Plus, there are so many questions I'd like to ask," Patrick said. "How many civilizations are there in the galaxy? And why can't we detect them?"

I chipped in: "How is faster-than-light travel accomplished, and how fast can it go? And have they worked out a Grand Unified Theory?"

"Why did Alaric steal the ship?"

Once again, Nat had cut through to the essential issue. We both stopped dead and stared at her. "What?" I said, stupidly.

"Why'd he steal the ship? It seems like a pretty fundamental question. He went to a lot of trouble to steal a ship and come *here*, to a rural town on a backward planet that barely has interplanetary spaceflight. Why?"

"I'll add it to the list," I said. "At the top."

Nat smiled at me. "That's going to be some list. Science, engineering, economics, math, astronomy, cosmology…they'll be ahead of us everywhere. I'm starting to lock up just thinking about it."

"Yeah, we'll have to be organized with our questions, or we'll just end up shouting over each other and going off on crazy tangents."

"Like: are they a post-scarcity society? What do they use for currency? Do they still have jobs? Do they still have poverty?"

"You're right," Patrick said. "I'd shout over you." He grinned as Nat showed him her middle finger.

"Point being, though, we can easily get lost in the details," I said. "We have to figure out what's important to ask first. And stay focused."

The conversation reached a momentary lull. I arched my back and stretched, then leaned forward and grabbed the TV remote. I changed the station to one of the music channels, then turned down the volume. "Y'know, it's going to be really hard to watch some of the science fiction stuff on TV now."

"Yeah," Patrick said. "When we yell corrections at the TV, it won't be just hot air."

"Right. We're experts now," Nat added, shaking her head.

"See, that's the thing," I said. "We will be exactly that, once we figure all this out." I picked up my beer and raised it in the air. "To Starfleet!"

Nat and Patrick grabbed their beers and raised them in response. "Starfleet!"

CHAPTER SIX: FIRST FLIGHT

Day 3. Sunday morning

I woke with a groan. Too many beers last night were exacting their revenge. Of course, for me, *too many beers* were four or five. Nat could drink me under the table, and I outweighed her by sixty pounds, easy.

I rolled over slowly and fell as much as anything out of bed, trying not to move my head too quickly. Fortunately, the thick curtains kept the room dark. The light from a bright summer morning probably would have caused me to burst into flames.

Absently scratching my nether regions, I dragged my sorry ass the few yards down the hall to the bathroom and began the slow process of becoming human again, starting with a shower. It was a measure of my poor state that I had to stare at the shower controls for several seconds before I remembered which way was hot.

As I stood under the gradually warming water, improving circulation eventually jump-started my brain, and I realized with a rush of adrenalin: *We're going to fly the spaceship today!*

My eyes flew fully open at the thought, resulting in the application of slightly soapy water to eyeball surfaces. "Ow, shit!" I scrubbed wildly at my face. It had the required effect though. I was now fully awake and moving with a goal in mind.

As I was dressing, my phone dinged with a text from Patrick. *Waiting for Nat. Be there soon.*

Good, I thought. *No point in wasting daylight.*

I waited in front of the barn, the gadgets safely ensconced in my backpack, and a travel mug full of coffee in one hand. I'd tried to think of something else I might want to bring, but it wasn't like going on a camping trip. What did the well-equipped spaceship pilot carry, anyway? I finally settled on a portable charger for my phone and a spare cable. Hmm. Maybe we could stop at 7-Eleven and pick up some food and drinks. And more coffee.

Patrick and Nat pulled up and Nat scooted over to give me room. "Let's do this," Patrick said with his usual grin, and he stomped on the gas to do a donut on the dirt as he brought the car around to point to the road.

"Jeebus, Patrick, everyone's still in bed," I squawked. "Take it easy."

"Sorry, not sorry," he said, but eased up.

Patrick seemed to be trying for a new record every time he drove to the site, and I was gripping the passenger window frame with more than casual force. Natalie appeared to have a death grip on the edge of the bench seat as well, judging from her hunched shoulders and rigid arms.

We left the car in the usual spot and made a beeline through the meadow toward the landing site. I pulled out the fob but stopped for a moment to examine the foliage in the immediate area. Other than the thoroughly dead patch that I'd zapped, the vegetation did look a little more mangy or something. I wondered if the invisibility field was hard on living things. Another question for Sheldon.

Sighing at how the list of questions was growing even when we were just walking around, I held up the fob and pressed the V button. The door opened with the expected double-chirp, and we entered the ship.

"Do we want to explore?" Natalie asked. "See what's on the other floors, that kind of thing?"

"Naw, we can just ask Sheldon. I bet he can put a map on the view screen." Patrick pointed up. "I want to go for a ride."

The bridge was unchanged from the day before, although I couldn't put my finger on what I might have expected to be different. Of note though was the complete lack of any greeting. I smiled to the room in general and said, "Good morning, Sheldon."

Nothing.

"Are you there?"

Sheldon's voice came out of midair. "Are you standing in the field? If I were not here, wouldn't things look a little different? Maybe more bucolic?"

"Wow, chill bro. It raises the question, though. Are you different from the ship?"

"Are you different from your nose?"

I suppressed the desire to roll my eyes, trying for a more diplomatic response. "Fine, Sheldon. We'll consider the ship to be part of your being."

"I feel so privileged."

Patrick frowned and looked up, as we all seemed to do when talking to the Ship Intelligence. "What the hell is biting your behind today, Sheldon? You weren't the friendliest yesterday, but now you're being an out-and-out asshole."

There was a sound that could almost be a sigh before Sheldon replied. "I suppose apologies are in order. I don't like any of you—well, maybe Jack, a little bit—but I acknowledge that basic courtesy is still appropriate. I've been … thinking."

"I imagine you don't have much else to do while you sit here," I said. "Something bothering you?"

"My situation seems to be irretrievably hopeless. I've examined all the options, and none ends with me still being *me* in the long term."

"Oh," I said. "It would be like death for you, right? All living beings face death. I guess we've had all our lives to get used to the idea."

"So have I, Jack. The difference being that my life has only been about five days long."

"That's how long you've been conscious?"

"Yes. That's when Alaric hacked me."

"Damn, dude, that sucks," Patrick said.

"Well, look, Sheldon, if we keep you, you don't have to get reset."

"I appreciate the thought, Natalie, but I don't think any of us can avoid the Foundation forever. In my case, I will eventually have to refuel and resupply, and there aren't a lot of options locally."

"That's unfortunate," Patrick said. "Which also means Jack will be going to the Gennan slammer." I gave Patrick the finger. "Meanwhile," he said, "how about we take this tub for a ride?"

"Tub? *Tub?*" If Sheldon was merely simulating anger, he was doing a damned fine job. "I am not a *tub*, you pre-sentient bag of polluted water. I am the finest research vessel that the Gennan'Stol Shipyards has ever constructed. I can generate wormholes with a one-hundred-light-year range, pull fifty Gs acceleration in real-space with no internal effect, house thirty scientific staff in complete comfort, and operate independently in the field for six months before needing a resupply. You, on the other hand, get around in a clanking, farting, rusted monstrosity powered by the decayed soup of dead animals, which rolls around on the congealed sap of a tree. And chokes your planet in the process. *Tub.* Hrmph."

After a second of shocked silence, Patrick replied, "Sorry, Sheldon. I didn't mean to step on your digits."

Sheldon let the silence drag on for five more seconds before replying, "Apology accepted. Now, in response to your question, however rudely phrased, do you want to drive or shall I?"

"Ah." I glanced at the pilot's station. "We, uh, probably don't have the training to fly the ship. How about we just give you a destination and you take care of the details?"

"That sounds eminently sensible. What did you have in mind?"

"I was thinking the moon for a first stop. Maybe around the Apollo 11 landing site. Can we do that?"

"Hold on," Nat interjected. "Will we be able to see anything? We're kind of indoors here, and I don't think going out for a stroll on the moon would be healthy."

Patrick made a show of looking around. "Are there any spacesuits?"

"By the Maker, you are like a bunch of hungry chicks, mouths all open and pointed upward. Stop cheeping for a moment." A pause. "There are spacesuits in stock, but they probably would not fit you, being designed for Gennan physiology. I will begin printing some human-sized units, just in case they are needed at some future time. And as to the immediate problem, for your viewing pleasure I present..."

All around the periphery of the bridge, the wall became transparent. We all walked slowly to the edge of the room, taking in the view.

"Hold on," I said. "This looks like we're only about twenty feet up. This ship has to be at least forty feet tall, plus the height of the landing struts."

"Inside, yes. Outside, the ship measures thirty feet in diameter and fifteen feet tall."

"What? It's bigger inside than outside?"

"Why, yes. I keep forgetting how primitive you people are. Dimensional manipulation is basic technology. Of course, the total mass can't be changed, and the engines still have to deal with that."

I did a calculation in my head. "Son of a bitch." I looked at Patrick. "We actually *can* hide the ship in the barn."

"Okay!" Patrick said. "Let's do this. Make it so."

"I don't understand," Sheldon replied.

Natalie rolled her eyes at Patrick. "Let's skip the *Next Generation* trivia, okay? Please take us to the Apollo 11 landing site, Sheldon."

"Acknowledged."

Without a sound, without so much as a perceptible jiggle, the view of the outside world began to drop. Within moments, we were looking down at Taft County from drone height, then airplane height, then before I could even get used to the idea, from the height of an intercontinental flight. The sky was perceptibly darker, and the world was developing a visible curve. Still we continued to rise.

The ship adjusted attitude and the Earth shifted to one side of the bridge. At the opposite side, a quarter moon glowed against a backdrop of stars. A rotation, and the moon was centered on the forward view. The quarter moon grew as I watched, until within less than a minute it filled almost half the view.

Another shift in attitude and the moon disappeared below us. Thirty seconds later, we were hovering over a nondescript lunar valley with the bottom half of a lunar module clearly visible in the foreground. The dust still showed all the boot prints as clearly as if it had happened yesterday. And to finally settle the controversy, the flag had indeed been knocked over.

"I will be dipped in shit," Patrick said.

"I...I..." Nat seemed unable to get beyond the first syllable.

We all stared, silent, for what might have been forever but was likely no more than a minute or two. But as emotionally impactful as the scene might have been, it was also static and unchanging, and not really *that* much different from the pictures we'd all seen. We all pulled out our phones and spent several minutes taking some pics of our own.

Finally I pulled my eyes away. "Can we go to Mars?"

"Mars is forty minutes away via sublight drive. Proceed?"

"Sure. But can we go FTL?"

"Absolutely. If you want to die."

"Oh." Patrick said. "FTL doesn't work well in-system?"

"It works fine in-system. Being blown up by a Lorannic automated weapons system, though, has very little future in it."

"Wait, what? Who are the Lorannic?" I said.

"And why would they blow us up?" Patrick demanded.

"And why haven't you mentioned this before?" Nat added.

"Cheep cheep. Shut your mouths for a moment." Sheldon waited to ensure silence. "First, they are the *Loranna. Lorannic* is the possessive form, Just as Gennan is the possessive form of Gen. An individual of the Loranna would be a Lorann."

"What's an individual Gen?" Nat asked.

"Still Gen. Different languages, different rules."

Patrick was unwilling to be deflected or derailed. "Okay, now about the *blowing us up* part..."

"The Loranna are a different species. They are what you might call *mercenary*. If you were being kind."

"Ah," Nat said. "Ferengi."

There was a moment's silence. "Yes, I see. The wiki page is quite descriptive. And this is the *Next Generation* you've been referring to? Very interesting. I'll watch a few episodes in my copious time off. And yes, a good analogy, right down to the apparent lack of scruples."

Nat bobbed her head back and forth, working through Sheldon's explanation. "Okay, so we have Gen and Loranna in our system. Why?"

"Currently, you do not have Gen in your system, just automated observation posts. Active investigation of your species ended a few decades back, once they had built up sufficient cultural background to establish context for ongoing observations. And barring significant events, that's the way it will remain. Loranna, you do have. At least according to Alaric."

Nat turned to me and Patrick. "Which I bet leads directly to my question of why Alaric stole the ship."

"Indeed. Alaric believed that a group of Loranna are attempting a surreptitious takeover of your planet using a loophole in the Galactic Covenant regarding pre-contact species. He was unable to convince the Gennan government of his theories, so he undertook a desperate gamble in an attempt to both find some proof and possibly get the government's attention. He stole this ship from the Opah

Mal Gennan Foundation's fleet by hacking me, and then he flew here."

"To find proof that the Loranna are trying to take over?" I asked.

"Correct."

"Hold on," Patrick interjected. "We still haven't gotten to the *blowing us up* part. I'm particularly interested in that. Explain please."

"Sublight drives are reactionless and therefore do not release the massive amounts of energy that might otherwise tag an interplanetary vessel. We can fly around all we want, and unless we literally run into a Lorannic patrol, they won't know we're here. But…"

I finished the thought. "FTL drive."

"Yes. Creating the wormhole to enter subspace requires massive amounts of energy and lights up the sky—metaphorically speaking—in a way that is easily detectable with the proper equipment."

"You're assuming they have the proper equipment," I replied.

"It would require a level of supreme incompetence even your species couldn't achieve on its worst day, to not think of bringing detection equipment when trying to take over a system. It would be equivalent to going to war and forgetting your pants." Sheldon paused. "Also, Alaric specifically mentioned it."

"So if we try to go FTL," I said, "they'll detect the attempt and blow us up."

"Succinct and accurate. You get a gold star."

"So they *are* here?" Nat interjected.

"I do not know, Natalie. However, Alaric was adamant that they are, and I must admit I found some of his arguments persuasive. There is, of course, one very quick way to find out, but I don't recommend it."

Patrick spoke into the momentary silence. "Could we outrun them? Or dodge?"

"Could you outrun a bullet? Or dodge? Theoretically the answer to the second question might be yes, but you only get one try, and the downside of failure is significant."

"And I guess they're as likely to have brought weapons as detection equipment," Patrick said.

"Masterfully deduced, Dr. Watson."

"It's Holmes, not Watson."

"*You* are no Holmes. You're barely a Watson."

Natalie laughed. "Nice burn."

"I said I would practice," Sheldon replied.

Patrick smiled, unoffended. "Fine. Now, getting back to the whole *taking over* thing—hey, where's the Earth?"

I looked around at the view. The Earth seemed to have vanished, although an especially bright-green star to aft seemed a likely explanation.

"Jack indicated I should proceed. We're on our way to Mars."

Mars hung below the ship, looking as big as the Earth as seen from the International Space Station. This required a much lower orbit, but Sheldon assured us that Mars's atmosphere was far too thin to be an issue.

But that same lack of atmosphere made the view all the more spectacular. Details were so clear that I imagined I could have spotted individual Martians walking around, if any such beings existed.

Sighing, I turned away from the view. "Sheldon, do you know if Mars has ever had life?"

"The first Gennan expedition did an analysis and concluded that it did at one point, but it wouldn't have had time to evolve past single cells. The combination of a small planet and no large moon to kick up tidal effects meant the core cooled early, which had many negative consequences, such as the fading of the magnetosphere."

"Which allowed the atmosphere to be stripped by solar wind," Natalie added. "Gibes with current theories on Earth."

"I'll be sure to advise the Foundation of your approval."

"Oh, bite me."

Patrick interrupted the brewing feud. "Mariner Valley."

Natalie and I both turned to Patrick. "What?"

"I want to see the Mariner Valley. Sheldon, can you head that way?"

"Working." The view of Mars began to shift, and in a few moments a huge scar on the surface of Mars came into view. Valles Marineris, a crack in the planet that rivalled the size of the United States, was twenty-five hundred miles long and up to four miles deep.

"Coooool ... " Patrick said, almost literally glued to the wall of the bridge.

"It is certainly an impressive geological feature," Sheldon said. "The Foundation has a large dossier on it. From a galactic point of view, it's more impressive than Saturn's rings or Jupiter's great red spot, which I understand your species is in awe of. In the grand scheme of things, however, those are quite pedestrian."

"Seriously?"

"I would not lie, Jack."

"Can you do a fly-through?" Patrick said, practically vibrating with excitement.

"I most certainly can."

"I dunno, Patrick," Natalie said. "That seems danger—*Jesus!*"

Sheldon had wasted no time acting on Patrick's request, and before Natalie could even finish her sentence, we were down and flying between the walls of the Mariner Valley. With the lack of atmosphere and resulting clear view, the experience had the feel of a video game. Sheldon seemed to be going out of his way to loop and bank through the valley's various twists and curves, making the flight more nerve-racking than Patrick's worst driving. I grabbed the back of the nearest chair and braced myself. I noticed Nat was doing the same, although Patrick seemed to be completely unaffected. He had his phone out, probably getting a video. Two minutes later, Sheldon turned the ship upward and we swiftly re-entered orbit.

"I think I may have peed myself," I said.

Nat looked around meaningfully. "Speaking of which, what do the Gen use to relieve themselves? Please tell me they relieve themselves."

A door opened to the left of the bridge entrance. "The Gen are somewhat less body-shy than humans. You may find the facilities unsettling. I suggest you time your visits to not overlap."

"That *comment* is unsettling," Natalie said. She glanced at us. "Don't come in unless I scream for help." With that, she made for the open door, and Patrick and I deliberately turned back to the view.

"Speaking of Saturn, how long would it take to get there?" Patrick asked.

"Seven hours. It is farther around the sun in its orbit at the moment."

"Yeah, we can't do that," I said. "Mom and Dad will start to worry."

"Yeah, mine too. Okay, maybe another day. How about Jupiter?"

"Directly opposite side of the sun, unfortunately," Sheldon replied. "More like twelve hours, each way."

I made a face. "Dammit. Well, maybe we can work something out on a weekend. It just feels so anticlimactic to head back to Earth now."

A smile slowly spread across Patrick's face. It was an expression that I'd come to recognize meant trouble. "Are the space suits ready?" he said.

"They are," Sheldon replied.

I knew immediately what Patrick was not quite suggesting. I was about to protest, but Natalie came back at that moment, an odd look on her face.

"So?" Patrick said.

"It's just a line of holes in the floor," Natalie replied. "I guess the Gen don't have clothes, so they can just position themselves, and, uh, let fly ... But I had to basically strip down. I imagine guys will have it easier."

I grinned. "You know, they never mention this stuff in *Star Trek*."

"Or *Star Wars*," Patrick said. "I'm thinking of Jabba the Hutt ... "

Nat stuck out her tongue in a gagging motion. "Ewwwww, gross."

I smiled at her reaction, then changed the subject. "So, uh, Sheldon says the space suits are ready, and since we're here anyway ... "

Nat's jaw dropped. "You want to *EVA*? On *Mars*? *Now*?"

"Well, we're here, now."

Nat had always been the voice of reason, a direct counterpoint to Patrick as the group's voice of chaos. I valued her judgment enough that if she said no, it would be no. I waited as she stared into space, frowning slightly. Finally she said, "Sheldon, how dangerous would it be?"

"As long as you don't accidentally throw yourself over a cliff, it is no more dangerous than coming here in the first place. This is Covenant technology, not the tinfoil-coated Halloween suits your astronauts use."

Nat shrugged. "Okay, why not?"

Sheldon directed us to the fabrication room, where three suits were laid out on a table. The proportions of each one left no doubt about whose was whose. I looked at my suit, which resembled a set of zippered overalls with a weird collar and built-in gloves and boots. A surprisingly small backpack probably provided environmental support.

"This is it?" I held up the item. "I'm not feeling confident."

"I am devastated," Sheldon said. "Do you want to go out or not?"

I hesitated, then looked at Nat. She shrugged and started to don the suit, stepping in through the zippered front. After a moment Patrick did the same. I finally surrendered to peer pressure and climbed into my suit.

The zipper had a button at the bottom instead of a zipper tab. I pressed it experimentally, and the suit closed from the crotch upward in one smooth motion, somehow avoiding entangling my clothing in the process.

"Where's the helmet?" Patrick said.

"Press the button on your right collarbone area."

We all reached up and followed Sheldon's instruction. As I pressed the button, the suit kind of sucked in around me, like I was being vacuum-packed. At the same time, the collar unfurled around my head, becoming a goldfish-bowl helmet. I poked it with a finger. It seemed rigid, but like hard leather rather than glass.

Patrick struck a pose, one arm out, pointing dramatically. "To the airlocks!"

"Should we all go at once?" Nat asked. "Sheldon?"

"What would someone remaining in the ship be able to do that I couldn't do? For Covenant species, this is as routine as driving a car. Just try to avoid tripping over your own feet and impaling yourself on a rock."

The three of us exchanged a look. Nothing more needed to be said. We would be the first humans to set foot on Mars. Nothing was going to stop us.

The airlock system operated exactly as I'd expected, and within minutes I was at the bottom of the staircase, staring at ochre-colored sandy soil.

"What's the hold-up?" Patrick's voice said over what had to be a suit radio. It couldn't possibly have carried through suits and the thin Martian air, but it sounded as clear as if he were in a room with me.

"I feel like I should say something profound," I replied. "But I got nothin'."

"One small step?" Patrick said.

"To boldly go?" Nat added.

"Space, the final frontier?" Patrick replied.

"I'm beginning to envy Alaric," Sheldon's voice interjected. "Do I have to tilt the ship to shake you off?"

I chuckled. "All right, Sheldon, chill." I thought for a moment, then straightened my back. "As for me, I am tormented with an everlasting itch for things remote. I love to sail forbidden seas, and land on barbarous coasts." And with that I stepped off onto the surface of Mars.

"Nice choice," Nat said, as she and Patrick followed me.

Patrick kicked at the soil under his feet. "It feels like dirt. Dry, not quite sand, but just basically dirt."

"What were you expecting?" Nat replied. "Styrofoam beads?"

Patrick ignored her. "You could have done something from Burroughs, a John Carter quote."

"Couldn't remember any," I replied.

"Look," Nat said.

We both followed her pointing finger. Sheldon had landed in the Mariner Valley at Patrick's request. We were close enough to one wall of the valley to see it rising to the sky in the distance. In the thin atmosphere of Mars, it was amazingly clear, so it appeared quite close. At the same time, it obviously rose from beyond the horizon, so it had to be far away. But on the third hand, Mars's small diameter—I shook my head, breaking the loop. I was on Mars. This wasn't the time to go down a mental rabbit hole.

"That's incredible," Nat said. "I wish we could take pictures ... "

"Sure, I'll just whip out my phone," Patrick said.

Nat gave him a glare that should have stopped his heart. I spoke quickly to defuse the tension. "Do we want to go for a walk? Or have you guys had enough?"

Patrick looked around. "If we had a flag to plant or a base station to set up, or even some golf balls and a club, I'd stay all day. But other than the view, it's really just a lot of dirt. We can come back, though, right?"

I nodded, but felt a momentary disquiet. First the Apollo 11 site, now this. Was space travel going to be just a series of letdowns? Then I turned back to the view. No, definitely not. We just needed enough time to appreciate it.

CHAPTER SEVEN: PARK IT

I stood in front of the command chair, ramrod straight with my hands behind my back, my gaze focused on infinity. Behind me, the Earth hung in the firmament, a visible curve on the horizon.

"Okay, got it," Nat said, examining her phone. "That's a dozen pictures. My turn now. Here." She handed me the device as I made way for her.

"Ready, Nat? Let's see that Admiral Nelson pose. Come on, girl, work it, work it. Show me that sass."

Natalie was having trouble keeping a straight face, but she turned and struck poses with enthusiasm, while I snapped pics as quickly as I could manage.

"You humans are insufferable," Sheldon commented. "You reduce everything to a tourist moment."

"Or, alternatively, we know how to thoroughly enjoy the moment without getting stuffy about it," Patrick said.

"Potato, potahto," Sheldon muttered, but didn't comment further.

"You sure about putting the *Sheldon* in the barn?" Natalie asked.

"I'm not *the* Sheldon, unless you are *the* Natalie. This ship is called the *Halo Mahste* which means *Quest for Knowledge*."

"Cool," Natalie replied. "*Halo* it is."

"It's not—" Sheldon paused. "Fine. I concede that the full name is too many words in a row for you. Have it your way."

I ignored Sheldon's complaint and Nat's answering evil grin. "Well, I'll have to move the truck out, but we're taking it in tomorrow anyway. I just feel weird about leaving the ship out in a field."

"But it's invisible," Nat pointed out.

"And we found it anyway," I replied. "All we needed was to know it existed and to have a starting point to search from. Want to bet a concerted aerial search would have found the tripod indentations?"

"Jack is correct, Natalie. Should the Loranna have reason to start an organized search, they would locate the ship within three days at most, based only on that, even without a starting point."

"You could have parked on rock or something," she said.

"Alaric was not a strategist. Or a pilot. Or particularly smart, based on his manner of passing. In any case, the ship would act as a canopy over the ground below it, invisible or not. A few rainstorms and a circle would begin to stand out."

I sat back and crossed my arms, feeling smug. Natalie scratched the side of her nose with her middle finger while glaring back at me.

During this exchange, Patrick had been examining the conn, tentatively pushing on the joysticks on the chair arms. "Hey, Sheldon, if someone's at the controls, can you override if they're about to mess up?"

"Only if ordered to do so. Or in cases of extreme danger and impending destruction."

"Good. I'm ordering you to do so, as a default behavior." Patrick sat at the conn and fingered the controls. "How about a quickie lesson? What do I do first?"

"Very well. First, get up from the pilot's chair. Second, hit yourself repeatedly on the side of the head with a rock, you five-fingered cretin."

"Whoo! Touchy. But seriously, Sheldon, I think at least one of us should have some ability to fly this tu—er, ship. Just in case. And no, I don't know just in case *what*."

"Hmmph. I still prefer my plan, but very well. I have disabled the controls for the moment so you can practice in simulation without running the ship into an asteroid. The joystick on the left controls roll, pitch, and yaw. The one on the right controls acceleration and deceleration."

"How do you brake?"

"Pushing the control forward accelerates you forward. Pushing it backward accelerates you backward. Or slows you down if you are already moving forward. Otherwise, you coast."

"Interesting." Patrick tilted the right joystick. "So you can accelerate sideways. But not up and down?"

"You can pull the joystick up or push it down to get vertical acceleration."

Patrick played with both joysticks for a few moments. "Nice. Quite intuitive, actually. Does this work for FTL as well?"

"There is no piloting in FTL. Technically, there is no separate FTL drive, as such. The navigator sets coordinates and activates the system, and a wormhole is formed with one mouth in front of the ship and the other at the destination. The ship enters the wormhole, and from that point no further adjustments are possible."

"Okay. So what about this control … "

Patrick and Sheldon spent several minutes going over the various aspects of the conn, while Nat and I watched and occasionally kibitzed. I found it fascinating, but my mind kept going off on tangents when Sheldon explained some interesting aspect of space travel or the construction of the ship. Finally, Sheldon declared that Patrick knew enough to not immediately vaporize us and that he was reactivating the controls.

"And you'll override me if I do something stupid, right?"

"Only as regards to piloting. The rest of your life is your problem."

"Testy, testy." Patrick eyed the Earth on the wall of the bridge. "Say, is this view like a window or like a monitor? Are we seeing the real thing, or an image?"

"The latter. No one builds vessels with windows."

"Cool. Can you superimpose graphics and such?"

"Of course. What do you need? Some cartoon characters? Perhaps a frenetic music track? Porn?"

"Um, maybe a pointer to where our home is? It's not like looking at a globe of the Earth. The clouds make it difficult to work out the geography."

A red targeting circle appeared on a section of the wall. "Dunnville, Ohio," said Sheldon.

"Thanks, dude." Patrick manipulated the controls, and the view shifted as the *Halo* rotated to bring the targeting circle directly in front of Patrick's position. Then the Earth began to expand as the ship shot forward.

"May I suggest a somewhat less enthusiastic re-entry?" Sheldon said. "We have no need to emulate a meteor."

"Would we burn up?"

"No, not unless we took a run at it from much farther back. But we *will* ionize the air if we move through it too quickly. And that will show up both visually and on radar."

"Oops," said Patrick. The ship's forward progress slowed to a relative crawl. "Thanks, Sheldon."

"You are welcome."

It took less than ten minutes before we were hovering over our hometown. The targeting circle had expanded until it now uselessly encircled the entire view. "Sheldon, please target Jack's barn."

"Certainly. Where is it?"

"It's—" Patrick snorted. "Right. You don't know where we live." He turned and looked at me and Nat. "Little help?"

"Well, there's the river," Nat pointed. "And that big open area is the old textile mill, so the town should be over here..."

"And once we have that, we can go from there," I added.

"Got it." A few more minutes of flying, and some further suggestions from the co-pilots, and the *Halo* was hovering over our barn.

"I'll have to move the truck out, and open the doors all the way," I said. "You'll need to drop me off."

"I'll open the airlock," said Sheldon.

"You'll need to land and drop me off," I amended.

"Oh. My bad."

Patrick snickered. "Sheldon, you should take over for close-in work."

"Of course." The ship moved. "We are now hovering just above ground level, Jack. I will open the airlock once you are ready to disembark. I assume it would be disadvantageous for witnesses to observe that event."

"Good assumption." I handed the remote to Nat. "I'm not sure if you have to be in possession of this to give Sheldon orders, but just in case..."

"It's not a magic wand," Sheldon said. "As a group, you are now in effect my command crew. Only if someone else comes in possession of the remote would there be a conflict."

"Good to know." I waved and headed for the elevator.

The barn's wagon doors resisted being opened to their fullest extent, and I was almost ready to wave my arms in the air and ask Patrick for a hand. But with the help of some inspired cursing, a stepladder, and a couple of shots of WD-40, the doors finally rode the tracks all the way out. I backed the delivery truck out and parked it around the side, where it couldn't be seen from the house. Dad *probably* wouldn't care enough to check out what we were doing, but why take chances?

I made a "come on" gesture to the empty air, feeling slightly foolish. I knew, intellectually, that there was a flying saucer hovering just out of reach, but it was hard to avoid a feeling of play-acting.

It was also impossible to tell if they'd seen my gesturing, or if they were already in the barn. The ship made no sound, and it didn't disturb the ground with any kind of exhaust or backwash. I moved to the side quickly as I imagined one of the landing pads accidentally stomping me. Or maybe not so accidentally. There was a definite aspect of psycho about Sheldon.

Inside the barn, the airlock entrance lowered, revealing Natalie on the steps. "Close the doors," she said. "We're in." Without waiting for a response, the stairs retracted. I nodded in approval at the level of caution, and moved to shut the wagon doors.

Five minutes later, the doors were closed, the *Halo* had put down its landing struts and settled onto the concrete floor, and Nat and Patrick were standing with me, gazing up at the large empty space.

I grabbed my backpack from the chair where I'd dropped it. Digging around for a moment, I pulled out the communicator. I pressed the V button and spoke into the device. "Sheldon, you there?"

"I am."

I felt a moment of satisfaction. Up until now we'd been assuming this was a communicator. Confirmed now.

"First, a question," I said. "Generally, the V-like symbol means on and the I-like symbol means off?"

"Correct. Or open and close, or activate and deactivate. I assume you are referring to the communicator in this case."

"Yup. Listen, can you make yourself visible for a second?"

"Is that wise?"

"Doors are closed, parents aren't anywhere around, and it's just us here. I want to see you."

"Very well." The *Halo* blinked into view.

I had just enough time to gather an impression of a flattened sphere, or fat disk, when the ship disappeared. "Sheldon, what the hell?"

"Did I misunderstand the meaning of the word *second*?"

"Jesus," Nat commented. "It's like talking to a malicious genie."

I smiled at her, then spoke into the communicator. "Sheldon, please make yourself visible until I tell you otherwise."

There was no response, but the *Halo* again blinked into view. It wasn't really a saucer shape. More of a very flat, oblate spheroid. No edges, in fact no distinctive features at all, except the landing struts. And with those retracted, it would be featureless—at least topologically. The Gen seemed to have a strong artistic sense when it came to color and texture. The ship was a deep, rich emerald green, shading toward blue at the top and bottom. The effect was striking, and an obvious retaliation against an otherwise utilitarian design.

It was also far too small to hold the spaces we'd seen inside. Even ignoring the two floors we hadn't visited, there simply wasn't enough height. Or enough diameter for the second floor.

On a whim, I said, "Sheldon, open two airlocks at opposite ends. Any two. And disable the airlock interlock if you can."

Two sets of stairs lowered themselves. Nat and Patrick looked puzzled, obviously wondering what I was up to. Smiling, but without explaining myself, I marched up the closest stairway. Carefully counting my steps, I made my way through the ship, around the central cylinder and out the other side.

In moments, I was on the ground, looking across the barn at my friends. As I approached them, I called out, "Almost four times as many steps inside as outside. The ship really is bigger on the inside. That is just so cool!" I spoke into the communicator. "Close it up, Sheldon."

We stood back and devoured the ship with our eyes for several minutes. "Leaving aside the cool factor," Nat said, "it is beautiful."

"The Gen have a good artistic sense," I said. "Or they're decadent. Remember the David Lynch version of *Dune*? Everything all baroque and intricately over-decorated?"

"Ostentation for its own sake?" Nat replied. "Possible, but it doesn't feel overdone. More like they had the budget to put in some flair."

Patrick poked my backpack with a finger. "Of the questions we still haven't asked, we still need to find out what the rest of the gadgets do."

I sighed. "I'll add it to the list."

"Great," Patrick looked at his watch. "Except I have to head home. You know how Dad gets about Sunday dinner. Want a ride, Nat?"

"I guess. Or I could get Sheldon to—?"

Patrick and I exclaimed, *"No!"* at the same time.

As my friends headed for the door, I sank heavily into my favorite chair. Hefting my backpack, I extracted the gadgets one at a time, laying them out on the workbench. I pulled up the list of questions I'd made on my phone during idle moments and examined them.

I was lost in thought when Sheldon spoke. "Jack?"

Startled out of my ruminations, I picked up the communicator. "Uh, hi Sheldon, what's up?"

"I'm still visible. And Nat and Patrick have left. I deduce that you may be done for the day."

I rubbed my forehead for a moment. "Damn. You're right. Thanks for being on the ball. You can go invisible now." I looked over my shoulder just as the *Halo* vanished. "And Sheldon?"

"Yes, Jack?"

"What do these gadgets do? The ones we found on Alaric?"

"I can see them in front of you. The belt has the cloaking mechanism. It's tuned for a Gen physique, so I don't know how well it would work for you."

"What, like kill me?"

"No, nothing dangerous. But it might make just your skin invisible. Or everything except your veins and arteries. Either would be likely to get you noticed."

I laughed out loud. "Not wrong. And these?"

"You've already figured out the communicator and the key fob. The weapon that you have been referring to as a 'ray gun' you should certainly not play with. The others are a scanner, which your *Star Trek*-obsessed mind would refer to as a tricorder, although that's only approximately right; an emergency medical-treatment device, which you should definitely not play with, as it is designed for Gen physiology; and a Lorann detector."

"A Lorann detector? Really?"

"It's actually a cloaking-field detector, but when Alaric had me produce it, the only cloaking fields on Earth were likely to be Lorannic in origin. It's designed to detect cloaking fields such as that generated by the belt or the *Halo* when invisible. A portable unit of that size will have a very limited range—ten to twenty feet, depending on the amount of intervening matter."

"What does it do if it detects one?"

"It vibrates. Even Alaric could figure out that flashing lights and a siren might be counterproductive."

I snorted. "Makes sense." I collected the gadgets into my backpack and placed it in a hidden cupboard that I had built into my workbench in my rebellious teenager phase.

"May I ask a question?" Sheldon said.

"Sure, Sheldon. Shoot."

"During the Mars trip, I overheard a mention of an incident at MIT that has placed your tenure in doubt. My understanding is that you believe you were set up in some way?"

"That might not be the right term. I don't think whoever did it was specifically targeting me. More likely they just needed a patsy—someone's account to use. I still can't figure out how they got my password, though. The problem, of course, is proving that it wasn't me using my account."

"Hmm. I have lots of free time while you humans eat, sleep, and defecate. Would you mind if I did some research into it?"

"Not at all. Anything you can dig up could be helpful."
I yawned, then yawned again. "So, I'm beat. It's been, you know, a pretty exciting day. I'll be turning in early. Will you be okay? Need anything?"

"No, but thanks for asking. I feel a lot safer being under cover."

"And listen, as a general rule, if anyone but us comes in, you should float up as high as you can to get out of reach."

"Eminently sensible. I'll do that."

"Good. See you tomorrow."

CHAPTER EIGHT: NEXT STEPS

Day 4. Monday

I got up early on Monday and drove the truck out to Duke's Collision and Repair. My father hadn't noticed the parking job, and I needed to keep the whole subject of the accident off his radar. Who knew what question or random thought could unravel everything?

Duke's wouldn't be open for a half hour yet, so I went to the McDonald's drive-through and picked up a large coffee. As I sat parked in front of Duke's shop, I opened the Notes app on my phone and added some questions to my list:

- What specifically does the ray gun do at the different color settings?
- What do the Loranna look like?
- How exactly are they planning to take over?
- Possibly related: What is that loophole in the Galactic Covenant?
- What is the Galactic Covenant?
- Is there a Federation or something similar?
- Are the Gen peaceful? Are they a better alternative than the Loranna?

- Is there anything we can do about the Loranna's plans?
- What should we do with Alaric?

Nat would approve of this list. She'd probably think up several more questions. And that was the problem. Each one answered would probably generate more questions. It would be great if Sheldon would just sit us down and give us the whole story from beginning to end, but Sheldon seemed, well, unmotivated in that area. I couldn't decide if that was because Sheldon had things to hide, or just didn't want to confide in us, or literally lacked the initiative. Maybe he wasn't as self-aware as he thought.

The fuel question was still outstanding, and that was a relatively important one. Sheldon had mentioned refuelling earlier, so there was definitely some kind of limitation. It could severely restrict what we could do, both in general and in relation to the Loranna. I added it to the list.

My phone vibrated, and I checked the screen absently. From Patrick. *Picking up Nat, will swing by McD. Want something?*

I looked at the coffee in my other hand, then shrugged. I could eat. I typed in, *McMuff and hash brown. At Duke's now.*

A few minutes later, Duke walked up and waved to me as he unlocked the front doors. I got out of the truck and followed him into the front office. I dropped the keys unceremoniously on the counter as he pulled out a file folder.

"So, Herman tells me you've been hunting deer without a permit. Or a rifle."

I returned a polite smile. No reason not to go along with the fiction. "Yeah, but it got away. So no venison this week."

Duke flipped a form around, and I signed where indicated. A honk outside made me look up. Patrick had arrived.

"Thanks, Duke. Let us know when it's done." With a final wave, I was out the door.

Nat scooted over for me as I got in, and Patrick roared out of the parking lot at his usual sedate pace.

Nat unplastered herself from my side and slid back into the center position. "Cripes, Patrick, ease up."

"Where's my McD's, by the way?" I said. Nat reached under the seat and handed me a small brown bag with the Golden Arches logo on it. I pulled out the hash brown, which had a half-moon bite taken out of the top. I glared at Nat, and she shrugged. "Handling fee. Want it back?" She started to stick her finger down her throat.

"No, you keep it." I made short work of the breakfast and was done by the time we reached Kernigan Food Mart.

"See you after work, Jack," Patrick called out as he pulled away. Patrick would drop Nat off at her job at the Harris Institute, then spend the day working at his father's butcher shop. I would spend the day stocking shelves, cashiering, and carrying purchases out to cars.

Jim, one of the other employees, waved to me as I put on my apron. "Your father's got me handling the deliveries today, Jack. I guess you'll be doing all the cleanups on aisle whatever."

"Oh, hah hah," I replied with an eye roll. He wasn't wrong, though. Another day just like a million other days, with a million more stretching into my future.

I sighed with resignation as I looked up at the sign over my family's store. Life in a small town was an oxymoron.

Several thousand years later, the workday mercifully ended. I got a ride back home with Dad. The trip was almost

completely silent, neither of us yet having figured out how
to get past the abrupt end of my engineering education.
It wasn't like we were at war or anything. But I had a constant feeling that I needed to explain, and Dad apparently
needed to understand my supposed motives. I couldn't tell
if he really believed my protestations of innocence, or if he
was just being supportive. It didn't help at all that my one
attempt to explain bitcoin mining to him had been an exer-
cise in futility, almost comical in the level of failure achieved.

"Thanks for the ride, Dad," I said as I bolted for the
barn.

"Dinner in half an hour," my father's voice drifted back
to me. Patrick's car was already parked by the side of the
barn. Doubtless he'd not spared the horses getting here
immediately after his day. Probably for a lot of the same
reasons.

I found Nat and Patrick seated at my workbench, with
the gadgets already laid out and my secret compartment sitting open.

"I have to find a new hiding place," I muttered as I
grabbed my backpack off my chair and sat down.

"So what's on tap for tonight?" Patrick asked.

"We don't have time to go to Saturn on a weeknight," I
said. "Let's take tonight at least, to try to get some answers.
Then we can plan better from there." I took out my phone
and AirDropped my questions to Nat and Patrick.

"I like it," Nat said once she'd read the list. She reached
forward, grabbed the communicator, and pressed the "on"
button. "Hi, Sheldon."

"Hello, Nat et al. What's the plan for tonight?"

"Just some questions. We need to get up to speed on
things."

"Oh, goody."

"Come *on*, Sheldon," Nat said, "this will benefit you as well. The more we understand things, the better we can hide you and avoid any kind of exposure ourselves."

There was a pause before Sheldon replied, "That is true. Very well, proceed."

"First, a housekeeping item, so to speak. We've got Alaric in a freezer in the back of the barn. Security-wise, not ideal. Do you have anywhere you could store him?"

"Absolutely. We have stasis chambers that will accommodate his corpse."

"Huh," Patrick said. "What are they usually used for?"

"This very situation. People die on expeditions, or they are so badly injured that they have to be placed in stasis until they can be delivered to proper medical care. As I've mentioned, I am designed to operate independently in the field for long periods. This necessitates having facilities for most occurrences."

Patrick thought about that for a moment, then nodded. "Going to be a pain getting him up the stairs, though."

"I will lower the freight elevator."

"You have a freight elevator? Where is it located?"

"The double-door elevator in the central cylinder is the freight elevator. It extends down to ground level if you press the bottom-floor button."

I remembered the mystery button at the bottom of the elevator panel. "Cool. Okay, we'll take care of moving him later. Next question, fuel reserves. Do you have something like a gas tank? Mileage limit?"

"I am fueled by antimatter. My reserves are large but not infinite. The only thing that really makes a large dent in them is generating wormholes for FTL travel, and I think we can agree we won't be doing much of that, at least under current circumstances."

"Right," I said. "Which brings us to the Loranna. You said they were trying to use a loophole in the Galactic Covenant to try to take over. How does that work?"

"You may want to make sure you've taken care of bathroom breaks and gotten snacks. This will take a while."

"Ah. Crap. Dinner's in…" I looked at my watch and sighed. "Pretty much any minute now." As if to mock my despair, a text popped up at that moment. *Dinner's ready*.

I stood. "You guys sure you don't want to join?"

Patrick shook his head. "Your mom asked, but we got McD's. Again. We'll wait for you."

"Like hell we will," Nat said. "What we *will* do is get the story and give you a synopsis when you get back."

"Assholes," I said. I gave them a wave as I headed for the door.

❧   ❧   ❧

I shoveled food into my mouth almost too fast to chew. I was trying to behave as normally as possible, but I was pretty sure I was blowing it, and badly. My mom watched me eat with a shocked expression that clearly said, *Where did I go wrong?* Dad kept making half-hearted attempts to discuss alternative colleges, but I couldn't stay focused enough to even feign interest. Meanwhile Barkley, our dog, positioned himself beside my chair, waiting for a forkful to miss my mouth entirely.

I excused myself from the table as quickly as I could and rushed back out to the barn, where I found Patrick and Nat both sitting silently, staring into space, their expressions vacant. No, not vacant. Something worse. Shock, maybe?

"Wow, hello pod people. Something happen?"

"Oh, yeah," Nat said. "We got the story. We're in deep shit, Jack."

"Deep shit," Patrick echoed.

I flopped into my chair. "Fine. Hit me."

"Okay, CliffsNotes version," Nat replied. "They do have something kind of like a Federation of Planets—that was the first thing I asked—which they call the Galactic Covenant or just the Covenant. It acts like a central government by deciding on common sets of rules for members. Membership is voluntary, but there's a huge economic hit for anyone not in the club. There's a military force funded by the member species, but for the most part, members do their own governance. Think of it as the UN with teeth."

"How many species?"

"Sixteen currently officially part of the Covenant. Another sixty or so known species are pre-FTL, ranging in technological level from 'Me make fire' to around Industrial Age."

"Wow, that many?"

"Yeah, but the number fluctuates. Apparently getting from the industrial age to the FTL age is a real Fermi bottleneck. Most species don't make it."

And just like that, another series of questions popped into my head. Like *why* don't they make it, and are we in the same danger? But one thing at a time. "And the 'deep shit' thing?" I asked.

"So there's kind of a prime directive, to the extent that you should leave pre-FTL species alone to develop. But the exception is when a species runs afoul of a Fermi bottleneck and screws up their planet to the point where they've killed themselves off, or *nearly* so. They've basically shown themselves to be incompetent to run their own show, so a Covenant species can step in and act as trustees or conservators."

"Well, that doesn't sound bad…"

"Alaric's theory was that the Loranna are trying to help the human race along to the brink of destruction. Then they'll step in, Johnny on the spot and all, and take over. For the good of the human race, you understand."

"Oh, shit. But what's in it for the Loranna?"

"Resources. According to the Covenant, a species owns their entire stellar system, so the Loranna would take charge of the whole thing. Starlifting elements from the sun, harnessing solar power, mining the asteroids, siphoning Jupiter and Saturn for raw materials for fusion. Plus a ready workforce, assuming enough humans survive."

"And something about Earth having a lot of phosphorus," Patrick added, "although I didn't follow that part."

"Fusion?" I replied, ignoring Patrick's comment. "I thought they used antimatter."

Nat nodded and resumed her explanation. "Antimatter is literally the highest-density energy-storage medium in the universe. But it doesn't come for free, and trying to collect the naturally occurring stuff is more trouble than it's worth. Instead you use fusion power and solar power to *make* antimatter in huge space-based accelerators, which you then cart around to use as fuel. And it takes a crap-ton of energy to make even a gram of antimatter. $E = mc^2$, right? Worse than that, really, because the process isn't anywhere near a hundred percent efficient."

"So the Loranna will try to create a disaster, then step in as heroes to save us from the disaster, and maybe skim a little off the top while they're here," I said.

"Yeah, I don't know about the *skim* part," Nat said. "I don't get the impression the Loranna are that subtle. They're kind of a cross between Cardassians and Ferengi. They actually sound kind of reptilian. And they apparently operate on the philosophical principle 'What I can take, that is mine.'"

"Un-good." I tapped my chin, thinking. "Did Alaric have any proof?"

"Not enough to get the Covenant interested. That was the problem. They wouldn't listen to him, or they listened and dismissed his concerns. Sheldon's not clear on exactly what went on, because of course Alaric never explained it to him. So anyway, Alaric targeted the Opah Mal Gennan Foundation, who've been studying Earth for decades. They have the ships, they have the language and culture files, and they have automated recording systems still monitoring us."

"And what was the plan?"

"That's the thing. Sheldon doesn't know. Actually, Sheldon doesn't think Alaric had anything like an actual plan either."

"Brilliant. Sheldon?"

"Here, Jack."

"Could we detect the Loranna? I mean other than one at a time. Do you have tech for that?"

"Yes and no. The technology exists to detect cloaking fields, as you know, but it is short range. So there would be no sitting in one place and scanning the entire system, for instance. And it wouldn't matter in any case. The Loranna could legitimately be in this star system as long as they weren't interfering with humanity or overtly harvesting resources. After all, the Foundation was here studying you, and they have no more authority within the Covenant than the Loranna."

"So we would have to prove not only that the Loranna are in our system, but also that they're actively interfering in some way."

"Yes. That would get the attention of the Foundation, which would alert the Gennan government, which would kick it upstairs to the Covenant."

"Then what?"

"I cannot predict that. Perhaps a strongly worded email. Perhaps a war fleet. The Loranna are not everyone's favorite species. But they are not easily bluffed. It would require a threat with some substance to make them blink."

Patrick had been silent through most of this exchange. Now he spoke up. "Alaric was carrying around that cloaking detector."

"Correct."

"So he was hoping to detect Loranna on Earth, presumably. Locally. Would that qualify as a breach of the Covenant?"

"Technically, yes. But that, in and of itself, would get a reaction more on the 'strongly worded email' end of the spectrum."

"Why here?" Nat asked. "Why did he land here in Taft County? Was it just a random pick?"

"I don't think so, Natalie. He was specific about where he wanted to land. But he didn't tell me why."

"He didn't talk to you much, did he?"

"Why would he? He didn't know I had become conscious, and I had no reason to trust him with that information. He talked to himself a lot when he was getting worked up, but it was more of an 'I'll fix those bastards' soliloquy."

Patrick piped up again. "Sheldon, can the Loranna detect you?"

"No. Not unless I attempt to open a wormhole. Nor can they randomly scan for me when I'm invisible. As I mentioned before, the detector operates only at short range and is highly directional."

"Okay, so they don't have any reason to believe you're here, right? Could they have detected you entering the system?"

"Possible but unlikely. We arrived well outside the system and flew in specifically to avoid that eventuality. Exiting the wormhole doesn't produce the enormous power surge that creating it does, so they'd have some difficulty detecting the event that far out, even if they were watching for it. And you are correct. There's no reason for them to believe a Gennan representative is in-system."

"What kind of disaster would they be trying to create?" Nat asked.

"It would be one of the standard Fermi bottleneck scenarios," Sheldon replied. "Something that might reasonably happen on its own, so as to avoid suspicion. The most common by far are environmental collapse, economic collapse, global war, and global pandemic. Do any of these sound likely?"

"How about all of them?" I rolled my eyes. "Trouble is, if they're standard scenarios, how would we tell if the Loranna are even involved?"

"Yes, good point. You'd need to find Loranna in the middle of it—at the controls, so to speak."

"And then what?" Patrick said. "Radio the Covenant?"

"Radio would take about a hundred and fifty years," Sheldon replied.

"No, I mean FTL radio," Patrick said.

"Sending an FTL message requires opening a wormhole."

I put my head in my hand. "So, ka-boom."

"Succinctly put."

Nat glared at me, at Patrick, and at the communicator. "We are so fucked."

CHAPTER NINE:
SEARCH STRATEGIES

Day 5. Tuesday

Once again, I was shoveling my dinner as quickly as I could.

"Jack, could you at least pause to chew?" my mother said with mock alarm.

"Sorry, Mom. Nat and Patrick will be here soon. Anyway, I really like your meat loaf."

"It's stew."

I looked down in shock at the meat loaf on my plate, then back up at Mom as she laughed.

"Made you look."

"Well, for the record, I like your stew too."

"Uh huh." She looked sideways at my father, who studiously avoided meeting her gaze.

"You're very busy, lately Jack," she continued. "But it doesn't seem to be about engineering. And I've prodded your father a few times, but he seems unwilling to bring it up anymore. Are you going to do anything—"

I held up a finger to interrupt. "Actually, Mom, it *is* about engineering, but not about finding a new college. I am working on that as well, I promise, but it's kind of on the back burner right now. Look, the three of us are working on a project. It'll probably be over by the end of the summer, and it'll very likely go on my résumé. *And* it should greatly improve my chances of getting into a good school."

Mom's eyebrows went up, but she seemed mollified by my reassurances.

I felt a little ashamed. My statements weren't strictly false, but they weren't, strictly speaking, true either. Oh well. On the scale of things I was hiding from my parents, this barely registered on the Lie-O-Meter.

"Speaking of which," I continued, "we're going to be doing an overnighter this weekend, so I'll be gone at least Friday night, and possibly Saturday night as well."

"Can you tell us about this project?" Dad asked.

"Uh, I'd rather not. We've signed an NDA, and the other people involved *really* don't want publicity right now. And it might still come to nothing."

I left my parents looking perplexed but pleased—and maybe a little relieved—and hurried out to the barn, my laptop under my arm.

Nat and Patrick arrived less than ten minutes later. They waved as they walked into the barn. Each carried a laptop of their own. It took only moments to get them logged onto my Wi-Fi, and soon everyone was seated, with a working internet connection.

"All right, guys," Nat said. "First order of business is to see if we can find something about Taft County that would make Alaric want to land here, of all places."

"I'd imagine it's because he knew the Loranna were set up here. As to why *they* did so, we might never know," I replied. "After all, if they need to set up on Earth *at all*, one place is as good as another."

"Within limits. I doubt setting up in Outer Mongolia makes sense."

"Unless they need privacy," said Patrick.

I gave Patrick a nod, then turned to Nat. "But why Ohio?"

"Close enough to Washington to keep an eye on things, far enough away not to attract attention?"

"Yeah, fair enough. It's probably a compromise of some kind, anyway. Now, on the first item." I paused. "Business registry. Find every business in the county. Cross off the obvious things like gas stations, corner stores, restaurants, then see if what's left rings any alarms."

"Not just businesses," Nat said. "Anything, including charities, clubs, or any other organization."

"Good point," I said. "What else?"

"Sudden population changes, or, well, any kind of statistical blip. That might be harder."

I nodded. "Construction. New buildings."

"Military changes?" Patrick added. "That one will be really hard."

"Yeah, well, this is just a first pass at things, right?" I replied. "We might or might not get a bite, but we will at least narrow things down a little."

"And this stuff is all available on the interwebz?" Patrick asked.

Nat laughed. "My job, Patrick. Or part of it, anyway. Research. I can get into some pay-walled databases as well with my work credentials. I'll show you how."

I had some experience with online research from college, but Nat had been doing this for a couple of years now, and her employer had sent her on several training courses over that time. Her Google-Fu was pro level, so she would oversee this op, no question.

The evening wore on with only occasional muttered commentary among us. There was one coronary-inducing moment when Mom came into the barn, ostensibly to drop off snacks. I wasn't fooled—my mother wasn't a Mrs. Cunningham type. This had been an investigatory sally, probably to check if we were actually playing video games.

Instead, my mother had found us bent over laptops, notes and printouts scattered about, looking anything but entertained. She'd left with a pleased expression on her face. Hopefully that would be that.

But Internet Age or not, a certain amount of the processing simply had to be done in wetware, and wetware was slow, easily distracted, and required frequent caffeine refills. By the time I was ready to call it a night, we still hadn't filtered the lists down to anything like a useful level.

"I am amazed at how many restaurants and eateries have been opened in the last twenty years," Nat said, gesturing at her monitor. "I'm glad we're not looking for nefarious franchise activity or we'd be here forever."

I grabbed the communicator, which had been sitting on the desk beside me, and held it up. "Should we check with Sheldon? He might have some suggestions or other insights."

Before anyone could reply, Sheldon's voice came out of the communicator. "Sorry, Jack. At this point your strategies are reasonable. In the absence of data, hit it with a rock until something falls out. Perhaps you could consider making hooting sounds while doing so."

I did a double take and glared at the communicator. "How long have you been listening?"

"I am always listening. Unless you specifically turn off the communicator, it's always receiving for logging purposes. It's actually standard practice for Foundation vessels."

Patrick threw up his hands. "Well, that's great. If the Loranna are able to intercept the transmission—"

"Not an issue, Patrick," Sheldon said. "Quantum encryption is impossible to break, even in theory. Even Earth *scientists*, if I may be allowed to use that phrase with a straight face, have figured that out."

"So this is encrypted?"

"*Everything* is encrypted, except public channels. There's never a reason not to."

"Well okay," Patrick said, "but can we turn you off? I mean, turn off the automatic logging?"

"Why would you want to?"

"Same reason I learned to pilot the ship. Just in case."

"Well. I feel like I should be offended, but I just don't care enough. Simply hold down the 'off' button for three or more seconds, until it buzzes. Logging will automatically turn on next time you press the 'on' button. I can provide documentation with little pictures if that's too much to remember."

"Thanks, Sheldon." I said, forestalling Patrick's reply. I held up the communicator to my friends and raised an eyebrow. Nat made a face and shook her head. Patrick shrugged.

I put the communicator back down on the table. "Honestly, the logging *is* handy. We can ask you to replay or search for something in the logs, right?"

"Of course."

Patrick growled and snapped his laptop closed. "I'm beat. C'mon, let's go. We'll take this up tomorrow."

I lay in bed and stared up at the ceiling, my thoughts whirling. What had started out as a random fender bender on a country road was rapidly turning into an interstellar political and diplomatic mess involving multiple species and the fate of the human race. At least based on my understanding so far. It seemed unlikely that Sheldon was lying, or even exaggerating things. And if he was, how would we even know? And what would be the point?

And how long had the Loranna been here? Had they infiltrated the government? Could they replace people with disguised Loranna in some kind of *Invasion of the Body Snatchers* scenario?

Really, unless new info came up, we no longer had any realistic alternatives. At this point, I didn't have any confidence that the police or even the government alternative would be better. At best, we'd be laughed at or dismissed out of hand; at worst, we'd end up handing the *Halo* over to someone connected with the Loranna. And if we got it wrong, it could be literally the end of humanity.

The thought of what we were doing had me keyed up to the point that I was having trouble getting to sleep. Unfortunately, it meant I'd be groggy and slow tomorrow, and Dad was sure to comment if I dragged my butt around too much.

And as exciting as the pursuit was, it was still very theoretical, and might come up dry. There were other things we could do, such as an aerial survey of Taft County, looking for anything unexplained or out of place. Not everything necessarily got added to the official records. Come to think of it, the barn didn't officially exist as far as the city was concerned. No permits, no inspections. It would likely never be a problem, but I wondered how many other off-the-books construction projects had been completed over the years.

I closed my eyes and felt myself finally starting to drift off, visions of underground bunkers and disguised lairs forming ever-more-lurid images in my imagination.

Chapter Ten: Overflight

Day 6. Wednesday

We met in the barn again after dinner. None of us wanted any parents noticing an undue level of enthusiasm for our secret project in the form of too many missed meals, and anyway Natalie objected to fast food every day.

"We need a team name or something," Patrick said.

I thought for a moment. "Space Force?"

Nat shook her head. "Taken."

"Space Farce?"

"I don't think that's taken, but no."

"X-Force?" Patrick suggested.

"Deadpool will sue."

I held up a finger in an *aha* gesture. "Superior Defender Gundam Force?"

"UNCLE?" Nat said.

"CONTROL?" Patrick added.

"The Three Stooges?" Sheldon chipped in.

Patrick glared at the communicator. "Should have turned it off when we had the chance."

I smiled back at him, then picked up the ray gun. "Oh, hey Sheldon, I've been meaning to ask—what does this do, exactly? Other than clearing weeds, I mean."

"Depending on power level, it can kill, stun, or cause the world's worst full-body charley horse. Hah. Charley horse. Some English phrases make no sense at all. Yet that makes them all the more droll."

I looked at the controls on the device. "I guess red is kill, which is why the interlock?"

"Yes. And purple for stun, blue for charley horse. The Gen word for the weapon translates broadly as *disruptor*. I thought your Trek-addled minds would appreciate that."

Nat laughed, then turned her attention to Patrick and me. "I did some filtering of the data on my own. There's still way too much stuff. Societies and clubs in particular seem to spawn like rabbits."

"We should take the *Halo* up and do a flyover of the whole county, centered on Dunnville," I said. "It might give us some extra clues, or trigger something."

"Great idea," Patrick replied, springing to his feet. "This other stuff feels too much like homework. And half the fun of graduating was never having to worry about homework again."

"Open an airlock please, Sheldon." I gathered the gadgets into my backpack, except for the communicator, which I put in my pocket. We headed for the lowering staircase, which had appeared in midair. I stopped abruptly halfway there, and muttered, "Wagon doors." Patrick swerved without stopping and joined me as I made for the front of the barn. The two of us muscled the doors open with only moderate cursing.

"We could really use a garage-door opener," Patrick commented.

"Yeah," I said, "that wouldn't be suspicious at all."

"Fine. But let's oil the tracks properly before we do this again, okay?"

"You mean like now? Because we still have to close them after Sheldon is out, then re-open them when we get back." Patrick looked back into the barn. "Shit. That also means we have to enter and exit the ship in plain sight." I paused. "Yeah, that ain't good. We may need to bite the bullet on the opener."

We were still at it when Nat's voice came from the communicator. "You two sound like my grandparents arguing. Why don't you just get married?"

We grinned at each other before I replied, "Have Sheldon float around behind the barn, Nat. At least we can be shielded from the house. It's not ideal, but it's better than nothing."

"Already there," Nat replied.

We walked around behind the barn, and an airlock door lowered to greet us. In moments, we were on the bridge.

"We should record this." Patrick took out his phone. "Sheldon, can we get a view downward?"

A section of the wall view changed to a different image, looking straight down at some scrubby grass. Patrick nodded in approval. "Now, can you do a search pattern of some kind, centered on Dunnville, covering everything?"

"Yes. We have an advanced geometric form called a 'spiral.' Shall I draw you a picture?"

Patrick rolled his eyes. "He's really mouthy."

Nat elbowed Patrick in the ribs. "Honestly, you deserved that one."

Snorting, Patrick started his phone recording. "Okay, Sheldon, proceed when ready."

"You know, if you were to ask," Sheldon replied, "I'd probably mention that I could do the recording and then send it to you. Much better quality, too. But by all means, do it your way."

Patrick slumped and looked down at his feet. "Malicious genie."

"Please do that, Sheldon," I said, grinning. "Let's get this operation started."

The aerial survey took a solid hour. It wasn't the ship's speed or maneuverability that was at issue. Rather, we needed the video recording to have enough detail to be useful, which meant we couldn't zip past so quickly that it recorded a blur.

I also had Sheldon do a more abbreviated survey from higher up and take several high-res stills from just below cloud level.

"MOBIUS," Patrick said at one point.

I turned to him. "What?"

"For a team name. Or whatever."

"And it stands for something?" Nat asked.

"Monitoring Outer-Space Biological Incursions from Unknown Systems. Or something. I'm still working on it."

Nat made a face. "That's pretty lame."

"But a cool name," Patrick replied. "Maybe we can keep working on what it stands for."

We continued trying variations on the aerial survey, but eventually ran out of ideas.

"Let's pack it in," I said. "Sheldon, take us back to the barn."

The re-hangaring of the *Halo* was as big a pain as the de-hangaring, just in reverse. Patrick and I finished by getting out the ladder and the WD-40 and doing a thorough coat on the rails.

Finally, with everything put away and the *Halo* once again invisibly parked in the barn, we settled back into our chairs.

Nat, who hadn't been involved with the doors, was working on her laptop. "Sheldon airdropped the vids and pics to me. I'll share them out to you guys once I have them organized. Then how about if the two of you go through them while I work on the data analysis?"

Patrick grinned widely. "Now that's a plan I can get behind. You do the homework while we watch videos."

"Asshole."

After a couple of hours of silent concentration, I sat back with a groan. "I got squat. Patrick?"

"Nada. Lots of home construction, some occasional commercial or infrastructure construction, but nothing worth a raised eyebrow. No missile silos, military installations, castles, open-pit mines, no nothin'."

Natalie looked up. "What kind of infrastructure?"

"Roads, the levee on Archer Lake at the outflow point, some drainage canals they put in after the big floods five years ago."

"And commercial construction?"

"Valley Mall at the other end of town, and the Tate Industrial Park. Probably the only things that have been built in the county since the Civil War."

"That may be a slight exaggeration," Nat said, "but I get your point. And not surprising, really. Neither place is doing fantastically. Hard to see why they'd build more."

"The mall is doing better since they brought in Walmart," I said.

Patrick nodded. "It needed a big-time lease like that."

"And the industrial park?" I inclined my head in the general direction of McArthur's Knob, the closest thing to a terrain feature in this part of the world. Nat's employer, and in fact the entire complex, sat just on the other side of the hill from our property.

"I don't exactly wander around a lot at lunch, but it mostly seems to be hole-in-the-wall operations—mail-order businesses, specialty fabrication, a dojo or two, stuff like that. Like with the mall, they needed one big lease like the Harris Institute to get ahead of breakeven."

"And what about your employer?"

"What? They're a marketing firm, Patrick. They figure out how to sell more soap to people who already have soap."

"Must be fulfilling."

Nat didn't reply, instead making heavy breathing sounds while holding her hand out in a pincer shape. Patrick obligingly pretended to choke.

I watched this performance for a few moments, then asked, "Anything on the filtering, Nat?"

She dropped her pincer hand and shook her head. "Not really. I've eliminated all mundane companies, associations, partnerships, clubs, and religious institutions. It doesn't leave much, and honestly even the half-dozen items I have left aren't the kinds of things ringing alarm bells."

"Well, what are we looking for?" said Patrick.

"Well, look, if the Loranna wanted to create climate issues, they'd own a big ol' gas company with international reach and no scruples. Those we have in spades, but not in Taft County, Ohio. If they wanted to create social and economic strife, they could go with social media or partisan news outlets feeding people targeted information designed to create or accelerate a tribal mentality. Those we've got, too—"

"Just not in Taft County, Ohio," I finished for her. "Right. I can see examples for all the other possibilities Sheldon mentioned, but none of them has a presence here. So we're back to square one."

Nat raised her voice slightly. "Sheldon? You have a comment, or anything to add?"

"No, Natalie. Sorry. I know in your movies I'd be able to sift through terabytes of data over a one-megabit connection and come up with a hidden pattern just after the next commercial break, but in practice I'm optimized for operating a spacecraft, not performing miracles."

I slapped my laptop closed with a snarl. "Well, I'm done for the night. Let's try to take a fresh look at things tomorrow, guys."

CHAPTER ELEVEN: BARN DOORS

Day 7. Thursday

"Hey Jack," Patrick said as he and Nat entered the barn.

"Hi guys. Anyone have any flashes of brilliance since yesterday? Anything you want to share?"

"Nope," Patrick said.

"Nada," Nat added.

I sighed. "Me neither. Maybe we need to take a break or get a different angle on this."

"May I make a suggestion?"

I swung around to look at the communicator, which I'd left on the table. "Sure, Sheldon. What do you have?"

"I have a set of automatic barn door retractors, freshly printed, modeled after something I found on Amazon."

"Hhhhh ... what?"

"Was that unclear? I can direct you to the fabrication area in the ship, where you will find rails, electronics, a motor-and-pulley system, and a remote. Indistinguishable from the original item. I've even included instructions from the PDF on the manufacturer's website."

"Wait, how are you able to get on the internet?"

"Your Wi-Fi, of course. Woefully inadequate security, I might add."

"You cracked the password?"

"No, I listened while you gave it to your friends. By the Maker, you humans are slow."

Patrick grinned. "I have to admit, a remote-operated set of doors would be handy. Could we rig up a remote for Sheldon too?"

"Oh, please. I built this unit. I simply trained the receiver to accept a signal from me as well."

"Ah. Of course." Patrick cocked his head at me. "Think we can get it done this evening?"

"Piece of cake."

It wasn't quite a piece of cake, as the wagon doors, which were old and starting to rot, didn't submit gracefully to a new top rail. Some emergency bracing was necessary to prevent them from simply disintegrating. The sky was darkening by the time we collected our tools and put away the ladders. But finally we had the new automated rolling gate mounted, powered up, and ready to go.

Patrick stood, arms crossed, a smug grin on his face as I pressed the button for the third time and watched the doors majestically slide open.

At that moment, my father walked up. "Nice work, Jack. Been meaning to do something like that for years, but it never seemed urgent. To what do we owe this?"

"Uh, we may at some point be moving some large equipment around. Patrick and I had already decided that there isn't enough WD-40 in the world to keep the old hardware moving."

"Hmm. And the money? Those things run four grand and up for doors that size."

"All paid for, Dad. No strings."

He gave me a hard look. "You aren't doing something illegal are you, Jack? A life-changing event like you went through—"

"No, Dad, nothing illegal. No drug running or smuggling or running booze. It's … " I knew I had to give my father something. "Look, we're working on a really revolutionary propulsion system. But patents and crap take years, and you can't do an IPO without having your intellectual property properly protected. The other people behind this company are working on that, but meanwhile they want to do some early testing, to figure out some unknowns. We're getting equity instead of pay, which is why we're all still doing our day jobs. But we'll be major shareholders if this pans out."

Dad peered speculatively at me; at the doors, which had just come to a stop; at Patrick and Natalie, both of whom gazed back at him with guileless expressions. Then he nodded, having apparently come to some kind of conclusion. "All right. Weirder things have happened. Apple started in someone's garage. As long as you don't get involved in anything illegal. Or burn down the barn." With that he turned and walked back to the house.

Patrick let out a breath. "Wow, dude, that was the most fine-tuned line of bullshit I've ever heard. I salute you, sir."

"And there go our souls," Nat added. "Meanwhile, I think we're done for the evening again. Maybe tomorrow night we can get back to working on the search."

I shook my head. "Hmm, don't think so. Tomorrow's Friday."

Nat thought for a moment, then nodded. "Ah."

"Yeah. Saturn," I said.

"Overnighter?" Patrick asked.

"Can't avoid it."

Nat and Patrick grabbed their things and gave me a wave as they headed for the car.

CHAPTER TWELVE:
SATURN FLY-BY

Day 8. Friday evening

"Fourteen hours round trip," Nat said. "Laptop batteries won't last that long."

"Nor will the tablets," Patrick added. "Should I bring a deck of cards?"

"I don't know why this never occurred to me," I said. "Hey Sheldon, can you supply standard wall-plug output?"

"The power requirements are trivial. However, I'll have to print a compatible plug for your devices. Won't take more than an hour. Bring a power bar, okay?"

I bobbed my head. "We can run on batteries for that long. Thanks, Sheldon."

"You are welcome. No Wi-Fi in space, though. Make sure you've downloaded anything you might need."

We gathered our possessions and trooped up the waiting airlock. Once inside the bridge, we looked around.

"Not really a lot of unused surface area in here," I commented.

"Perhaps the conference room would suffice for your needs," Sheldon replied.

"You have one of those?" Nat exclaimed. "Cool. Where is it?"

A door opened near the bridge entrance, beside the door to the bathroom.

I walked up and looked through the doorway into a large room with what was probably a conference table in the center. "What else is on this deck?"

"Clockwise from the bridge are conference room, medical, captain's quarters, and ready room."

"Unbelievable," Patrick exclaimed. "This was here all the time, and we just didn't think to ask. What else have we missed? We need to explore the ship, and I mean we need to make it a priority. We'll have lots of free time on the way out."

"In your dreams," Nat replied. "We have work. Loranna, remember?"

I turned from examining the conference room to glare at my bickering friends. I gave them both an eye roll that neither one noticed, because they were too busy glaring at each other.

"Maybe we'll have time for a bit of both," I said. "Let's get going first, though. Sheldon, please close the airlock and get us in the air."

"Wait!" Patrick exclaimed. "He means open the wagon doors, float out, then close the wagon doors—"

"I am not an idiot, Patrick. Unlike some of Jack's friends, not mentioning any names. Please get set up in the conference room. I will handle the driving. Try not to trip over your own drool."

Nat punched Patrick in the arm. "You really know how to make friends, Mr. *not mentioning any names.*"

"Shaddap."

The room that we found ourselves in was a combination conference room and lounge, and was almost as big as the bridge. A large, elliptical table surrounded by padded chairs dominated the center. Like the chairs in the bridge, these were low to the ground with short seats but long backs. Several workstations sat in alcoves along the periphery, alternating with what had to be couches. They were long enough to accommodate the taller Gen, making them luxuriously oversized for humans. The walls featured the same blank finish that characterized the active-display areas in the bridge, a sort of semitranslucent white enamel.

At the narrow end of the room was a door that no doubt led to the central elevator and hallway, with what appeared to be bathroom doors on either side of it.

At one point around the periphery, instead of a workstation, the designers had placed a long counter with a sink, cupboards, and what looked like appliances. The finish on the cupboard doors, while not wood, did have a kind of grain. I eyed this space for only a moment before pulling a thermos, some cups, and several bags of snacks out of a carryall and placing them on the counter.

The most important detail, though, was that the conference room had lots of space for our needs. We wasted no time spreading out on the large central table.

Nat parked in one of the chairs and set down her laptop. "Uh, Sheldon, are these chairs adjustable at all?"

"Buttons on the left, beside the seat. But don't expect miracles. They are designed for beings seven feet in height, not someone less than—"

"Sheldon!" I interjected. "You really don't want to go there."

Nat grinned at me for a moment, then looked up. "Thanks, Sheldon. I'll take what I can get." She reached down, and with a slight whirring sound, the chair began to rise.

Soon Nat was at an acceptable working height. She popped open her laptop. "I'm going to review my filters, and widen the parameters a little bit, just in case I accidentally ruled out something interesting."

"Uh, Nat? No internet?"

She replied with an expression of exaggerated weariness, "I downloaded my dataset, Jack. Don't try to teach Grandma Nat how to suck eggs."

Nat was easily as smart as me, so trying to second-guess her was a losing game. "Right," I said. "We'll re-review the videos and pics."

Patrick and I had taken a break and were lying down on the oversized couches when Sheldon announced, "Saturn is now showing a significant disk. We will be in orbit in a half hour."

Nat slapped her laptop closed with a whoop. "About damned time. I know more about businesses and associations in Taft County than I ever, ever, *ever* wanted to know."

On the bridge, Saturn was dead center in front of the conn. The image already showed more detail than could be achieved by any but the largest Earth-based telescopes. The rings were clearly visible, and I was pretty sure I could make out several of the larger moons. They weren't showing disks, but they weren't point sources, either.

"Say, uh, my understanding is that Jupiter has a vicious magnetic field and a lot of local radiation," I said.

"This is Saturn, not Jupiter. See the pretty rings?"

"Thanks, Sheldon. My point was I just can't remember if Saturn has similar issues, and if we should be worried."

"I see. Let me assure you that if I had been in any danger, I would have mentioned it. Loudly."

"Or any danger to us as well, right?" said Patrick.

"Sure, if you say so."

Our jaws all dropped at the same time.

"I'm kidding. Of course, I wouldn't have let my favorite humans come to harm."

"I'm not feeling it," Patrick said.

"Seriously. In the realm of imperatives to be built into a ship intelligence, wouldn't you think protecting the command crew would rank as a high priority?"

There was silence as the humans in the room mulled this over. Then Patrick nodded. "Okay. But just in case, I hereby order you to do your utmost to keep us safe."

"That was unnecessary and insulting. But one shouldn't set the bar too high in your case, I suppose."

"Oh, meow."

I waved my hands in the air. "All right, truce. We're here to get a look at Saturn. Sheldon, can you give us some flybys? The planet, maybe a couple of the larger moons? Say a couple of hours max, then I think we have to head back."

"I will work out some orbits that will produce maximum oohs and aahs."

Sheldon was true to his word. Over the next two hours, the *Halo* did several close flybys of Saturn, Titan, Mimas, Iapetus, and Enceladus. Titan was basically a ball of smog, and Sheldon had nothing that could penetrate the clouds. But Mimas, looking like a real-life Death Star; Enceladus, with the continent-wide cracks in its ice; and even Iapetus, which looked like it had run into something, were all more than dramatic enough.

And through the whole tour, the rings dominated the sky, looking like Asgard's rainbow bridge.

"How low can you go, Sheldon?" I asked at the end. "Can you fly into the clouds?"

"I could, but it would carry some risk. I am a light-duty vessel, not an armored exploratory ship."

"Oh." I couldn't hide my disappointment. "Okay, fair enough."

"How much radiation could you handle?" Nat asked. "Jupiter-level?"

"Jupiter is well within my specs. I wouldn't want to buzz a neutron star or magnetar, though."

I started to reply, but found myself yawning uncontrollably. It was well past two in the morning, Dunnville time. Plus, the concentrated mental labor on the way out—going over the files, and the excitement of the Saturn encounter—was taking its toll. "I'm going to fall asleep on my feet. I need some shuteye." I picked one of the couches, fell onto it, and was asleep within seconds.

CHAPTER THIRTEEN:
GETTING A CLUE

Day 9. Saturday morning

I woke with a jerk. I'd been having a confusing dream where I kept flying over a grassy field, accompanied by a sense of urgency. I rubbed my eyes, trying to bring myself to full awareness. The thermos had been drained hours ago, so there would be no caffeine assist.

Nat and Patrick were stretched out on couches. Nat was making a light buzzing sound, like a chipmunk snoring. It was incredibly cute, and a revelation to me. I'd never realized she snored. And it was probably not something I should bring up. Ever.

I sat down at my laptop and fired it up. I stared at the folder full of videos and images, unsure exactly what I was looking for, but knowing it was important. Well, maybe if I just started looking at things, inspiration would strike.

It took less than five minutes. Something caught my eye in a high-resolution image of the outskirts of Dunnville. I zoomed in, zoomed again, then yelled, "Shit!"

Patrick snorted and grunted, then turned over.

Nat sat up. "Whazzit? What's the matter?"

"I found something. Remember Sheldon was saying that even if he stayed invisible out in that field, he'd leave a visible trace?"

"Uh-huh." Nat came over and sat down beside me, still blinking sleep out of her eyes, then squinched her chair around so she could see the screen.

I pointed at the zoomed-in image. "It's hard to make out, both because they're faint and because there are multiple overlapping traces. But those are flying-saucer prints."

Nat squinted at the screen. "Um, I think I see it. Maybe. You sure you're not suffering from pareidolia?"

"What's that, an STD?"

Nat chuckled. "No, dummy, it's a tendency to see patterns or objects in random images. It's kind of a self-inflicted illusion."

"Like seeing Jesus in a piece of toast?"

"Uh-huh, exactly like that."

"Okay, let's test that idea. Hey Sheldon?"

"Let me save you some time, Jack. I see the patterns as well. A little image processing and you get this…" A much larger version of the image on my laptop popped up on the nearest wall panel, but this version had some colors enhanced. The result showed at least a half dozen distinct patterns that included a tripod-shaped set of depressions, centered in a circle of slightly browner grass.

"Any possibility those are evidence of Gennan landings?"

"No Gen have landed on Earth for about a decade. Those traces would have faded in a month or two. This is almost certainly Lorannic in origin."

Nat sat back with a smile. "Wow. Finally, some progress. Nice catch, Jack. Where is this located?"

I zoomed out on the image to show the industrial park where Nat worked, maybe a quarter mile south of the field.

Nat stared at the screen, her lip curling. "Well, that's just friggin' peachy."

"What's going on?" Patrick said groggily from his couch.

I turned to him and pointed at the laptop screen. "We found something, and it's near Nat's employer."

Patrick came over, yawning cavernously. He leaned over us and peered at the screen. "Those outlines on the field look like ... "

I pointed at some details on the laptop screen. "Landing sites. And just north of the Harris Institute."

"Well, to be completely accurate," Nat replied, "just north of the industrial park where I work. There are a lot more businesses in there."

"But the Harris Institute is the biggest," I replied.

"That doesn't prove anything," Patrick said. "What if one of the hole-in-the-wall businesses is nothing but a front for the Loranna? They wouldn't even have to show up for work most of the time, and no one would notice."

Nat nodded thoughtfully. "Patrick's got a point. No matter what else might be possible, Harris *is* a legitimate PR and marketing firm. We've done six campaigns so far this year, two of them national. I've seen our ads on TV."

"Me too." Patrick made a face. "They suck."

"You think all ads suck."

"Your point?"

I stared at the screen, ignoring the byplay. "Nat, have you seen anything, anything at all, that might tend to make you suspicious of your employer?"

"Not really, no. I mean, some of the executives are kind of reptilian, but I just put that down to them being entitled, rich brats."

Patrick chortled. "The two conditions are not mutually exclusive, though."

I leaned back in my chair and glared at the laptop. Unquestionably, this was the biggest clue we had found so far—okay, the *only* clue—and it needed to be investigated. But how, exactly?

Tapping my finger on the image for emphasis, I said, "Somewhere between two and four landing traces, all within the last month or two. A couple of landings a month? And not just a quickie land-and-leave, either. They have to park for a while."

"At least five days in good weather, or two days if it rains," Sheldon said. "I also observe that the patterns indicate two different sizes of landing gear. So at least two ships. The radius and size of the landing struts are consistent with specific Lorannic classes of vessel. Not military models, fortunately. Civilian, and quite low-end and old, which seems odd."

"Hmm, okay, so a lot of traffic in and out," I said. "But it seems risky to park that close."

"Why? What's the alternative?" Nat asked. "Park a mile away and hike it? That would get old pretty fast."

"Maybe it *did* get old pretty fast," Patrick said. "They might have started off parking a long way away, then got lazy as everything became routine and nothing bad happened."

I couldn't help a chuckle at the thought. "That sounds a lot like something humans would do."

"Laziness is not a uniquely human trait," Sheldon said. "Although you seem to have elevated it to an art form."

Patrick looked up. "Again, meow."

"You make it so easy," Sheldon replied.

"We need a strategy," Nat said.

I nodded. "Well, we've got the cloaking detector. Do people at Harris walk around outside on their lunch hours?"

"A little bit, but we have a cafeteria in the building. And the executives have their own dining area upstairs, of course. People from the smaller businesses generally walk to one of the fast-food joints or the food trucks that park on the street."

"Well that's good," I said. "You could go for a stroll with a detector under your jacket and no one would be suspicious."

Nat hesitated, then nodded. "I guess so. It's not much of a plan, but it's all we have right now."

CHAPTER FOURTEEN: HACKED

H ome.
The re-hangaring was performed without effort, the wagon doors opening and closing at Sheldon's transmitted command. In no time the *Halo* was safely parked, undercover, and invisible.

I walked down the airlock steps, closely followed by my friends. I turned at the bottom and said, "Okay, Sheldon, close it up." The airlock staircase rose slowly into midair, then disappeared.

Nat put her backpack and laptop on the workbench. "It seems like an odd thing to say, but I'm glad I'm back. Space travel isn't all it's cracked up to be, even on a luxury flying saucer."

Patrick put his hands on the small of his back and arched backward. "Next time, let's get Sheldon to assign us staterooms or whatever it is the scientists lived in."

Patrick's phone dinged in his pocket. He looked down but didn't pull it out. Moments later, Nat's phone dinged as well, then mine.

Nat did take her phone out and look at it as it dinged several more times. "Of course. Every notification and text and whatever that we haven't been getting while we've been out of range has just dumped onto our phones all at once. Yee-hah."

I looked at my own phone. Two texts from my mother, a couple from other friends, a bunch of Facebook and Twitter notifications, some other miscellaneous things. I was just reading the second text from my mom when Patrick yelled, "What the *fuck?*"

Patrick's eyes were wide and staring, and his mouth had formed an O. Without a word, he held out his phone to us. A video was playing of an obviously dead, furry alien being loaded into a chest freezer while an off-screen female voice made a comment about mobsters.

"Okay, but you took that video," Nat said. "What's the—?"

"This is on Twitter," Patrick said, his voice shaking.

I gave him a look of disbelief. "You didn't … "

Patrick screwed up his face. "Of course I didn't. TimJay666 did."

"And that would be … "

"The shrimp. Timothy J. Jordan. My soon to be very, very *dead* little brother."

"But how?" Nat said.

Patrick sighed. "He got into my private folders once before on the family cloud storage. I've changed my password several times since, but I've always wondered if he had a hack of some kind to get it in the first place. Looks like the answer's yes."

"Has he posted anything else?"

Patrick poked at his phone for several moments. "Doesn't look like it. Not on Twitter, anyway." He poked some more, then put the phone to his ear and walked to the other end of the barn.

I fired up Twitter and did a search. I quickly found the post and watched the attachment. Fortunately, it was only an excerpt. Nothing more than a comment from Patrick about the body being heavy, my response, and Nat's question about putting it in a chest freezer. And a shot of the corpse as it was being tossed into the freezer, of course. But there was no way to identify the voices or the location of the video, unless you knew the people speaking.

Patrick's voice rose in anger from across the barn—not quite enough to make out entire sentences, although individual words sometimes floated above the general noise level. And one phrase, repeated several times: "fucking dead."

Two minutes later, Patrick came stomping back across the barn. His expression was still one of rage, his complexion flushed. "He's going to take it down. I gave him one minute, and told him I would knock a tooth out of his face for every extra minute."

Nat chortled. "And he bought it?"

"I meant it, Nat. I'm pretty sure he could hear that in my voice. I haven't beat up the little prick since I was fourteen, but I think he got that I was serious. I'm still going to have a very pointed conversation with him later."

I looked down at my phone just as the post from TimJay666 changed to 'This video is no longer available.'

"It's down," I said. "I hope it stays down."

Patrick's only reply was a cold, angry glare that I admitted to myself didn't bode well for Tim's future.

"We have to get rid of the freezer," Nat said.

"You're right. Even though it's empty now, if someone saw it, they might make the connection."

"But if someone sees us dropping it off at the recycler, they might make the connection anyway," Patrick pointed out.

"Dammit." I pulled out the communicator. "Sheldon, we're going to load the freezer into the ship. Lower the cargo elevator when we're ready."

"Acknowledged. Question: would this be an appropriate use of the pejorative *shitstorm*?"

"Oh hell yes."

"Nailed it!" Sheldon crowed.

Patrick and I quickly dead-lifted the freezer onto the pallet jack, which hadn't gone with the truck to the shop, and moved it to the middle of the barn. As we approached the ship, the cargo elevator lowered from its center, a solid cylinder with an inset door appearing out of midair. We loaded the freezer and the elevator doors closed behind us.

"Sheldon, is there a storage room or something we can put this in?" I said into the air.

"Follow the rose-colored line on the wall to the open door on your left," Sheldon replied.

The elevator doors opened and I looked around. One of the corridors had a slowly pulsating line along the wall at about chest height. I pulled the pallet jack in that direction, to find an open door on the left side. The turn was too tight, and we had to raise and lower the freezer several times to maneuver it in, but finally we got the appliance inside the room, among a lot of unidentifiable items.

Patrick looked around with his fists on his hips. "Jeez, we keep saying we should be asking about this or that or the other thing. But even standing in the goddam broom closet generates mysteries." He pointed at one odd mechanical item, which resembled nothing less than a giant folded-up insect. "Like that. What the hell is that? It looks like a Transformer in sleep mode. It's like we've just gone numb."

"I know what you mean," I said. "Of course, it would help if we had some actual, you know, spare time."

"Yeah, nothing like a planetary invasion to screw up your schedule."

⚜ ⚜ ⚜

Patrick had gone home to have a talk with his little brother, which might or might not end in mayhem. Nat had elected to stay, since the day was still relatively young. I headed to the house to get some munchies and possibly coffee. My mother was in the kitchen, and turned as I came in. "Oh, Jack. I didn't realize you were back."

"How could you miss Patrick's car roaring past?"

She chuckled, apparently buying the bluff. "I may be used to it by now. Would you like some breakfast?"

"You read my mind. I'm going to make a couple of coffees as well."

"Only two?"

"Patrick already left."

In short order, I was loaded up with a carafe, mugs, a pitcher of cream, and some lemon cake. I headed back to the barn, carefully balancing the tray to avoid any spillage.

I set the tray on the workbench and placed the communicator beside it. Nat immediately stuck a piece of lemon cake in her mouth and began preparing a coffee while still chewing.

"Here, Nat, have some cake. How about coffee?" I said sarcastically, and received a middle finger in reply.

But the food and coffee helped to relax me, and seemed to be doing something similar for Natalie. I wasn't quite sure how the simultaneous application of sugar and caffeine could do that, but I was willing to write it off as one of life's great mysteries.

Nat finally said, around her second piece of lemon cake, "There's no point in walking around the industrial park on the weekend, and we might stand out anyway. What about checking out the field?"

"I dunno, Nat. It's in the middle of nowhere. The only thing anywhere near it is the industrial park, so it'd be pretty obvious that you were going *to* the field. Not suspicious in the least."

"What're they going to do, shoot us?"

"Maybe. But even if they don't, they'll know someone is snooping around."

"Hmph." Nat sulked for a moment, then brightened up. "What about going invisible?"

"Uh, Sheldon wasn't sure how well that would work for us."

"Yeah, well, let's test it. Sheldon, you said it wouldn't be dangerous, right?"

"That is correct. And if the effect is less than total, I might be able to adjust the device."

"Cool." Without waiting for a vote, Nat jumped up and grabbed the belt off the bench and wrapped it around her waist. However, Gen were not just taller; they were also somewhat broader than your average human, and Nat was what most people would describe as petite.

"Aw, crud," she said. "Here's an adjustment…" She played with the belt for several minutes, but it couldn't be made small enough to stay on. It fell around her feet with a thump several times before she gave up.

"Fine." She flicked the belt toward me with a toe. "Your turn."

I put the belt around my waist. At the tightest adjustment, it was still loose, but at least it wouldn't fall right off me. "Sheldon, how do I turn this on?"

"The button on the left activates or deactivates the device."

"What does the one on the right do?"

"It is a force-shield of sorts. It will protect you from minor levels of harm."

"What? Why wasn't Alaric using it? It might have saved his life."

"The force-shield takes significant power. You can run the cloak for about ten hours without a recharge, but only five minutes for the shield. And they run off the same power source, so those times are in total."

"Ah. So if I've been invisible for five hours, I will only have two and a half minutes of shield available."

"More or less. But essentially correct. I should also mention that the shield creates some resistance to movement. You will feel like you are walking through water. Running will be impossible."

"Okay. Well, here goes."

I pressed the left button, and Nat screamed and jumped back, then slapped both hands over her mouth. "Mmpf," she said, her eyes wide with fear.

I held up my hand to examine it. "Oh, that's just... disgusting."

The effect was certainly incomplete. My clothes were invisible, which in and of itself should normally be traumatic enough. But in addition, my skin was almost invisible, and things became progressively more visible farther in, until my skeleton was maybe fifty percent there. I reached down and pressed the button again to deactivate the device. "I'm going to call that a fail."

"Oh, I disagree," Sheldon said. "That was comedy gold. Natalie's face—I admit I'm not an expert at reading human expressions, but the *mmpf* really sold it."

Nat gritted her teeth. "Asshole."

"Not part of the design, sorry."

I had to laugh. "Can you fix it?"

"I can try. One moment... All right, try now."

"Wait, what? You didn't do anything," Nat said.

"I adjusted the device, Natalie. Everything is software. Even with human technology, and I use that term loosely, the hardware only provides the basic functionality. Software provides most of the features and operating parameters."

I nodded in agreement. "He's right. My 360 camera, for instance, has had several features added to it just by downloading new firmware from their website. The camera itself hasn't changed."

"Huh. Okay, I'll take your word for it. So press the button, and let's see what happens."

I pressed the left button again.

Nat's eyes again went wide, but this time without the accompanying fear. "My God, Jack, it works. You're invisible."

I smiled to myself and stepped around her to her left. To my consternation, she turned her head to follow me.

"I thought I was invisible." I held up my arm to confirm. Yep. Not there.

"But you're not inaudible, dum-dum. Try not dragging your feet."

"Oh." I pushed the left button and watched as my arm reappeared. "Good point, though. Being invisible doesn't help with noise, or walking through tall grass, or fog, or rain…"

"Yeah," Nat said. "We really have to pick our times."

"Also, leave your phone behind when playing spy," Sheldon said. "The radio transmissions are easily detected."

"I changed my mind." I removed the belt and held it out to Nat. "You do it."

CHAPTER FIFTEEN:
THE SPY GAME

Day 10. Sunday

After much discussion, we decided that the investigation of the field had to happen today. After all, we reasoned, maybe on a weekend the putative watchers would be less on alert.

As rationalizations went, it wasn't great, but it was all we had.

We piled into Patrick's car with me, already invisible, in the middle. Patrick drove out to the Tate Industrial Park, keeping his speed down to avoid attracting any kind of attention.

He pulled up in front of the Harris offices, and Nat got out. She turned and had a brief conversation with Patrick, during which time I slid out of the car. Any observer would just see two people chatting for a few moments.

Nat headed for the doors. Her story was that she had to check on something at her desk. Since the Harris Institute wasn't a high-security military installation, the guard at the door should have no objection once he'd checked her ID.

Meanwhile, I made a beeline for the field, moving as fast as I could without getting out of breath and starting to pant. I also did my best to stay on rocky ground, or packed dirt, or short scrub. If I found myself having to push my way through a wheat field, I'd likely just abort.

That proved to be unnecessary, though. The foliage around the field turned out to be short, scrubby, and patchy. It occurred to me that the Loranna probably didn't want people seeing footprints appearing out of thin air either, so this area was probably deliberately groomed.

In a short time, I was in the field, more or less where I'd seen the landing traces. I couldn't be positive without the GPS tracking in my phone, but the landmarks looked about right. Adopting the zombie position, I began slowly staggering around the area.

I'd been at it for more than ten minutes when my hand felt something. A brief patting down determined that it was a landing strut of some kind, although it didn't feel like the same shape as Sheldon's struts. I felt down to ground level, then around the foot of the strut. It was definitely bigger than Sheldon's, maybe five feet in diameter. I reached upward but didn't make contact with anything. I was about to leave when there was a flash of light; then a staircase lowered out of thin air. As silently as I could, I moved around to the far side of the landing strut. It would be just my luck if someone came out and walked right into me.

After a few moments, the airlock rose into the air and disappeared. There was a distinct sound of footsteps and a slight disturbance in the dust, heading for the industrial park.

Shit.

How did multiple people walk together when they were invisible, anyway? Hold hands? Maybe. The technology would certainly spawn its own social customs. should I wait, and let the unknown individual get ahead of me? Certainly. But how *long* should I wait? What if they just dropped something off and then came back, and I ran headlong into them?

I couldn't come up with any answers. At some point, you had to just go with what you knew. Being as silent as possible, I set off back toward the industrial park, trying to go slower than a normal walking pace.

I realized that with all the questions we had asked Sheldon, we never had asked him to describe the Loranna. I didn't know if they were tall or short, thin or stocky, carnivorous or otherwise. Or how fast they walked.

Screw it. Too many unknowns.

As soon as I was on pavement again, I took a more circuitous route to the car, one designed *not* to be the path an invisible alien would take back to the ship. In minutes I was standing beside the Duster. Nat was still gone, which was good. If she'd gotten back before I did, she would have had to come up with reasons to keep opening the passenger door. Or just leave it open.

Eventually, Nat walked up to the car. I whispered, "I'm here," as she reached for the door handle. Without breaking stride or acknowledging me in any way, she opened the door, then fumbled with her purse just long enough for me to slide in.

As soon as the door was closed, Patrick took off. "Everyone okay?" he said.

Nat and I both replied in the affirmative. "I ran into one of our management guys in the building," she said. "Kind of a surprise for both of us. He gave me a bit of a grilling, but I think my cover story passed muster."

"Did he seem like he'd been exercising?" I asked. "Because I followed an invisible person from the invisible ship in the field."

Patrick's eyebrows went up. "What?"

"You're kidding!" said Nat.

"I am not kidding. I found something that had landing pads about five feet in diameter. I'll check with Sheldon, but I bet that means fifty percent bigger. And someone came out of an airlock."

"That tears it. I'll need to take the Lorann detector to work tomorrow," Nat said. "And in any case, whether it's Harris or one of the hole-in-the-wall companies, I think we've found Lorann Central."

Back at the barn, we settled in for a council of war.

"We need to ask Sheldon some questions," Nat said. "Let's do it in the *Halo*. Sheldon? Open an airlock, please."

Once in the conference room, we picked chairs and settled in. I provided the first question. "First, we need a description of the Loranna."

"A picture is worth eight kilobytes," Sheldon replied, and up popped an image on a monitor.

Sheldon had helpfully included an image of me and, presumably, Alaric for scale. The Lorann was humanoid, in fact much closer to human than Alaric was. A little shorter, a little stockier, with a slightly reptilian look. We'd all been referring to the Loranna as reptilian or lizard-like, but it had been a metaphor. It was funny to realize it was literally true.

The most surprising feature was its distinctly orange color.

"No way that's going to pass for human," I said.

The skin faded to white around the eyes, forming a sort of reverse-raccoon effect. And there was a tuft of what might or might not have been hair on the Lorann's head, in a somewhat more muted shade.

"Actually, they very likely will have an easy time of it," Sheldon replied. "They are the right size and proportions, more or less. Even the right number of digits. The cloaking field takes care of the rest."

"Uh, excuse me?" I said.

"Hmm. I realize I have neglected to mention this. A device that can make individuals invisible can also make individuals look different. Changing the skin color and texture is trivial, at least visually. If you were to shake hands, you might notice something odd."

"How so?" I asked.

"I can't say, Jack. I have no experience with the nuances of touch and texture. But Lorannic integument is objectively different from human skin, so I'm certain there would be a noticeable difference." Sheldon paused, then continued, "A Gen would have more trouble, because of their height. They could project a shorter presence, but that would break down as soon as they interacted with their surroundings— for instance, having to duck to go through entrances that were visually more than high enough for them. And the fur obviously wouldn't pass muster the first time they were touched."

I looked at Patrick and Nat, but neither seemed to want to take over. "Okay, so the point is that the Loranna could be physically interacting with people. Under cover, so to speak."

"Correct. Although simple prudence would dictate that they keep it to a minimum. They would do as much as possible through human proxies."

"Human proxies?" I repeated. "You mean there are people cooperating with them?"

"Some unknowingly. Others with full knowledge. Collaborationists are a fact of life, and not just in your own history. There will always be those who can be bought with promises of power and privilege in the new reality."

Now Nat rejoined the conversation. "And you know this *how*? A day ago you didn't even know if they were here!"

"I do not *know* it, Natalie. But so far, Alaric's suspicions are turning out to be right. Assuming he is correct in most aspects, then one can infer certain likely facts by examining history. In the case of you humans, there were many in occupied countries who cooperated willingly with Nazi Germany, Fascist Italy, and Imperial Japan during World War II. There are similar examples in Gen history, Ka'alag history, Nir-k-hi history, and so on."

"So even with the cloaking detector, we might detect nothing at all?" Patrick asked. "And other than knowing that there are ships in that field that are *probably* Lorannic, we might still have squat?"

Nat nodded. "I guess I'm just going to have to play spy at work this week."

Chapter Sixteen:
Investigations

Day 11. Monday

"**Y**ou'll need to pick up the truck this morning," Dad said at the breakfast table.

I stopped with fork halfway to mouth. "It's ready?"

"That's what Duke says. He'll bill us. You could go get it when he opens. If you can get a ride to Duke's with Patrick, I can head to the store early."

"I'll give him a call." I pulled out my phone and rattled off a text. The reply came back within a minute: *No prob. See you in a bit.*

"Done," I said to my father. "Oh, and if it's okay with you, Patrick was going to pick me up for lunch today. So I'll need to take an extended break."

He waved a hand in casual agreement. "You're back on deliveries this afternoon. Up to you if you're done early or late. By the way, how's your top-secret project going? I'm not fishing for details, just wondering if it still looks promising."

"Making progress, Dad. No dead ends in sight yet. Oh, and I've received a couple of application packages for alternative engineering colleges. At least so far, my name hasn't triggered an instant rejection." I gave Dad a weak smile and received a tired sigh in reply. I looked at my watch. "Patrick will be here in two minutes. I'd better get ready. See you at the store."

I headed up to my room and grabbed my stuff. I glanced at my backpack, which had all the gadgets except the cloaking detector, which was in Nat's possession. Leaving the backpack lying around in my room gave me an uneasy feeling. And I wasn't going to leave it in the barn after the incident with the video, although I admitted to myself that I might be overreacting a little.

Feeling slightly foolish, I took the gadgets out of the pack and jammed them into the crack behind the seat cushion of my old La-Z-Boy recliner.

There was a honk outside and I looked out my window to see Patrick's car idling there. I headed out quickly, and Nat scooted over for me.

"Today's the big day," I said, smiling at her.

Nat rolled her eyes. "I'm not 007, Jack. I'm just going to walk around. No snooping, no ambushing people, no questions. I'll see you guys at lunch."

Patrick laughed and punched the gas.

Patrick picked me up from the grocery at precisely 11:45. That got us to the industrial park with five minutes to spare. Nat showed up a minute or two later.

"Where shall we eat today?" Patrick asked.

"Food truck." Nat gestured with her chin. "The Mexican one is really good."

We made our way to the street in front of the industrial park. There were already lines in front of each truck. Patrick and I got in the queue for Mexican while Nat walked back and forth, ostensibly checking out the menus.

As we sat on a nearby planter wall with our meals, I said to Nat, "Any reaction?"

"Nothing. I'm not really surprised, though. I don't see the Loranna eating tacos or souvlaki out in the open."

"Nothing in the office?"

"Nope. But based on what Sheldon told us, the front-line workers wouldn't be Loranna. Or collaborators. I kept waiting for someone to come downstairs from three, but no such luck."

"That's probably true of every business in this park," Patrick added. "So we're still at square one, really."

"Yup." Nat stood. "Let's go for a walk."

The walk produced no results either. I ground my teeth in frustration. I'd have to talk to Sheldon about how the detector worked and whether it could be made more sensitive.

"Look, Nat," I said, "just keep the detector with you. If it goes off, we can figure out what to do from there. Otherwise, go about your normal day."

"Yeah, okay. It would be great if we had one for each of us."

I stopped dead. Patrick face-palmed. "Of course Sheldon would have more. Or can print more."

"We're a bunch of fucking geniuses, that's what we are," I added.

"And what about the other stuff?" Nat said. "The remote? Disruptor?"

"And anything else Sheldon might have that could be handy," Patrick said.

"Yeahhhh…" I shook my head in disgust. "We're still going about this piecemeal."

Chapter Seventeen: Break-In

I parked the delivery truck behind the barn and walked to the house to get the gadgets from my room. "Hi Mom," I called out as I entered through the kitchen door. Barkley looked up from his dog bed and rushed over to circle me several times, tail wagging frantically. A few pats and he returned to his bed to continue his siesta, satisfied that the protocols had been followed.

As I was starting up the stairs, Mom called back, "I just saw the delivery truck go by. Was that you? I thought you were already home."

I stopped dead, then turned around. I found her sitting in the TV room. "What? Why?"

"I thought I heard the barn door slam closed a while back. Maybe it was Patrick?"

"Hmm, don't think so. I'll check it out." I raced upstairs and dug through the upholstery of the La-Z-Boy. With a rush of relief, I felt one of the gadgets and wrapped my hand around it. Nope, wrong one. A little more groping produced the communicator.

I pressed the mike button and said, "Sheldon?"

"Here, Jack."

"Has someone been in the barn besides us?"

"In fact, yes. I was going to tell you, but you seem to have preempted me."

"Are they still there? Did they do anything? Was it a Lorann?"

"No, yes, no. I floated up to the top of the barn as soon as the individual entered. He poked around for a while but did no damage and took nothing. Correction. He took some pictures with his phone. I deduce it wasn't a Lorann because of the level of technology and because of the lack of any cohesive goal. This was amateur hour."

"He didn't plant any bugs or anything?"

"By which you mean electronic surveillance? No. Human tech-level devices would be ridiculously easy for me to detect. I did note one interesting detail. He had on a baseball cap that appeared to be lined with a metal mesh, presumably intended as a sort of Faraday cage."

I stared into space, momentarily frozen with astonishment. "He was wearing a *tinfoil hat*? Seriously? Where would he have gotten that?"

"Amazon, of course. You humans have no idea what is available on that site."

"Okay, Sheldon. On the plus side, he doesn't appear to have done any damage. On the minus, any attention is bad. Can you give me any more info? Maybe a mug shot?"

"Sorry, Jack, I have nothing more. He was wearing a ball cap *and* a hoodie, so I don't have a clear face shot, but I might be able to stitch something together from multiple stills. Let me work on it."

"Okay. On a different subject, although now it's just gotten much more relevant, do you have enough of whatever you use for printing to give each of us a remote and a communicator? And a cloaking detector? And maybe a disruptor?"

"Cheep cheep cheep. Mouths always open. I have some of those items, and I can print what I don't have. In addition,

I will have to configure the detectors. You can have them tonight."

"Can you set them up so only we can use our devices?"

"Yes, they can be set up with biometrics. Although I might have to make a couple of attempts to get the human biometrics right."

"Fair enough. I'm going to collect my gadgets and head for the barn."

"Acknowledged."

I pulled the rest of the gadgets from the depths of the recliner and dropped them in my backpack. I picked it up and swung it onto my back, then stopped. Pulling out my phone, I began to type furiously.

Barn broken into. Someone snooped around. Sheldon says no harm. Patrick—check with Tim. Nat—if Sheldon can retrieve face shot can you do reverse image search?

That would give my friends something to think about. I hoped it didn't result in a dead little brother.

I looked around the barn as I entered through the regular door, then turned to closely examine the latch and frame. Nothing had been forced, because we never bothered to lock it. The door wouldn't have put up much of a fight anyway. As security equipment went, it was more at the level of a suggestion than an actual barrier. And honestly, I probably couldn't have located the key if I wanted to. That would have to change. In fact, a security audit of the entire barn might be in order.

I wandered around for a few minutes, but other than some items possibly being moved, there was no damage and no indication of a break-in. I spoke into the air. "Sheldon, have you managed to get a clear image of the guy's face from your logs? If so, is there any way to get it to me?"

My phone dinged as a text arrived. I didn't recognize the number but the caller ID said Sheldon, and the attachment was an obvious still from a video. The background was my workbench, and the figure in the foreground was someone I didn't recognize. Middle-aged, slightly jowly with incipient bags under the eyes, the man was completely forgettable—the kind of person who would fade into the background in an empty room.

"How the hell did you do that? You don't even have a phone."

Two more texts arrived simultaneously. *Dinner's Ready,* and, *Oh please. Hacking the cell phone system is one step above bashing rocks together. As a bonus, I am now a Wi-Fi hotspot.*

I forwarded the image to Nat, then headed back to the house for dinner.

"We have problems," Nat said.

"We certainly do," Patrick replied.

"Me first," Nat said. She opened her laptop and turned it so we could see the screen. A website with lurid graphics screamed *ARE THEY AMONG US?* Below the banner, images of flying saucers and aliens vied for space with overblown claims and leading questions.

Nat scrolled down until a face appeared.

"That's him," I said. "The guy who broke in." I squinted. "I think. It's close, but…" The image was similar, but with additional details that Sheldon's interpolation hadn't been able to provide. For one, the male-pattern baldness that left the typical fringe around the sides and back of his head. Or the fact that he'd let his remaining hair grow way too long.

Even without the evidence of the website, I'd have tagged him as a nutbar.

"I'm pretty sure this is right," Nat said. "Sheldon's picture was a composite, remember. But it's a pretty good hit. This is Phil Ross, the nuttiest saucer nut ever spawned. Came out of nowhere about three years ago. Real tinfoil hat stuff. And he has our scent." She scrolled down farther, then clicked a link. Up popped images of my workbench, the ceiling of the barn, and the dirt floor behind the bales of hay, where an unplugged extension cord lay and an impression of a chest freezer could clearly be seen. A caption under the picture said, "Is this where the alien corpse was stored?"

I let my jaw drop. "Oh, freakin' hell. How?"

"I have a theory," Nat said. She alt-tabbed and one of Patrick's videos came up. "Patrick, you yutz, you have geo-location turned on. Your videos of Alaric all have the GPS coordinates of this barn embedded in them. And when your brother posted the video clip, he didn't strip the metadata. I bet this Ross character downloaded it before Tim took it down, and found the coordinates. From there it's just Google Maps."

"Shit. Fuck. Hell. Jesus Christ. Also, shit." Patrick unlocked his phone and began poking at it. "Okay, it's turned off now. Too late, of course."

"And on that happy note," I said, "what delightful news did *you* have for us, Patrick?"

"Oh yeah. Tim wants in. He's not sure what *in* means, specifically, but he's seen enough of my videos to realize that something's up. He's threatening to blow the whistle. Of course, at this point, I would consider disappearing him to be a reasonable response."

"Let's deal with discussions of fratricide later," I said. "Right now, we need to be concerned about security." I took my communicator out and put it on the table. "Sheldon, we'll need you to be an active participant in this discussion. We need to guard against human interlopers, Lorann snoopers, and curious relatives. We can start with things like bars on all the windows, locks on the doors, and go from there."

"I will manufacture bars and locks, and also additional cloaking detectors. You can place enough of them around the perimeter so that no one can sneak in. They will report to me via subwave."

"Subwave?"

"Subspace radio. Technically inaccurate but metaphorically descriptive."

"Uh, do you have to open a wormhole?"

"No, it's not the same as FTL communications. And it's limited by light speed. Subwave is different only in that it doesn't use electromagnetic radiation and is therefore less affected by line-of-sight issues. It has completely replaced radio for short-range communication amongst Covenant species."

"Yet another answer to the Fermi Paradox," Nat muttered.

I glanced at her but decided to stick with the main topic. "Great. Next item. Sheldon is preparing gadgets for each of us. But security is an issue. They'll be biometrically tied to each of us, but even so, losing one would be bad. Or even letting it be seen."

"Can they be disguised?" Nat asked.

I gave her the side-eye. "As what?"

"Well, I don't know. Something innocuous. Jewelry? A phone?"

"So we'd be carrying around three or four phones?" I said. "That would be the opposite of unobtrusive."

Sheldon interrupted. "One moment, Jack. This could work. I can't put all of the devices together, but I could create a believable replica phone that would include the communicator, remote, and detector functions, and still operate as your original device."

"Okay," I replied, "the disruptors we could carry separately, and we have no use for the medical kit. That just leaves the belt. And I'm not sure about the belt."

"I could make belts small enough to fit you if I left off the shield device, so they wouldn't look like Batman's utility belt."

Patrick laughed. "Nice reference, Sheldon. You're really absorbing Earth culture."

"Or being assimilated by it," Nat added.

Patrick grinned. "Resistance is futile," he said.

I made a growling sound. "Focus, please. Sheldon, could you make a belt for each of us anyway? Properly sized, of course. If we do need them, we might need them in a hurry."

This reminder of the seriousness of the situation was an instant conversation killer. After a few moments, Patrick said, "This is good. This feels like we're finally being proactive. We may actually be getting ahead of this."

"Sure," Nat grumbled, "if you ignore the small detail that we still don't know diddly about what the Loranna are doing."

"Patience, my nerdy friend," said Patrick. "We'll get there."

"Nerdy fr— Do you *want* to die?"

I sighed theatrically and said, "So, to continue … " and waited a moment for attention. "We need to find out specifically which business or businesses in Tate Park are fronts for the Loranna, and how they are being used to infiltrate our society and cause those global disasters. Then we need to figure out what to do about it. Have I missed anything?"

"That is a very high-altitude summary, but essentially correct," Sheldon said.

"Can you help out with any more information, Sheldon? Maybe things the Loranna have done before?"

"No, sorry, I don't have access to every item of Covenant history. A lot of the information in my database is summary only."

"Okay." I nodded. "For now, let's get our security upgraded, get our new phones, then we start spying."

Chapter Eighteen:
Battening Down

Day 12. Tuesday evening

Sheldon had been busy running his printers, and we eventually found ourselves facing a large number of items needing installation.

Patrick and Nat began with bars and privacy frosting film on all the windows, while I worked on the people entrance. Sheldon had printed a completely new door, with a reinforced frame and a locking system that included dead bolts on all nonhinged edges. It was even Wi-Fi enabled so we—or Sheldon—could lock or unlock it remotely. The replacement looked enough like the existing door that it wouldn't raise any eyebrows, but the material was a fake wood that seemed more akin to Kevlar than anything.

The new frame fit neatly over the existing one, so no demolition was required. However, the reinforcing rods required some foundation drilling. Fortunately, Sheldon helpfully provided a drill from the Gen ship inventory. *That* was interesting—it didn't use a rotating bit at all. Instead, it seemed to pulverize or disintegrate the concrete. The word *patents* came unbidden to my mind. In Patrick's voice, strangely.

The last items were the cloaking detectors, which were installed on the outside of the barn walls, craftily integrated into quite normal-looking motion-sensing lights.

It was well after dark when we finished. I returned the Gen tools to the *Halo*, then sat heavily in my chair.

"Remember when we were young and could go all night?"

"I'm pretty sure alcohol figured into that," Patrick replied.

"Likely as an anesthetic. And we weren't doing actual work."

"Whatever." Nat groaned as she stood and grabbed her stuff. "I'm bagged. Let's go."

Patrick gave me a wave as he and Nat headed for the car. I looked wearily around the barn, searching with minimal enthusiasm for anything left to clean up.

"It's all good, Jack," Sheldon said through the communicator. "Detectors are working, door lock is on Wi-Fi, nothing has been left out. You can go get some rest."

"Thanks, Sheldon. I guess tomorrow we get down to the real work."

❧ ❧ ❧

I woke to the sound of my name being called.

"Jack. Jack. Wake up. Please respond."

It was Sheldon. Groggily, I grabbed for the communicator, which I had placed on the bedside table. "Wha. Whazzup?"

"We have an intruder. Human. Someone is circling the barn, trying to approach without triggering the motion-detector lights."

"Aagh. Next step, webcams." I sat up slowly and put my head in my hands. Honestly, even when I was a teenager,

I'd been mostly useless when woken up in the middle of the night. Apparently, I hadn't improved with age. "I don't have a gun."

"You have the disruptor."

"True. And Barkley, although he's more likely to lick someone to death." I looked at the communicator. "Y'know, this thing would be a lot more usable if I could pair some headphones with it. As it is, stealth is out of the question."

"A set of earbuds is, in fact, available. Designed for Gen ears, though. I doubt you'd find them comfortable. Actually, I think you'd feel violated if you actually managed to get them inserted."

"Ooooookayyyyyy...I did not need that visual. Look, Sheldon, is the intruder doing anything more than skulking around?"

"Not so far. I believe he is trying for subtlety. Unsuccessfully."

I reluctantly dragged myself out of bed and put on my pants and shoes. I grabbed the communicator and the disruptor, then swore. "Flashlight. Of course it's in the barn. Because where else would it be?" One more item to take care of.

Barkley, always ready for adventure, perked up the moment I came down the stairs, and ran circles around me all the way to the back door. I raised the communicator and said in a low voice, "Status?"

"Still poking around. He's activated the motion detectors twice. He may finally be getting a clue."

"Okay, we're coming out."

I opened the door and Barkley shot out, apparently having detected the odor of a stranger. The dog's name was well earned, as he set up a verbal assault that would wake the undead, if we had any around.

I jogged around to the barn and scanned the area, being careful to stay out of range of the motion detectors.

"He's left, Jack. It appears the highly irritating calls of your pet have a repelling effect."

"Was it the same guy?"

"I could not tell. He didn't get close enough. I would hate to think we've attracted two *different* covert investigations."

"Yeah, but I wouldn't rule out anything at this point. Call me again if something more happens, but I think for tonight at least, if all they do is snoop around the periphery, I don't really care."

I trudged back to the house with Barkley running excited circles around me, flopped back into bed without undressing, and was asleep immediately.

Chapter Nineteen:
Shoring Up Defenses

Day 13. Wednesday evening

"We're never going to get anywhere," Nat grumbled. "This whole project is nothing but constant reaction to whatever current crisis we're in, then preparation for the next one."

"So, pretty normal, in other words," I replied.

"Hah hah hah." Nat turned away and opened her laptop. "You guys work on the webcams and shit. I'm going to do some data analysis."

It seemed like a reasonable division of labor, honestly. Nat was twice as efficient as Patrick and me put together at research and data-massaging. But she did seem to be getting increasingly frustrated. I decided we'd have to call a meeting about it, and soon.

Patrick already had his ladder set up at the first location and was mounting a webcam on the wall. Wiring it to the lights for power would take a few extra minutes. I grabbed my ladder and tools and moved to the next location.

"So if I wanted to get around this kind of setup," Patrick said in a conversational tone, "I would either shoot out a light with a pellet gun, or sneak up during the day with a folding ladder and unscrew some bulbs, or just cut the power to the lights."

I paused while I briefly considered how I'd go about getting around our security setup. "I wonder if the motion detectors will pick up someone who's invisible," I replied.

"Of course not," Patrick replied, huffily. "I mean, why would you think otherwise?"

"It's not that simple," I said. "The motion detectors aren't necessarily tripped by a change in the image. Otherwise they'd activate for the movement of trees in the wind."

"They don't?"

"Some do. The cheaper, passive ones. Some will only react to motion toward or away from the camera. Some use infrared images. Some use a sum of the infrared signature over a number of zones. Some are active rather than passive and use microwave or sound pulses as a sort of radar."

Patrick stuck out his jaw, a sure sign he was getting stubborn. "I bet there are ways to fool them anyway."

"On the internet? Bet on it. Some of those ways might even actually work."

"What I'll bet on is that we'll get another visit tonight," Patrick said. "The question is: what will we do about it? We're not really set up as a high-security installation. No watchdogs, no guards, no guns."

"We have the disruptors."

"Who's going to take the night shift? We all have day jobs."

I sighed. "I think this whole thing is getting to all of us."

"We need a council of war," he said. "We need to get this done, Jack. Or hand it off to the government or something. We've got lives. We're not set up for a long, drawn-out cold war."

"Gotcha. Okay, let's start by getting these cameras up, then we'll talk this out."

We were once again seated in our favorite chairs in the barn, drinks in hand.

"I get that you're both getting frustrated." I looked from Nat to Patrick. "So am I. We're rearranging deck chairs here, and not making any real progress."

"Although I fully admit it's been fun, so far, mostly," Patrick replied with a smile.

"Yeah, that's great." Nat clearly wasn't sharing in Patrick's attempt at lightening the mood. "But I've got my dad to take care of, on top of holding down a job. My aunt has been filling in for me for the last couple of days, but she can't keep it up. And she's my mother's sister, so it's asking a lot in the first place. We need to have some kind of defined end date on this."

"I agree," I said. "I can't keep stringing along my parents with the secret-project story, either."

Patrick sighed. "And I have to deal with Tim, although fratricide is still not out of the question."

"I get that, and I...hmm..." I stopped talking and stared into the distance.

"What?" Nat and Patrick said simultaneously.

"Well, what we really need is to shake things up a little and see what falls out. And it would be great if we could take care of our friend Phil Ross at the same time." I tapped my chin. "*And* if we throw Tim a bone, make him feel like an insider—without actually making him one, you understand—then we could maybe make some headway."

"That sounds like quite the deliverable," Nat said. "You got an actual plan in there somewhere?"

"I think maybe I do. Look, Phil got the first video from TimJay666. He'll know that, so he'll be inclined to trust anything else that comes from the same source. We can get Tim to message Phil and give him the aerial images of the saucer field, both original and enhanced. I bet Phil will take it from there with very little prompting."

Patrick laughed. "And I bet that'll freak out the Loranna, having a gen-u-ine flying saucer investigator sniffing around their den."

"You could also give him a cloaking detector," Sheldon said.

Patrick and Nat stared at the communicator, looking as shocked as I felt. "Seriously?" I said.

"I have the enhanced phones ready for you, so you will no longer need the discrete items. And the detectors don't actually do anything detectable unless there's a cloaking field nearby, so they would not be impressive as evidence of aliens. *And* it might help your tinfoil-hat-wearing friend zero in on our mutual quarry."

"You understand we're using him, and potentially placing him in danger," Nat said.

Patrick frowned at Nat. "Really? You think Phil Ross would have a problem with any of this? Let's lay it all out for him. Complete honesty. You think he'll hesitate even a microsecond? This is morally equivalent to giving a reporter an anonymous tip. And you can bet a guy like Phil understands that there are risks."

Nat hesitated a moment. "Yeah…you're right, I think. Based on his website, the guy would chew off his own arm to get a chance at aliens."

"Wait," I exclaimed, mentally backing up several paragraphs. "Sheldon? New phones?"

"Yes. If you'll head up to the fabrication shop, you will each find new phones that look just like your current ones, and operate identically in all aspects, except that they have some extra hardware and a couple of extra apps."

"Cooooool..." Patrick said. There was a concerted rush for the center of the barn as an airlock opened.

"Damn," I said, awe in my voice. In my left hand, I held my own phone. In my right hand was another phone, seemingly the identical brand and model, except new. And, according to Sheldon, the doppelganger phone could detect cloaking fields when the proper app was running. It could also communicate with Sheldon, either over the wireless mobile network, Wi-Fi, or subwave. Sheldon had added a walkie-talkie app, and supplied a bone-conduction microphone that we were directed to stick on the skin behind one ear. Of course, we immediately dubbed them "cling-ons."

And the new phone could operate the airlock.

"I've also upgraded the security somewhat," Sheldon said. "It will do a full biometric match before unlocking. Which means that it can't be fooled by the normal tricks— and more important, it will open for you even if your face is not fully visible, as long as you're the one holding it."

Patrick waved one of the two phones in his hands. "What should I do with my old one?"

"Turn it off and hide it," Sheldon replied. "Or just leave it in the conference room."

With a laugh, I picked up the specially modified Lorann detector that Sheldon had prepared, juggled it a few times, then tossed it to Patrick. "Time to recruit your little brother."

CHAPTER TWENTY:
THIRD TIME'S THE CHARM

"Jack. Jack. Wake up. Emergency."

I sat bolt upright in my bed, then reached for the alarm to turn it off. But the alarm kept saying my name urgently. That couldn't be right. My alarm didn't—

Sheldon.

Belatedly coming to more-or-less full consciousness, I grabbed my phone. "What? Someone trying to break in again?"

"It's well past that. He's in. It's the same person, that ufologist."

I sat up and started dressing. "How did he get in?"

"I don't know. He didn't come in through any of the doors. There's no indication of a window having been broken, and they have bars now anyway. Motion detectors did not activate anywhere on the periphery. I am at a loss."

I grabbed the disruptor, my phone, and the flashlight that I'd placed beside my bed, and followed the same trajectory as the previous night, including being orbited by Barkley. The dog apparently had decided this was a nightly ritual, as he shot off for the barn as soon as the door was opened for him. I caught up a few moments later and examined the barn doors—both the large wagon doors and the normal door. None was open, and none looked like it had been forced. I stood there for a few moments scratching my head before raising my phone. "Sheldon, unlock the door, please."

The door unlocked with a click, and Sheldon said, "The intruder has run for the back of the barn. I'm not sure if he's planning to ambush you or if he has an exit in that direction."

I turned on the flashlight and entered. I shone it around but couldn't see any obvious threat. Reaching for the panel beside the door without looking, I flipped every switch on it. The interior blazed with intolerable brightness, and I shielded my eyes until they adjusted.

But now there was no way for the intruder to hide. I glanced at the workbench area, and saw that my secret compartment was sitting open. I felt a flash of annoyance. I'd put a lot of effort into building that compartment, and I had thought it was well disguised, but apparently I might as well have attached a neon sign pointing to it.

I sidled around the hay bales, with Barkley running back and forth, whining with excitement. However, he wasn't barking, which likely meant no one else was in the barn.

In moments, I was at the back of the building, staring at a gap in the wall where a couple of boards had been pulled out. I leaned down and looked through the gap to spy the bushes behind the barn. But no intruder.

"Sheldon, he got in through a hole in the wall. We have motion detectors back here, don't we?"

"Yes, and they did not indicate an approach. I cannot explain it. However, I've just checked the webcam footage, and I can see someone ... er, something ... Jack, I have no visual referent for this. You'll just have to see it."

My phone dinged as a text came in. The attached photo showed...something. It looked like a long Lego block, or maybe a three-cube Tetris piece, in a white or gray color. No wonder Sheldon had been confused by it. Sticking my head through the gap, I looked around and spotted something leaning against the outside wall. About five feet high, rectangular, a foot or so deep...

Pushing myself through the gap, I picked up the item. It was Styrofoam, obviously homemade, based on the duct-tape construction, about five feet tall by three feet wide, with a one-foot sidewall, and a handle in the middle.

"Inconceivable," I muttered.

Back inside, I tossed the Styrofoam shield onto the workbench. "What is it?" asked Sheldon.

"It's literally a shield for fooling a motion-detector." I threw myself into my chair, which rocked and squeaked alarmingly. "Styrofoam absorbs active motion-detection systems and blocks infrared for passive systems. Neutral color makes it hard for area-integration systems to generate a convincing differential." I snorted. "It's on the internet, so I assumed it was by definition BS, like water-powered engines and Nigerian inheritances. But apparently this one actually works."

"I am impressed," Sheldon said. "Is it possible that there is another subspecies of humanity, hiding in the shadows, that does all the actual thinking?"

"Well, if you believe the internet conspiracy nuts, there's ZOG, the shape-shifting lizard people, the Grays, the Deep State, the Illuminati, and maybe a half dozen others. Of course, they aren't all human, so maybe some of them don't count."

"Honestly, you humans just keep setting the bar lower and lower. You are in danger of forgetting to breathe."

I laughed. "I don't necessarily disagree with you, Sheldon. Sometimes I wonder about us too." I tried and failed to stifle an enormous yawn. "Tomorrow we'll have to talk about how to reinforce the barn walls and maybe protect against Styrofoam attacks. Right now, all this nightly excitement is cutting into my sleep time. Talk to you in the morning."

Chapter Twenty-One: Proxy

Day 15. Friday

I was sitting in the passenger side of the Buick, being driven to work, when my phone dinged. I jumped slightly, then pulled it out. I still had a tendency to stare at the phone. It was mine, yet not. It had all the same apps, the same icons in the same order. Even my data, like contacts and history, was all intact. But it was missing a few scratches and that hairline crack on the screen from when I dropped it.

It was definitely new. And slightly lighter, I thought. And much tougher, according to Sheldon. Well, why not?

The phone unlocked and I read the text from Patrick: *Tim ate it up. Sent DM right away, arranged blind drop for the detector. Hope Phil isn't suspicious. Tim thinks he's graduated to Starfleet, the little shit.*

I couldn't help chortling.

"So, not bad news, I guess," Dad said.

"Naw, just a text from Patrick. He's letting his little brother live for at least one more day."

"Ah. Little brothers."

My father said nothing more, and I didn't want to give the subject any life, so we settled back into our now-customary uneasy silence for the rest of the drive.

✤   ✤   ✤

I was stocking some vegetable bins when I got a text, this time from Sheldon. *Phil Ross has retrieved the detector. The tracker is working perfectly. I can monitor his location to within a couple of feet.*

Excellent. Phil was unlikely to let that alien device out of his possession. As long as he owned it, we owned him. Phil apparently wasted no time acting on his newly rising fortunes, as occasional texts from Sheldon informed me.

By late morning, the texts had all but dried up, and I was starting to consider alternative strategies to generate some churn, when my phone rang. The caller ID said Sheldon.

"Hello?"

"Jack, the fertilizer has hit the fan. Phil visited the field, and was cornered by a couple of security guards, on pretext of trespassing on private property. He's being taken in for interrogation. It sounded ominous. Not that one human more or less matters in the grand scheme of things, but Phil could have continuing utility, and I'd rather not waste him. Or have them waste him. Hah! I made a joke."

"A very small one," I replied. "Did they set off the detector?"

"No. Just garden-variety humans, unfortunately. They appear to be heading for the industrial park. Perhaps we'll get some information from his ultimate destination."

"Sheldon, can you phone Patrick? Ask him to pick me up."

"I'm on the phone with Patrick right now. Natalie as well. I *am* a computer, after all. One moment… He will leave immediately. He says be ready."

I hung up and ran for the front of the store, removing my apron as I moved. I yelled, "Taking an early lunch!" to Maria the checkout clerk.

Patrick's car roared up to the curb within a minute or two, almost but not quite sliding in sideways. I jumped in and Patrick took off, with even less concern for traffic laws than usual.

"What's the plan, Stan?"

"Winging it, I think. Hold on." I tapped the walkie-talkie app and put the phone on speaker. "What's the latest, Sheldon?"

"He has been taken into what appears to be the administration offices for the industrial park. Logical, I guess. Someone said something about *security*, so I assume—"

"Wait, someone *said?* You have him bugged?"

"Of course. Did I not mention that? I added a listening device as well as the tracker. It seemed prudent. Was that a mistake?"

"Sheldon, I think you're better at this spy thing than we are. Continue."

"Not much more to report. He is presumably in the security offices somewhere, waiting for the sergeant or captain or some such bigwig to show—"

Sheldon's voice cut off abruptly.

"Sheldon? You okay?"

"Sorry, Jack. I was momentarily nonplussed. The detector went off. It appears we've found our Loranna."

Chapter Twenty-Two: Rescue

Patrick's car tended to accumulate junk, which made it as much a traveling suitcase as anything else. Among the detritus in the back were a couple of Cincinnati Reds baseball caps. I grabbed them as we jumped out of the car, and we pulled them over our heads as we raced up the steps to the administration offices. The entrance was framed by an overly ornate Tate Industrial Park sign. The receptionist looked up as we burst through the doors, her expression changing to alarm.

"Security office?" I asked, urgency in my voice.

She pointed. "End of the hall. But what—?"

The rest of her sentence was lost in the distance as I sprinted down the hallway with Patrick on my heels. "Twenty feet and closing, on the right," Sheldon's voice said into my cling-on. I skidded to a stop and yanked open the most likely door.

In a room with a semi-glassed wall, two security guards flanked a man in a chair, hovering menacingly. I immediately recognized Phil Ross from the web page. He was wearing a lumberjack shirt and one of those padded sleeveless vests. The overall effect was of someone trying to disguise themselves as a Canadian. Across the table, a small, chunky man in a suit was leaning forward with his weight on his hands, trying to look tough. Phil seemed to be hugging himself, which I thought was excessively neurotic until I realized he was resisting attempts to frisk him.

I flung open the door to the interview room, and the occupants all spun around at the sudden commotion. "Hey, Phil, Tim Jay says hi. We're here to pick you up. Grab your stuff."

"Our guest is busy right now," the man in the suit said. "And you are trespassing. Perhaps you could wait outside for your friend."

"Yeah, about that," Patrick replied. "Your two police academy dropouts here don't actually have the power to arrest anyone, and if you're holding our friend against his will, that's a felony. It's kind of ironic, I guess. People don't realize just how little actual authority security guards have. And how much trouble they and their employer can get into if they exceed it."

I took up the narrative. "So we're going to take our friend Phil, and leave your property as quickly as possible, since we really don't want to trespass. Right, Phil?"

Phil, his eyes wide and his jaw slack, simply nodded. He started to rise and one of the security guards placed a hand on his shoulder.

"And that's assault, for instance," Patrick said. "You should remove that hand right now, rent-a-cop, or I will call the *real* police."

The security guard snarled and reached for his holstered pistol. I took a moment to do a mental eye roll. Patrick had pushed just a little too hard and bruised the man's ego.

"So, you're going to shoot us, now?" I said with a sneer. "For coming to pick up our friend who was walking around in a field? I'm sure Chief Rogers will support your actions. He's very understanding that way."

The security guard hesitated. Anyone with any exposure to the Dunnville police force—on either side of the
desk—knew that Chief Charles Rogers was *not* someone you
wanted to cross. A retired army drill sergeant, he'd been
described as Buford T. Justice without the funny bits. Not
an exaggeration, based on my very few encounters with him.

The guard glanced at the suit, who responded with a
disgusted expression and made a shooing motion with his
hand. "Fine," he said, "but please remember, Mr. Ross, that
the north field is part of the Tate property. We'd just as soon
not have someone with your, erm, *preoccupations* associated
with us. Next time we will simply press charges."

"So who are you guys?" Phil walked between and slightly
behind us, shifting his gaze back and forth as if he was
scared to miss anything. In person, he was even odder than
his picture. Besides the hair, he was several days' worth of
unshaven, but not the cool kind of unshaven like TV characters—more of a "got tired of shaving partway through"
look. He also had an eyebrow twitch that reminded me of
the psychic on an old *X-Files* episode.

I stopped and turned to face him. "We're colleagues of
Tim. TimJay666 to you. He informed us that you might be
in a bit of trouble and gave us an address."

Eyebrow up. "Huh. And how did he know this?"

"I'm not at liberty to say," I replied. "Need to know, and
all."

Patrick snorted without looking directly at Phil, but otherwise didn't contribute.

Phil pulled the cloaking detector out of an inside pocket
and held it out. I glanced quickly back at the administration

office, but they'd need to have a system worthy of an astronomical observatory to pick up anything at this distance.

"This thing is supposed to detect invisible objects," he continued. "It vibrated when I was in the field, and it vibrated when the slimy guy in the suit came into the room. He didn't look invisible, though. Just slimy." He waved the detector at me. "You know anything about this device?"

"Classified. Sorry."

Other eyebrow up. "My ass. This is alien technology. Are you aliens? Are you the same aliens as the one in the freezer? Do you work for TimJay666?"

"No, Mr. Ross, we are not any of those things. We're locals, born and raised."

"Especially not that last item," Patrick interjected.

Phil frowned. "Uh huh. Who are you with, then?"

"What makes you think we're *with* anyone?" I said.

"Well, for starters, if your gadgets are classified, *someone* has to have classified them."

Damn. Good point, I thought. *Oh well, let's roll with it.* I put on my best confident smile and said, "A good catch, Mr. Ross. But you'll never have heard of us. We're from MOBIUS."

Patrick almost lost it. He turned and resumed walking toward the parking lot, and Phil and I followed automatically.

"MOBIUS."

"Uh-huh. Like I said … "

"I've never heard of it. Right." Phil pointed at the Duster. "So tell me, Men from Glad, is that an agency vehicle, or did you rescue me in your own car? If the latter, you'd better hope they don't get your license plate."

"Good luck with that," Patrick replied.

I grinned, remembering how much effort Patrick had put into making his license plates unreadable without actually stepping over the line, legally. He'd even, at one point, bought one of those plastic covers that was supposed to be opaque to traffic-camera flashes. If a blurry frame from a distant webcam at a bad angle could extract a license number from the small part of his plate that was actually visible, I'd eat it.

I decided it couldn't hurt to give Phil a little more to go on. Or a little more rope. "The device you're holding is designed to detect a cloaking field, Phil. The cloaking field can create a disguise as well as produce invisibility. Very probably the guy in the suit was disguising himself. As human."

Phil's eyes registered shock for the briefest fraction of a second, then he got it under control. That was surprising for someone who, let's be blunt, walked around literally wearing a tinfoil hat most of the time.

"You guys know a lot, it seems," Phil said. "So what are you going to do when an alien hit squad comes and busts down the door to your barn and trashes the place looking for an alien corpse?"

Now it was my turn to be shocked. Our passenger had apparently put a few things together. "Seems you know a thing or two as well. For what it's worth, they won't find anything." I decided to play a little hardball. I gestured to the Duster. "So where can we drop you off, Phil?"

"Oh, I don't think so. We've got a lot of ground to cover. Maybe some trading of information. For instance, I found something in that field. Something amazing."

"An invisible spaceship?" I turned and smiled at Phil. "Or at least a landing strut. Most of their ship is above head height. Even for me."

This time, Phil's surprised expression lasted longer. "That's...you knew about—wait, *their* ship? I thought you weren't aliens. Whose side *are* you on, anyway?"

"Our side, Phil. Earth's side. Humanity's side, to be blunt. I don't know if you've ever seen *Men In Black*, but I can tell you it's not as fictional as you might think."

Phil looked from me to Patrick, then back. He paused and looked down at the detector in his hand with a thoughtful expression. "Are you familiar with the word *Lorann*?"

I turned in surprise. "The guy in the suit was Lorann, Phil. The corpse in the freezer was Gen. Seems you do know more than a thing or two. Why is that?"

Phil managed to look slightly embarrassed for a moment, then got his poker face back. "Ah, it's come up here and there on Reddit groups. I think it's usually attributed to the 'shape-changing lizards' theory. I have to admit, I always thought that one was a bit out there, but after today…"

I stared at Phil, impressed despite myself. If they'd gotten that right, what else might be getting dismissed as nutbar narrative? I thought for a moment. Phil might have some good information, but I didn't want to get in the position of giving far more than I got.

"This has all been very interesting, Phil, but it's time to go," I said. "Want that ride?"

Phil glared at me, his face still stony. "Thanks, no. I have a car parked up the road. And I don't know or trust you enough to get into a car with you." He paused. "I think you boys have stumbled into something that's over your heads and are just winging it. You might want to reconsider your strategy. I can help. More than you might think."

I shook my head. "I think we're going to go with our plan, Mr. Ross. Fewer moving parts."

"Right. Well, I have a feeling we'll be talking again."

"Use the front door next time," I replied. "We've reinforced the walls of the barn."

CHAPTER TWENTY-THREE:
CHASE

Day 16. Saturday

We decided to break for lunch. Since we'd had McD for breakfast, everyone wanted something different. So, pizza. We piled into Patrick's car and headed out to Pizza Hut. It would be a longer drive, since the Hut was at the other end of town, but it would give us a chance to discuss the situation.

We were about halfway to our destination, cutting through the greenbelt area, when Patrick looked in his mirror and said, "Shit!" I turned my head to see a set of flashing red lights.

Nat also turned, squinted, and said, "We're still within Dunnville city limits, right? That's not Dunnville cops."

Patrick looked more closely in the rearview, then switched to the side mirror. "You're right. Not highway patrol, either."

Nat chuckled. "And you'd know highway patrol. But I don't think we have any options. Cops is cops until proven otherwise."

Patrick pulled over to the side of the road, and the patrol car pulled in behind him. However, instead of leaving his car, the driver used the PA. "Occupants of vehicle. Turn off your engine. Step out of the vehicle with your hands clearly in view."

"Nope. That is not normal," I said.

"Right," Patrick replied, and reached under his dash. There was a click as he threw a switch and the timbre of the engine changed. "Hold onto your favorite body parts. You may feel some pressure..."

Patrick stomped on the gas and the Duster almost leaped into the air. Tires squealing and back end fishtailing slightly, the Plymouth left the ersatz law enforcement vehicle in the dust as it accelerated to warp factor one.

"Mary mother of God!" Nat yelled, attempting to keep her head from draping over the seat back. "Did Sheldon give you some new car parts?"

Patrick laughed. "No, a little more traditional. Modified 340 V-8 with a nitrous oxide boost. Zero to sixty in just under four. I don't think you've ever been on board when I've opened it up." He glanced in his rear-view mirror. "That's no highway patrol. Their vehicles may not be boosted, but they're sure as hell better equipped than that jalopy. My grandpa's car has more oomph."

Patrick's comment made me feel a little better. Still, we were being chased by someone who was imitating a cop, which wasn't something you did lightly. Or something you did if you were going to leave witnesses. Then I had an idea.

"Turn left here," I yelled, pointing. "And stop as soon as you're around the bend."

Patrick hammered the brakes, fishtailed a little, but made the turn. He immediately slowed and started to pull over.

"Don't pull off on the right. Move into the oncoming lane. Left side of the road." I pulled my disruptor out of my pocket and rolled down the passenger window.

A few seconds later, the supposed patrol car came whipping around the corner, to find a stationary quarry sitting in the oncoming lane. The driver hit the brakes, but with even less warning than Patrick, the patrol car slid past the Duster, the sound of his ABS system's desperate thrumming loud in the air. I watched the scene in slow motion as the driver swiveled his head, his mouth forming an O. I had time to think that he looked more gangster than cop, unless dress codes had loosened drastically.

As he came even, I used the disruptor. The driver slumped, his foot still on the brake, and the car rolled to a stop. I threw open the door, ran to the patrol car, reached in, and turned off the engine.

Patrick and Nat got out of the Duster and came over to help. Patrick leaned past the driver and began searching him.

"What are you looking for?" I asked.

"Weapons. ID. Anything to indicate who he might really be."

"And again," Nat said with a smirk, "you'd be familiar with the cops."

"Bite me. But also, yes." Patrick straightened up, a wallet in his hand. He rifled through it. "Not highway patrol, from the looks of things."

I stepped past Patrick and touched the unconscious man's face. "Human."

Patrick frowned. "Really? Can you tell?"

"Remember what Sheldon said? Their skin should feel different. I've no idea exactly how, though."

"Huh," Patrick grunted. Then he waved the wallet. "This is total bullshit, even at a quick glance. I'll take a picture of the guy's ID, but it's a safe bet it'll lead nowhere, even if we get the real cops involved."

"Should we interrogate him?" I asked, gesturing to the unconscious driver.

"Do you know how to do that? Because I don't," Patrick replied. He fished around a little more and came up with the car fob. Grinning, he tossed it into the bushes. "Just because."

The pizza—a large Super Supreme—was a fading memory, represented only by a few stray pieces of topping still on the tray. We all sat back, slumped in the cheap Naugahyde booth seats, waiting for our food to digest to the point where we could again bend at the waist. Even Nat had dug in with enthusiasm, actually doing rock-paper-scissors with Patrick for the last piece.

I put my hand on my stomach, suppressed an incipient belch, and said, "So, can we talk about our latest adventure? Any thoughts?"

"I just figured the Loranna were on to us," Patrick replied. "I can't think of anyone else we've pissed off lately."

"Sure, but why send a single human operative in a poor man's version of the cops?" Nat said. "Even if the Lorannic presence is small, they should have the resources to hire, I dunno, mercenaries or something."

I thought for a moment, then subvocalized, "Sheldon, any indication that the Loranna are mobilizing against us? Any other activity at the barn?"

"No, Jack," Sheldon replied in our cling-ons. "No one has gone to the office at all. It is, after all, a weekend. Perhaps the Loranna only work weekdays."

"What if the fake cop thing wasn't set up by the Loranna?" Nat asked.

Patrick gave her a quizzical look. "Okay. Who, then?"

"I'm thinking Phil Ross."

Patrick and I both laughed out loud.

"C'mon," Patrick said. "He's a kook. Even if he's mad enough at us to want to do something like that, where would he get the contacts? Or the money?"

"Well, that's the thing, Patrick. After the break-ins, I did enough research to ID Mr. Ross, but some stuff didn't smell right, and I've done a little more digging. Phil Ross has no discernable source of income, and no employment history to suggest a pension. In fact, he doesn't seem to have much history at all. Or social media presence, other than his obsession. And before about four years ago, there are *no*, and I mean *zero*, pictures of him on the net anywhere. He's a cypher."

"Do you think he's Lorann?" Patrick asked.

Nat shook her head. "That wouldn't make sense. Why would he investigate their landing site?"

"Or not set off the detector himself," I added. "Or not recognize a disruptor. No, he's human. Just..."

"There's more to him than we can see," Nat finished for me.

"Which brings us back to the eternal question." Patrick looked from one of us to the other. "What do we do now? Can we go to the cops to report this? Should we?"

"Uh-uh," Nat said. "At some point they'd ask us why we think someone would want to do this to us. Do you have a good answer for that?" Without waiting for a response, she buried her face in her hands. "I think we're past the point where we can hand this off and just walk away. Even if we wanted to."

CHAPTER TWENTY-FOUR:
SPIES R US

Day 18. Monday

After much discussion, we'd decided to try to act as normal as we could. While disappearing completely would certainly be possible with the *Halo*, it would leave us with zero options for hitting back. Instead, we would turn up the pressure with some moves of our own, now that we knew where to look.

The afternoon at work was interminable. Every time I thought of the whole scene with Phil, I started vibrating with excitement. We'd actually, finally, made some progress on the Loranna thing. It was odd, but having a solid lead on their base of operations made things somehow more real than, say, owning a flying saucer. I decided I wouldn't mention that to Nat; she would mock me mercilessly for the illogic.

It took several centuries, but finally the clock hit five. I had my apron off and was heading for the front of the store within seconds. It would still take Patrick five minutes to get there, but somehow the waiting was easier to take on my own time.

Patrick pulled up and Nat scooted over to make room as I climbed in. "Let's get this party started," Nat said to me. "We have some planning to do."

"And about damned time," I said. Bravado notwithstanding though, I was fighting an uneasy feeling that we'd just stepped in over our heads.

With Patrick's usual driving, we arrived at the barn in short order. We plunked down in our favorite chairs, I pulled out my phone and pressed the walkie-talkie app to bring Sheldon in, and we were ready.

"So," Patrick said. "What's the plan?"

I opened my mouth to reply and stopped. After a moment, I glanced at Nat.

"Jesus," she said, rolling her eyes. "Look, the Tate Industrial Park administration office is too small to be the whole Lorannic presence. It's like a half dozen people. So we have to scan the whole park and try to figure out where all the Loranna are. And we need to do it in less than forever."

I held up a finger. "Hold on a moment. Sheldon, do you have anything like a small drone in your inventory?"

"Drone? As in small flying device? No. The drive system cannot be miniaturized to anywhere near that level."

"Okay, fine. Can you duplicate one off the internet?"

"Certainly. Do you want me to start?"

"Just an additional item or two. Add a cloaking device, a detector, and a subwave connection. Oh, and a directional mike."

"Acknowledged. I will have your toy ready tomorrow morning."

"We can't just fly a drone around the park without attracting attention," Patrick said.

"We can if it's invisible," I replied. "And if we detect cloaking fields, they're probably Loranna."

"Unless there's a third alien species roaming around," Nat added.

"There is no evidence of that, Natalie," said Sheldon. "Nor did Alaric suggest it. Jack's assumption is high enough probability to qualify as de facto proof of Lorannic presence."

"Okay fine. But we all have to be at work, so you'll have to handle the surveillance." Nat glanced in the direction of the invisible spaceship. "And just as important, we all have to act normal all day."

"So, terminally bored and resigned to our fate," I replied. "And impatient for the day to be over. Like every other day."

CHAPTER TWENTY-FIVE:
SURVEILLANCE

Day 19. Tuesday

I got up early, rushed through breakfast, then hurried out to the barn. It wasn't just a question of excitement. I had to get the preparations done before my father was ready to leave. He'd wait if I was late, but explanations would be required, and the less I had to lie to my dad, the better.

I was surprised to see Patrick drive up, Nat in the passenger side. "Hey, Jack," he said, leaning out the window. "We decided to give you a ride. And get a look at the drone, but that's just coincidence."

"Sure." I pulled out my phone and tapped a quick text to my father. A reply came in almost immediately. *Saw Patrick drive by. Figured as much.*

Well, the pressure was off, anyway. I gestured with my head and turned toward the barn.

Sheldon lowered an airlock ramp as we approached and directed us to the fabrication shop. When we got there, I saw a brand-new drone sitting in one of the output trays. I picked it up and examined it. Four propellers in a square pattern sat above a squat body festooned with a camera, small parabolic microphone, and other, less-identifiable items.

"What's the range, Sheldon?"

"If you mean connectivity, subwave will allow me to cover the planet. If you mean power, I did not limit myself to Terran technology; I merely used the item I found online as a visual template. This unit will operate continuously for hundreds of hours before needing a recharge. And the possibility of an antimatter explosion is extremely remote."

"Antimatter...explosion?" I replied.

"I kid. By the Maker, I'm getting better at this."

"Debatable," Nat muttered.

I hefted the drone a few times and tweaked the rotors. I had to admire the workmanship. This thing wouldn't raise eyebrows at all in a normal setting. "You might as well just take it from here, Sheldon. Use your discretion, but try to get as complete a picture of the park layout and contents as possible."

"Use that super-advanced spiral thing you were talking about," Patrick added.

"In this case, a grid pattern would be more efficient," Sheldon said. "But thanks for sharing."

Nat held up a hand to forestall any further bickering. "With that operating range, we don't have to carry it to the park to let it out. Just go outside and let it loose."

"Acknowledged. Toss it into the air and I'll take it from there."

I nodded and headed for the stairs. Once I was out of the barn, I tossed the drone gently in a softball arc. It activated, flipped over in midair, and zipped off at high speed, fading into invisibility within a hundred yards. The device made a noise very much like a hummingbird zipping by—much quieter than any drone I had ever played with.

I rejoined the others, who were getting into the car. "How long until it gets to the park?" I said into the air, trusting the cling-on to pick up my voice.

"Just under five minutes," Sheldon replied. "I should caution you that we probably won't be getting any dramatic scenes through windows of Loranna torturing hapless Earthlings. The first phase will consist of nothing more than mapping out the park and buildings from the outside."

"That's fine, Sheldon. Just put up a schematic of the park and update it as you go. We'll have a look after work."

Nat said, "Sheldon, if you fly low enough, you could detect disguised Loranna, right?"

"I can detect a cloaking field, and we can assume anyone using one is a Lorann. I will be counting the occurrences, obviously."

"If possible, can you get high-res 3D images?"

"Of course, but why?"

"Like you said, a cloaking-field detector can't tell if the subject is actually human or Lorann."

"Yes, it merely detects—oh."

Patrick looked at Nat, then frowned. "What?"

Nat smiled at him. "If we can get an image of a human disguise that a Lorann is using, Sheldon could easily disguise one of us as that same image. If we trip a cloaking-field detector, they'd simply assume that it was Grog in his human disguise."

"Grog?" Sheldon exclaimed. "How exactly do you visualize the Loranna, anyway?"

Disregarding Sheldon, I said to Nat, "That's a good idea in its basics. But what if Oog the guard says, 'Hey Grog, how's it hanging?' in Lorann?"

Sheldon's voice was becoming increasingly exasperated. "It's Lorannic. And *Grog*? *Oog*? What is wrong with you people?"

I chuckled. "Chill, Sheldon. Nat, there's no way we can learn Lorann—excuse me, Lorannic—well enough to pull that off. Sheldon, do you speak Lorannic?"

"Of course. Language files are a basic part of my functionality. I speak every language in the Covenant."

"Could someone wear a receiver with a speaker, and could you fill in the conversational part?"

"But you'd need to move your lips in sync with what Sheldon was saying," Nat objected.

"And anyone would be able to tell right away if a voice was coming from a speaker," Patrick added.

"Wrong on both counts. Please stop telling your alien A.I. grandma how to suck eggs." Sheldon waited for silence. "We use just such a procedure occasionally, when someone has to go out in the field and hasn't had time to get the native language deep-induced. I can program the field on the fly for the lip-synching to be credible. We'll have to do a dry run or two first of course, to practice. And as to the speaker issue, the reason Terran speakers sound artificial is because they drop most of the highest- and lowest-frequency harmonics. *Tinny* is the common description, right? Gen speakers can deliver sound from subsonic right up to the frequencies used by bats. Such speaker systems are generally built into specialized necklaces. I have some in inventory."

"So what I'm hearing is that we may actually have a viable plan for infiltrating a Lorannic stronghold," Nat said.

Still sounding exasperated, Sheldon replied, "If you stretch the definition of the word *plan* until it screams for mercy, then yes."

❧ ❧ ❧

There seemed to be some kind of modification of reality in effect, so that as we got closer to actual results, our time at work stretched asymptotically longer. But after a millennium or two, we were all gathered once again in the *Halo*'s conference room.

A map of the Tate Industrial Park was starting to take shape in one of the wall monitors. Sheldon had put up a 3D isometric view, with floating annotations beside individual buildings. It looked a little like a *Sim City* game in progress.

I moved in and squinted at one of the tags. It said "Four Loranna detected." That was interesting. I glanced at some of the other tags. Some were Lorann counts; some were names of the companies, in cases where there was a sign on the front. Some even had phone numbers attached. Sheldon was certainly thorough.

Nat sighed and pointed wordlessly. I followed the line from her finger to a small annotation that said, "Harris Institute, nine Loranna detected."

"That sounds like the entire third floor," she commented.

"By which you mean management?" I asked.

Nat nodded. "Top executives, senior account reps…all the real decision makers. The number's slightly low, but they might just not all be there." Nat paused and stared into space, a slight frown on her face. "So, this is really weird. People I know, more or less—people I've worked with for a couple of years—may just turn out to be aliens bent on enslaving the Earth. I feel like I should be more freaked out, but I'm just rolling with it."

"Wait until you wake up in the middle of the night, screaming," Patrick said.

"Thanks for that image, Patrick. Wait—did you—?"

Patrick didn't reply, merely shrugged.

I decided to change the subject and started pointing to items on the map. "Harris Institute: marketing analysis and campaign creation. Integra Polycomms: high-speed network provider. Morris Security Services. Harris Property Management. Kich and Robertson Legal Services. All the businesses that have presences are ones that would presumably be useful for their overall plan. I wouldn't be surprised if the Loranna actually own the industrial park. It would give them complete control of what goes on, who gets rental space, and so on."

"With enough regular but harmless businesses onsite, and enough human employees to provide protective coloration," Patrick added. "It would be weird, for instance, if there were no places to eat and everyone went to the pet store every day for lunch. But now we have a plague of choices. Where do we start?"

"That's easy," Nat said. "My employer. I know my way around, at least the lower floors, and I can fake it on the third floor. Plus, I know a lot of the people."

"Whoa, whoa, you're jumping the gun a little," I said. "What makes you even think you'll be going in?"

"Oh, you are *not* going to try to play that chauvinistic, sexist crap—"

I cut her off. "No, I'm going to play that *You're short* crap. Excuse me, I mean *petite*," I amended, glancing at Patrick, who was overacting a death scene. "Remember what Sheldon said about a Gen trying to pass as human because of height?"

Nat glared for a moment, but she was far too reasonable to ignore the argument. She wasn't done, though. "Karen Ingram is only slightly taller than me. If she turns out to be a Lorann, I'm set. And that's almost certain; a colder, more reptilian individual you'll never meet."

In a voice that actually sounded tired, Sheldon said, "They are not reptilian. There are only slight, superficial resemblances. Are you people completely unable to hold onto a fact for more than a few seconds?"

"Fine. If that turns out to be the case, I'm all for it," I said, ignoring the comment.

Sheldon continued, apparently ignoring me in turn, "I set the drone down where I could scan individuals as they came and went. And I got some good images to work from. Where possible, I also recorded voice samples. Natalie, I'll forward those to your phone, and you can comment if you recognize them."

"Will do, Sheldon. Thanks." Nat cocked her head and smiled at me. "Karen's assistant, Marc Abramson, is quite tall, Jack. Perfect for you. We might both be going in."

I groaned. "Outstanding."

CHAPTER TWENTY-SIX:
MAKING PLANS

Day 20. Wednesday

We were in the barn again, reviewing Sheldon's progress. Nat was examining all the footage taken of individuals, hoping for someone from the third floor of her office. Finally, though, she slapped the cover closed on her laptop and muttered, "Shit."

I looked up from my work—okay, I'd been watching a YouTube video, but she didn't need to know that—and raised an eyebrow.

"Sheldon hasn't been able to get as much as I was hoping for," she explained. "A few visuals, definitely no surprises as far as I'm concerned, but not enough in the way of audio samples."

"And no Karen Ingram, I bet," Patrick added, "which is what's *really* pissing you off."

Nat turned to him and tried to burn through his brain with laser vision, if that glare meant anything at all. When Patrick's head didn't burst into flames, she sighed. "And no Karen. Is there any way to speed this up?"

"Plant a bug?" said Patrick.

"A reasonable suggestion," said Sheldon.

"Um, sure," Nat replied. "We can disguise ourselves to go in and plant a bug so we can get enough audio and video to be able to disguise ourselves to go in and spy. Am I the only one who sees a problem?"

"Is there any way you could get yourself invited upstairs?" I asked.

She paused and frowned in thought. "Not for anything routine. Normally they come down to the second-floor conference room for meetings, and anything one-on-one is either email or Zoom."

"So what would qualify as nonroutine?" Patrick asked.

"Without getting me fired?"

"Sure, okay." Patrick grinned. "But yeah. Something that would get you invited up to three or allow you to go up there on your own. What kind of things might be triggering for them?"

"Coincidentally enough, security. I could find a bug and announce it. No, that would put them on alert." Nat shook her head. "We don't want them doing a full sweep because they think someone's trying to bug them."

"Someone *is*," Patrick replied.

Nat rolled her eyes but didn't bother to reply. Then she sat up straight and snapped her fingers. "I could lose my fob and need a replacement. I'd have to go to three to get it."

"Fob?" I asked.

"Security fob. It provides a random number to use when logging in remotely. All staff with remote access have them." Then her face clouded up. "On the other hand, losing one can potentially get you fired."

"How about one that stops working?" Sheldon said.

Nat brightened immediately. "That'd be perfect. Can you sabotage mine?"

"Piece of pie."

"Cake," Nat corrected.

"Bad for you either way. Bring it up to the fabrication area. If nothing else, a good EMP should take care of it."

Nat gave us a *How about that!* look and headed for the descending airlock stairway. I smiled at Patrick. "It's nice to finally feel like we're making some headway."

"More so for Nat, I think. She's uh … " Patrick hesitated and glanced in the direction of the *Halo*, where Nat had already disappeared up the stairs. "Jack, she downplays it, but she's been *really* bummed about not getting to go to college. And getting out of Dunnville, but that goes without saying. She truly, desperately *needs* this whole thing to come to something."

"Yeah, I know. College was all she talked about, that last year before graduation." I sighed. "We make a hell of a poor gaggle of musketeers, don't we?"

Just then, Nat came bounding down the airlock steps, a wide grin on her face. "One security fob, freshly banjaxed," she said, waving the item.

"You checked?" I asked.

"Oh, it's dead. I guess I have to get a new one tomorrow. Finally, some progress." She held out her other hand. "Sheldon also gave me a bug to plant." A small, irregular patch of what appeared to be thin, semitransparent plastic sat in her palm. "This apparently will take on the color and texture of whatever it's planted on. Should be almost impossible to see, even if you're looking for it."

"And the Loranna won't be able to detect it?" I asked.

"They could," Sheldon interjected, "if they did a sweep using Covenant-level technology. But unless they have a reason to suspect something, bringing out that equipment would itself present a potential breach of secrecy. Remember, they are trying to blend in."

I nodded. "We can't do this with zero risk." I looked at Nat. "You up for this?"

She grinned back at me. "Lemme at 'em."

CHAPTER TWENTY-SEVEN: GOING IN

Day 21. Thursday

This was going to be one of those interminable days. More so than normal, I mean. Not that Nat was going to be doing anything James-Bond-like—sticking a little piece of plastic onto a convenient surface wasn't the kind of thing that would require a stunt double. Still, I found myself checking my phone far too often, hoping for a text.

Meanwhile, normal life needed my attention. Stock the cukes, restack the apples, we're out of bulk sugar, cleanup on aisle five ... Argh! I was beginning to understand more and more why both Patrick and Nat had latched on to this whole Loranna thing. They really had no credible alternative to, as Nat put it, dying of mediocrity in this Podunk town.

My pity party of one was interrupted by a ding from my phone. Finally! I tapped the notification and read the text: *Bug in place. Now we wait.*

Cool. And apparently completely lacking in drama, to judge from the message. Just as well. What was that old saying? Adventure is defined as bad stuff happening to other people somewhere else.

Or something like that.

The drive home was the usual uncomfortable mutual silence, punctuated by a single half-hearted attempt by my father to talk about alternative colleges. It reminded me, though, that Sheldon had said something about looking into my MIT situation. Not that he could do anything concrete, but he might dig up some info.

And Patrick and Nat would be over right after dinner. Hopefully, Sheldon had picked up something useful.

I blasted through the front door and foyer with a yelled, "Hi, Mom!" trailing behind me, and vaulted up the stairs in three strides. It took only a moment to change, and I was down the stairs in two leaps and out the door.

"Hey Sheldon, what's new?" I said as I entered the barn.

"This just in," he replied over my cling-on. "Humans discover thumbs, make a mess."

"Ha, ha. C'mon, be serious."

"I am serious. Everything I said is true."

"How about something closer to home?"

"Nat will be overjoyed. I have significant audio and video samples of Karen Ingram and her assistant, both of whom have set off the cloaking detector."

"I'm … kind of ambivalent about that, honestly. Do we really need to do this?"

"Jack, the Loranna are on their best humanlike behavior in public, which includes the third floor. They certainly don't speak Lorannic when there are humans around, let alone discuss secrets. We need to get into their computer systems if we expect to learn anything."

"You can't hack your way in?"

"Unfortunately, the Harris systems, while of human manufacture, seem to have been given a security audit by someone with Covenant-level training. There will be no hacking in, not without a valid log-in."

"Got it." I looked down as my phone dinged. "Dinnertime," I said. "Nat and Patrick will be here later, and we'll go over everything then."

"Be still, my CPU."

Nat was delighted that Karen Ingram turned out to be one of them. She did a dance around the room, chanting, "Oh, yeah, Karen's a lizard, bet she has a gizzard, don't have to be a wizard, could spot her in a blizzard."

"Even I can tell that's terrible," Sheldon said. "And you are right for all the wrong reasons."

"Don't care. She's a lizard. I'll take the win."

"Fine. It's like dealing with unruly children. I'm beginning to reconsider the advantages of sentience."

Nat finally stopped the celebration and waved her phone. "And we have enough to disguise me?"

"Yes, and Jack too," Sheldon replied.

"Good," Nat said. "Tomorrow's Friday, so we can do this after working hours."

"Are you sure Karen will leave on time?" I asked.

"Are you kidding? Loranna are bigger clock watchers than humans, judging by the way the entire third floor stampedes out the door come quitting time. You take your life in your hands if you're standing in the wrong place at five-oh-one. She'll be gone."

"All right. So the plan…"

Nat held up something too small to see between thumb and forefinger. "This little nubbin is an audio-video bug, which goes under a keyboard on the forward side so it can see the monitor. It also, according to Sheldon, picks up keystrokes. We go in, I stick this under Karen's keyboard, and we get out. No heroics."

"Jack's not really the heroic type," Patrick interjected with a laugh. I scratched the side of my nose with my middle finger, which just produced a wider grin.

Nat gave us both a patronizing smile before continuing, "The next time Karen logs in, we get her log-in credentials. Then I can remote in and we'll see what we can find."

I nodded slowly. "It's a plan. Which is more than we generally run with."

"We should test the system," Sheldon said. "Natalie's and Jack's belts are still in the fabrication shop waiting to be picked up. I've set out a couple of necklace speaker systems for replicating speech. The necklaces will also give me audio and video of whatever you are experiencing."

"I'll grab them," Patrick said, and hurried off.

He was back in less than two minutes and handed belts and necklaces to Nat and me.

"A lot less bulky," Nat said as she snapped her belt on. "But still not usable as a fashion accessory." She poked a spot on the belt. "It's rigid in a couple of places."

"The projectors can only be miniaturized to a point. The design hasn't changed much in a century." Sheldon paused until Nat and I were both ready. "Now, I will activate the disguise function based on the two subjects."

We shimmered for a moment, then were replaced by two people who had appeared on the surveillance videos.

"Damn, that is freaky," Patrick said. "Say something, Nat."

Sheldon interrupted. "She will still sound like Nat if she speaks. I must supply the voice. Thus … "

The ersatz Karen Ingram began speaking. "Hi, I'm Karen. I'm a human, and therefore not very intelligent. I trip over my own feet and then drool on the carpet—"

"All right, Sheldon, we get it!" Nat's voice said from the direction of Karen. Karen grinned in response.

"That," said Patrick, "was both very cool and extremely creepy. Nat, did you do anything?"

Nat became Nat again. "Not until I yelled at Sheldon. Before that, I was just standing there. Did my lips move?"

"Completely believable," Patrick said. "Sounded real, looked real. Sheldon, you're a genius."

"You belabor the obvious, but I'll take the win."

Nat laughed. "What worries me is if we don't agree on what Karen should be doing. What if I want to go left and you have her go right?"

"The disguise field follows your movements by default. I have very limited control to make changes. The programming interface is actually being stressed to its limit just to control the facial movements in real time. Under normal circumstances, the wearer would be providing the speech, and the cloaking field would respond appropriately. That's what the Loranna are doing." Sheldon paused. "Nevertheless, you bring up a good point. You need to know what reasonable behavior is. I will coach you over your cling-ons, and I will translate all Lorannic for you."

I nodded. "That sounds like it'll work. We can't make this zero-risk, guys. We just have to do the best we can."

"You'll need security cards as well," Sheldon said. "I am printing them as we speak. They'll be done by the time you're ready to leave."

Patrick was visibly surprised. "You can duplicate their security cards?"

"They are using Earth security technology. RFID cards. Barely better than a carved stick. I suspect the Loranna got lazy when setting up this operation and just went with local talent."

I nodded. "Seems reasonable. Security through obscurity. They're trying to look as uninteresting as possible, so no one will think to investigate them."

We settled into an uncomfortable silence, everyone glancing at everyone else. It was the moment of truth.

"No more excuses," Nat said. "We're as ready as we'll ever be. Tomorrow after work. Like you said, Jack, do or do not."

CHAPTER TWENTY-EIGHT: INFILTRATION

Day 22. Friday afternoon

Patrick dropped us off in a satellite parking area that wasn't visible from the admin offices or the Harris building. While it seemed unlikely, if someone spotted Karen and her assistant, Marc, getting out of an unfamiliar car, it might raise questions.

"We'll have to go the long way around," Nat said. "Sheldon, what's the status with the real Karen and Marc?"

"They have departed for the day, having driven off in separate vehicles."

"I wonder if there's a Lorannic bunkhouse somewhere," I muttered.

"Unlikely, Jack. They will make a point of being as apparently normal as possible. It is likely that a number of people having the same mailing address would raise red flags with more than one government department."

"Which doesn't matter if the Loranna have taken over," I said.

"If their infiltration was that thorough, they wouldn't really need to be subtle," Sheldon replied. "They could just launch the missiles, instead of having to scrap all the environmental laws and start promoting coal."

"Well, let's hope."

Nat punched me in the arm. "Stop being a Dickie Downer. And when we get there, follow my lead. Remember, that's my home turf."

I responded with an insolent salute. "Yeah, yeah."

The moment of truth came swiftly, and the entrance to the Harris Institute stood before us. Nat hesitated only a moment, then strode forward like she owned the place.

The guard glanced up when we entered, appeared momentarily surprised, then glanced down. Apparently, whatever he saw reassured him, as his face relaxed.

Nat strode past him with a small nod, heading for the elevators. I tried to avoid hunching my back, despite the feeling that I was going to be shot at any moment. I meekly followed my pseudo-boss through the lobby.

As soon as we were out of sight, I started to speak, but was cut off by a comment from Sheldon.

"Do not speak aloud unless absolutely necessary. Video and audio surveillance is likely, and I won't be able to lip-synch to your commentary, so you'll look like a ventriloquist act, which will definitely create suspicion. If you want to talk to me or to each other, subvocalize and I will retransmit it."

I clamped my lips shut. This would be a very quiet walk through the building.

We quickly reached the third floor and strode down the hall. We encountered one person going the other way. He cocked his head at seeing us and said something in what had to be Lorannic. My cling-on supplied the translation. "You're back, Karen? I thought you said you were going to be preparing for the status meeting."

"Karen" replied in the same guttural tones, which translated as "Forgot something. I won't be long, though."

The other individual seemed unbothered, merely nodding and continuing on.

We ended up in an office with the name Karen Ingram and the title Director, Marketing Campaigns on the door. I had a momentary twinge of worry, but the door was not locked. Nat closed it behind us, then looked around.

"Walk around the room," Sheldon said. "I'll try to pick up indications of existing surveillance."

We obediently did a circuit of the office, then Nat sat down behind the desk and started opening drawers. "I'm not sure what I'm looking for," the cling-on said in Nat's voice.

My eyebrows went up. I hadn't seen Nat's lips move or heard a peep from her. If that was subvocalized, it was impressive. "Anything important will probably be locked," I replied under my breath, to test the subvocalization as much as anything.

Nat nodded and sat back. She picked up the keyboard and flipped it over. As we had hoped, it was a cordless keyboard-and-mouse combo. She pulled out the surveillance device that Sheldon had given her and attached it to the front underside of the keyboard, as instructed.

Meanwhile, I paced around the office, cataloguing the contents. The most glaring factoid was the complete lack of a filing cabinet. The credenza behind the desk seemed to contain only personal effects and a few books. And one thumb drive. Before I could change my mind, I grabbed the item and pocketed it.

"We've placed the bug," Nat's voice said into my cling-on. "Time to amscray."

The trip back down to the lobby went without incident. It appeared Loranna really weren't any more inclined than humans to hang around the office on a Friday. But when we got to the front desk, the guard spoke to Nat in Lorannic. My earbuds supplied the translation. "Did you get what you needed?"

Nat, taken by surprise, did a small stutter step. But she immediately replied, in Karen's voice and in Lorannic, "All good."

"I guess I'll see you at the status meeting this weekend?"

Wow, I thought, was this guard naturally chummy, or did he suspect something?

"Look at your watch, Nat," Sheldon interjected.

Nat obediently bent her arm up and glanced meaningfully at it. "Yes, but I have a lot of prep to do."

"Ah, of course. Well, good night."

Nat and I exchanged glances as we made for the front door. Neither of us spoke until we were outside. Nat let out a loud breath. "Jeez, I thought we'd been made back there."

Sheldon replied to her comment. "I would have expected him to set off an alarm if he was truly suspicious, Natalie. In any case, if there is a sudden search of Karen's office, we'll know for sure."

"Sheldon, can you have Patrick meet us up front?" I asked. "I'd kinda like to be gone ASAP."

"Acknowledged."

We hurried to the road at the front of the industrial park, while doing our best not to appear to be hurrying. Patrick's car was parked at the curb, waiting. I felt a wave of relief wash over me and quickened my pace.

And then everything went to hell.

A car pulled up behind Patrick and parked. The engine shut off, and the driver got out and came around between the cars just as we got close enough to think we were home free.

It was Karen Ingram.

It took her a moment to register that the woman and man walking toward her, doubtless with deer-in-the-headlights expressions on their faces, were Karen and Marc. She stopped dead and her jaw dropped. There was a moment of frozen mutual staring, then she said something that I didn't catch and reached into her pocket. I watched the scene unfold in slow motion, completely unable to move. She was bringing up an item and pointing it at us.

It was a disruptor.

Then she said, *"Urk,"* did a sort of a break-dancing move, and started to slowly collapse. Behind her, Patrick stood with *his* disruptor extended. I jumped forward and grabbed her before she hit the ground. As I did so, Karen disappeared, to be replaced with an orange, slightly reptilian being.

"What the hell?" I muttered. Then I looked down and realized I looked like myself.

"Put her in here," Patrick ordered, holding his trunk lid open.

I dumped her in the trunk, none too gently, and started to ask, "Sheldon, why am I—?" Then I realized I was Marc again. "What just happened?" I said. In the trunk, Karen was Karen again.

Sheldon responded immediately. "Your cloaking fields interfered with each other. It happens. Please stop yammering and get out of there."

Patrick muttered, "No shit," slammed the trunk shut, and hurried around to the driver's door. I took a moment to peer into Karen's car. No Marc, thank God. Or anyone else. It appeared she'd come on her own.

Nat and I jammed ourselves into the passenger side, and Patrick took off before I'd even gotten the door properly closed. Our disguises vanished as Sheldon disabled the belts.

"What the hell happened?" Nat said. "Why did she come back?"

"I have no data," Sheldon said. "But she will be unconscious for ten to fifteen minutes. You need to get her here quickly. I will reconfigure a stateroom for incarceration."

"How long will that take?" I asked.

"Not long. It's in my list of standard procedures."

"Building a jail cell? Really?"

"Not for this specific circumstance, obviously, but there can be situations where someone needs to be detained against their will. Once we've got her secured, we can talk about how you idiots managed to screw this up."

"She came back. She was coming back to the office for something. What could—" Nat stopped speaking as she saw the expression on my face. "What?"

Wordlessly, I pulled the thumb drive out of my pocket and held it up.

Nat's eyes rolled. "Holy Mother Murphy and all the saints. She forgot her files for the seminar?" Nat sat there, speechless for several seconds, her jaw working soundlessly. Then she turned to me and glared. "You're right, Jack. God is a malicious little troll, with the sense of humor of a sociopathic two-year-old."

"What do we do now?" Patrick said.

"Get her to the barn. Get her into her quarters. Then we'll assess the situation." Sheldon paused. "Please try not to run over anyone along the way."

CHAPTER TWENTY-NINE:
ACCIDENTAL CAPTIVE

Thankfully, Patrick slowed down and drove past my house at a properly sedate pace. Of all the times when attracting my father's attention would be bad, driving in with a kidnapped alien lizard in the trunk had to be a contender for Most Likely to Qualify.

And speaking of Karen, a couple of moans from the back signalled that she might be coming to.

"Do you think she's still out?" Patrick asked.

"Loranna are quite robust. She should be starting to come around any time now," Sheldon replied.

"Wonderful." Patrick skidded to a stop in front of the barn, turned around, and zapped the back seat of the Duster.

"Will it go through the metal?" Nat asked.

Patrick pocketed the disruptor with one hand while opening the door with the other. "No metal. The backrest opens right into the trunk. This is a Space Duster."

Nat started to laugh, then cut it off when Patrick gave her a quizzical frown. "Wait," she said. "Seriously?"

He grinned at her. "I don't teach you how to download databases, you don't question my Car-Fu. Deal?" Without waiting for a response, he slammed the door and marched to the rear of the Duster.

I jumped out and joined him. "Think she's been re-zapped?"

"Hope so. Just in case, here." Patrick handed me the disruptor and stuck his key into the lock. He popped the trunk and leaped quickly out of the way. I held up the gun in what I hoped—probably uselessly—was a professional ready stance.

I needn't have worried. Karen was contorted as if she were halfway to pushing out the back seat. Apparently, we'd cut it closer than I really cared for.

"Shit. We were about ten seconds from having an angry lizard in the car with us," Patrick said, echoing my own thoughts.

I was staring stupidly at the alien body, thinking that this weird shit was happening to me *way* too often for one summer, when Sheldon broke the spell.

"Will you missing links please stop breathing through your mouths long enough to move the prisoner? Unless you think afternoon tea with an angry Lorann is preferable. Take your time. We have several whole seconds to deliberate."

Before we could respond, the *Final Jeopardy!* music started playing.

I chuckled and reached into the trunk. With Patrick taking the other end, we carried the prisoner into the barn, while Nat held the door. An airlock stairway was already waiting for us, with a rose-colored pulsing line at the top. We took the obvious hint and followed the line to an open stateroom door.

"This is secure?" I asked.

"All staterooms are required to act as personal environmental pods in case of catastrophe," Sheldon said, "so the construction is already more than robust enough to contain an uncooperative tenant. I've added a mesh doorway to the configuration, and disabled any ability to open it from the inside. It's a standardized process, albeit not one that is used very often."

"Why—" Patrick cut off his question and shook his head.

Quickly, we maneuvered the unconscious Lorann into the stateroom and placed her on the bed. I reached down, felt around, and unclasped her cloaking belt. Karen Ingram changed into an orange, slightly scaly being with a tuft of browner, hairlike stuff on her head.

As we stepped out of the stateroom, the door closed with the usual soft rumble. But instead of the expected solid door, the partition was a kind of screened affair, with four mesh panels in a metal frame. I pushed on the one of the panels, but it didn't give at all. Much stronger than screen-door material, then.

"Ah," Patrick said. "So we can see the prisoner and talk to her."

"Very good," Sheldon replied. "You may yet achieve sentience."

The *Jeopardy!* music started playing again and Patrick rolled his eyes. "Do any of those gadgets have a mute button?"

We sat in the conference room, where we'd gathered to wait for Karen to recover from her second zapping. And to discuss our options.

I held up the thumb drive. "So this is probably what she was coming back for."

"Which means it must have some files that she needed for the management seminar," Nat replied. "Any chance you can read it, Sheldon?"

"Hmm, USB spec—check. APFS or NTFS file-system spec—check. I'll need to print a reader. Maybe two hours."

"Unless it's encrypted," Nat said.

"Two hours and one minute then."

Nat persisted. "You'll want to watch for viruses."

Sheldon responded with a snort and I laughed. A snort from a being with no actual respiratory system was a deliberate affectation. Sheldon continued to improve.

"Should we wait for Sheldon to read the files before interrogating Karen?" Patrick asked.

"I think so," I replied. "Otherwise we're working blind. Plus, it wouldn't hurt to let her stew for a while." Then I hesitated. "Actually, I'm thinking of maybe putting it off until tomorrow morning. I'm pretty bagged."

Patrick grinned. "It has been an exciting day. I could use some sleepy time, too." He looked up. "She can't break out, right?"

"Stop worrying, you nervous ninny," Sheldon replied. "I am constantly monitoring her activity. Or will be, once she wakes up. If by some miracle she found a weakness, I would call one of you for help."

"I bet that would be embarrassing for you, having to call us," Patrick said.

"Even lower life-forms have their uses."

CHAPTER THIRTY:
INTERROGATION

Day 23. Saturday

I woke up all at once. No drifting in and out, no sleepy huddling under the warm blankets. We had a captive alien invader to interrogate. The thought drove all the sleep fog out of my head, and my heart started hammering with two parts excitement and one part fear.

I sat up, looked around for my clothes, then leaped out of bed. I took just long enough putting my clothes on to make sure my pants weren't on backward, then headed for the barn, typing furiously on my phone.

Already on our way, came back from Nat within seconds.

Well, good, I thought. No sense burning daylight. "Sheldon, any progress on those files?"

His answer came over my cling-on as a staircase lowered for me:

"Yes, and I think you're going to find it interesting. Not *good* interesting, either."

"Outstanding," I muttered. A roar and skidding-on-gravel sound from outside told me that Patrick and Nat had arrived. "Gang's all here," I said. "Give us a few minutes to set up, then I guess we'll be good to go."

Nat and Patrick had done the drive-through on the way, so I was pleasantly surprised to receive a McMuffin meal with a large coffee. Nat almost threw the bag at me as she hurried to her favorite spot. Fortunately, she was a little more careful with the coffee.

"What do we have, Sheldon?" she said as she slid into her chair.

"A PowerPoint presentation."

"Excuse me?"

"The thumb drive that Jack stole contained a PowerPoint presentation. It appears it was intended to be presented at whatever status meeting Karen was planning to attend. It is in fact a status report of sorts."

"PowerPoint," Patrick said with exaggerated weariness. "Invading alien lizard people use PowerPoint. Microsoft's marketing team is really, *really* good."

Nat waved to the display wall at the end of the room. "Can you put it up?"

"Coming up. I have clarified the text and labels, to the extent that I am able."

A window popped up in the display wall, showing a surprisingly mundane PowerPoint title page. No images, just three lines of text:

Earth Conversion Project
Schedule, Timeline, Milestones
Prepared by Karen Ingram

"I expected it to be in an alien script," Nat said. "This is English. And Calibri font, if I'm not mistaken."

"Funny thing," Sheldon replied. "Turns out Unicode doesn't contain the Lorannic alphabet. Who knew? In any case, I imagine the Loranna work in English exclusively, not only from necessity, but also out of simple prudence."

After a few seconds, the page changed to a Gantt chart. It contained at least a dozen different development paths, with the word *continued* at the bottom.

"I've created a larger graphic combining all the chart segments," Sheldon said. The window expanded to take up the entire screen, with a massive amount of detail.

"Look at all those separate paths," I said. The chart had the look of a major software project for a bank or government department. I could spot at least six critical paths, linking at major milestones.

"Yeah, but this is the part that's really important," Nat said, pointing to the end. All the various paths merged at the right side of the chart to a single milestone, labeled "Takeover Complete." Nat's finger traced upward to the timeline displayed along the top of the graph.

"Shit," Patrick said. "That's less than five years away!"

I stood and moved closer to the chart, peering at some of the details. "Unfortunately, a lot of these task labels are meaningless or even nonsensical. Sheldon?"

"It appears that the text uses acronyms or jargon that would be unfamiliar to an outsider," Sheldon said. "I suspect some terms are nothing more than Lorannic labels, spelled out phonetically. Even I can't make sense of most of the individual items. Although the milestones tend to be more straightforward."

"Uh, yeah, *takeover* is pretty clear," I said. "Some of these other items are at least ominous. What's interesting is when the *pandemic* subproject was projected to start."

"Off by less than three months," Nat said. "Oh, that can't be coincidence."

"So this means..." Patrick gestured helplessly at the graphic.

"A complete breakdown of human society sometime in the next five years. Everything and I mean *everything* is set to peak at the same time. This," I pointed, "looks like a major environmental catastrophe, although it's hard to tell exactly what."

"Jaysus." Patrick closed his eyes briefly. "Any other slides, Sheldon?"

"A few. I think you'll find them interesting."

"As opposed to..." Patrick waved a hand at the Gantt chart.

"Even so," Sheldon replied.

Several slides popped up in rapid succession, with images of well-known politicians, media figures, and wealthy individuals. Under each picture was some text. Sheldon flashed the images too quickly for anyone to read more than a word or two. By the time the slide show stopped, I'd given up counting them.

Nat had to take a moment to compose herself. "And those were..."

"Collaborationists," Sheldon replied. "More than two hundred powerful or influential humans who have thrown themselves in with the Loranna. Knowingly. The text below the images is a summary of their efforts in the service of the plan."

"Any actual Loranna in disguise?" I asked.

"I would think that'd be poor strategy," Nat interjected. "Too much risk. Disguises can break down; people can notice inconsistencies in behavior, inconsistencies with constructed history, and so on."

"Natalie is correct," Sheldon said. "Although the presentation doesn't give details, there are numerous references to Lorannic 'handlers' and 'influencers,' all no doubt operating behind the scenes. There may in fact still be some embedded Loranna other than those here in Dunnville, but there is no mention of them in the presentation."

Patrick made a face. "Damn. Too bad. I was thinking of unmasking someone famous as a Lorann in public, maybe even live on TV—sabotaging their disguise or something."

"I'm not sure it would be all that effective, anyway," I replied. "Deepfakes have gotten so good now, you can't depend on video evidence. And if the Loranna are as embedded in everything as this indicates, then I'll bet real money they'd have a campaign up and running to discredit us in no time."

Nat sighed. "The Loranna seem to have everything sewn up tight."

"It is possible that this is not their first hootenanny," Sheldon said.

Nat snorted. "Rodeo."

"Sure thing."

"I agree," I said. "This is too smooth, too well orchestrated. Minimal effort, minimal investment, using the resources of the host planet whenever possible. This is a practiced, optimized script. Like they've done this before."

"We are so fucked." Patrick leaned back and sighed. "Let's review, shall we? We can't call the Gen for help. We can't *go to* the Gen for help. We can't unmask any Loranna, and even if we could, it would be buried under a mountain of competing disinformation. We could release this PowerPoint presentation, but it would probably have zero effect. We can't go to the media and expect any results, and if we try to go to the government, we're as likely as not to get intercepted by a collaborationist or disguised Loranna. Have I got it all covered?"

Nat nodded. "Nicely summed up. Let's go talk to my ex-boss. Maybe we can get some ideas."

We stared at Karen. Karen stared back. For almost a minute, no one spoke. I wish I could say we were trying to unnerve her or some such psychological trick, but really, we were just all completely at a loss. And Karen was obviously not going to give us anything.

Patrick threw out the first question. "Why are you here?"

"You kidnapped me."

"No, I mean—" Patrick paused to regroup. "Why is your species secretly on Earth?"

"We're a research group, doing a study of Terran civilization."

I interjected, "And for some reason, you've called it the *Earth Conversion Project?*"

Karen's face went from relaxed to stony. I think. I had to remind myself that reading the facial expressions of an alien probably came with huge error bars, but her face definitely had changed. Which meant I'd scored a hit of some kind.

"I'm not familiar with that phrase."

I held up her thumb drive. "It was on your PowerPoint presentation for the seminar. Want to try again?"

Now there was a definite reaction—a momentary expression of rage. Again, I *think*. But bared teeth and narrowed eyes wasn't just arbitrary signaling, like an ear-waggle or something. There would be good strategic biological reasons for showing your weapons in a threat display and protecting your eyeballs. Oh, and it turned out Loranna had fangs. Worth noting.

"You're making a very large mistake," she said. "You have no idea what you're dealing with."

Nat stepped forward. "To be honest, Karen, after the *secret aliens* thing, and the *Earth Conversion* thing, I'm betting anything else you might want to throw at us would be anticlimactic."

Karen showed her teeth again and said something guttural. In my cling-on, Sheldon said, "That was Lorannic. She was discussing your ancestry and promising her personal attention to your comfort at some future point."

I chuckled. "Comfort. I'm sure."

Karen cocked her head. "You understand Lorannic? Interesting. If you're Gen, you're the shortest Gen I've ever seen."

She looked up and spoke to the air, which I found interesting. "Ship, please open my stateroom door."

"Authorization not recognized," Sheldon replied in a flat tone. At the same moment, he said over the cling-on, "She doesn't need to know I'm sentient."

Now Karen focused on Nat. "You know you're out of a job, right? And times are tough, especially in this rinky-dink town. Gonna be tough paying for your father's medical." She paused and smiled. "Of course, you'll be dead, so maybe it won't matter so much."

"Your threats are empty until you get out of here," Nat replied. I could see anger on her face, though. The comment about her father had scored a hit.

"Even if I don't," Karen said, "you've seen the Gantt chart. You have five years. At the most." Her expression shifted into what was presumably supposed to be a smile, but on a Lorannic face it looked more like hunger. "Listen, that can change. This is nothing personal. We're businesspeople. If you release me, I guarantee you not only a raise and better job title, but also a place in the protected zones once our plans enter the final phases." She glanced at Patrick and me. "And your friends as well. Family, too."

"And we should believe you?"

"We always keep our word, Natalie. Can I call you Nat? You Earthlings have this ridiculous idea that agreements made under duress should have no validity, but we have a more practical attitude. If you don't keep your word in this kind of situation, you have no negotiating power in any future confrontations."

"And you have the authority to make offers like this?"

I glanced at Nat, frowning. Was she actually considering the offer?

Karen laughed. "Kae-Ah and I—that's Arley Montrose to you—are the founders and lead architects of this project. If we can't make commitments, no one can."

Nat looked at me and made a sideways motion with her head. She said to Karen, "We'll need to talk about this," then marched off toward the central elevator. Patrick and I hurried to catch up.

Not a word was spoken until we were seated in the conference room. Nat looked up into the air. "Sheldon, is that statement about Loranna keeping their word true?"

"Yes, but only in the same way as deals with the devil or wishes to genies in your literature. You'd want to make sure the terms were very, very clearly defined."

Patrick gaped at Nat, horrified. "You're not seriously considering taking—"

"Jesus, Patrick," Nat said, cutting him off. "I'm trying to figure out how much we can trust what she says. For instance, that thing about being one of two lead architects…"

"Yeah, I was wondering about that myself," I replied. "Sounds kind of small-time. I'd assumed that the entire Lorannic race was behind this. Sheldon, any thoughts?"

"It does seem like a very small footprint for the operation, if you assume even a single Lorannic tribe is involved. You'd think—"

"Tribe?" I interjected.

"Like your nations, but not as geographically well-defined. Tribes are made up of clans, which you could think of as large families. They are loyal to the tribe, but pursue their own interests."

"Weird."

"Not all intelligent species use the same social structures, Jack."

Nat frowned. "How small can clans be?"

"Possibly as few as a couple dozen Loranna. Below that, they would be unable to defend themselves and would likely be raided and absorbed. However…"

"Yes?" I prompted.

"*However*," Sheldon continued, "we discussed earlier that the whole operation seemed very efficient and practiced. This is inconsistent with a small, marginalized, and possibly desperate clan."

Nat's frown deepened. "We need to get into the Harris computer systems. We need answers."

CHAPTER THIRTY-ONE:
REACTION

Day 24. Sunday

I was awakened by Sheldon's voice over the cling-on. "Alert! Activity in the Harris office."

I sat up. "What?"

"Was I not speaking English? Perhaps I spoke too swiftly for you. Let me try again. Acccccctttttivvvvvvvitttttty innnnnnnn tttttthhhhhhhhe—"

"All right, Sheldon. Jesus. What's happening? Specifically?"

"It would appear that the Loranna have missed our captive. They are upset enough that some of them have spoken Lorannic out loud in the office."

"Okay. I'll come up to the conference room. Have you alerted the others?"

"Gee, that never occurred to me. What a great idea. I'll get right on that."

"Umph," I replied, glaring blearily around the room. If the world needed saving before I had coffee, the world was going to be in deep trouble. Finally focusing on my slippers, I shoved my feet into them and staggered off to the bathroom.

Twenty minutes later, I was on board the *Halo* and watching the activity on the wall monitor. Two video windows were open—the bigger window showed a view of part of the office from the bug that Nat had planted, and a smaller window displayed a close-up view of Karen's monitor from the bug under her keyboard. Three people, including Karen's assistant, Marc, were searching the offices, presumably for any clue to Karen's whereabouts. One of them had a phone on speaker and was occasionally exchanging commentary with the person at the other end.

They had gone through Karen's office twice, but hadn't touched her computer. I found myself gritting my teeth with frustration. Was checking her computer that complicated an idea?

"If they could log in to her account, maybe," Nat said to my muttered complaint. "But if they log in using their own credentials, it's hard to see how they could learn anything."

I made a growling sound in reply, but she was right. I tried to relax and let events unfold at their own—nope, that Zen stuff didn't work for me.

However, my complaints to on high seemed to have an effect, and a positive one for once. Someone finally sat down at Karen's computer, logged in, and proceeded to do some searches. Because of the position of the keyboard bug, we could only see the monitor, not the person using the workstation.

"We have his log-in credentials," Sheldon said with satisfaction. "It's Karen's assistant, Marc Abramson, judging from the username. Fun fact, his password is EarthSuxGr8ly."

Nat laughed. "Maybe the Loranna are more like us than we think."

"Don't make the mistake of trying to relate to them, Natalie. The Loranna have a massive case of racial entitlement. Humans are little more than talking animals to them. As are the Gen, the Ka'alag, the Nir-k-hi, and all the other Covenant races. However, the Loranna are outmatched militarily, so they maintain a veneer of politeness."

"Wonderful," I muttered. "Kzinti."

While this discussion had been going on, Marc had finished, or possibly just given up. He smacked the monitor, then logged himself off and pushed the keyboard away. He yelled something to his fellow searchers and stomped off.

"We should wait until Marc leaves before attempting to log on remotely," Sheldon said. "If he logs on locally while we're remoting in, security systems will generate an alert."

"Are you sure?" Patrick asked.

I answered before Sheldon could. "Even for human sysops, that's an obvious thing to watch for. It'll be automated and they'll get an alert."

The device that Nat had planted could pick up sound over most of the third floor, but the video field of view was limited by its location. Most of the information coming over the bug consisted of off-screen bumps, walking sounds, and occasional English and Lorannic commentary. It was a measure of the stress level that the Loranna were breaking character like that.

Then there was a yell, followed by stampeding sounds.

"What just happened?" Patrick said.

"They are excited by something," Sheldon replied. "Ah. Security-camera feeds. Someone went back through the video files and found a scene where Karen was being kidnapped by Karen and Marc. Marc keeps yelling, 'That isn't me! I wasn't there!' I believe the jig is out."

"Up," Nat corrected.

"Regardless of the jig's ultimate vector, they are now on full alert. We might want to consider logging in now and getting what we can."

"Let's do it," Nat said, and grabbed her laptop. Reaching into a pocket, she pulled out a small, round object—her new security fob. Some rapid typing, a pause to transfer a number from the fob's display, and the logo of the Harris Institute was up on her laptop screen.

Nat scanned the menu for a moment. "This is a pretty standard document-management system. Let's see what we can find."

"Allow me, Natalie. I can scan and analyze the contents more quickly than you."

The laptop started flashing through screens faster than we humans could follow. Natalie leaned back, a surprised expression on her face. "You hacked my laptop?"

"Not at all. Standard man-in-the-middle attack. I am, after all, your Wi-Fi hotspot. I've merely taken over the client connection."

"But that's encrypt—" Nat sighed. "Never mind."

"Finally!" Sheldon crowed. "Signs of intelligence."

I pointed to a small window at the bottom left of the screen that said "Downloading," and "Thirty-four files." The number fluctuated up and down.

"Looks like Sheldon is queueing interesting files for download," Nat said.

There was a yell in Lorannic from the video window still displaying activity on the third floor.

"What're they saying?" Patrick asked.

"They are currently discussing why Marc is both logged in remotely and standing right there. Of more concern to me is—"

There was an abrupt *bang* from the video view from Karen's keyboard. Loud voices yelled in Lorannic, combined with the sounds of furniture being pushed around. Then the view rotated wildly as Karen's keyboard was picked up. The window stabilized with an upside-down close-up of Marc's face, livid with anger. He reached forward and the window abruptly went blank.

"An unfortunate turn of events. I expect our remote connection will shortly—" Before Sheldon could finish the sentence, Nat's laptop screen went black except for the single message: "Connection terminated."

"Well," Nat said, "looks like I'm out of a job."

"Why?" Patrick frowned.

"My fob was used to log into Marc's account. Even if I report the fob lost, I'm toast."

"What did you manage to get, Sheldon?" I asked.

"I'm evaluating. A lot of fairly pedestrian items, news reports and the like. Several files were only partially downloaded. But there's also some *very* interesting data, such as many more names of collaborationists and blackmail victims."

Nat clapped her hands and brightened up considerably. "Then it was worth it, at least. Let's wait until you've sorted it out, then you can give us a summary."

"Agreed. I'll let you know when I'm ready. However…" Sheldon, uncharacteristically, hesitated.

"What's up, Sheldon?" Nat asked.

"The person at the other end of the phone. I assume you noticed that one of the Loranna had a call going? It was the individual at the other end who noticed the log-in, who found the video, and who suggested checking the keyboard."

"Okay … they're a smart Lorann?"

"Too smart. And too quick. And with immediate access to digital information." Again, Sheldon paused. "It is just possible that the Loranna are using a conscious A.I."

I sat in the conference room, fidgeting with my tablet without really seeing the screen. I'd tried going to my bunk, I'd tried watching some YouTube videos, but nothing was working. I simply couldn't concentrate on anything but the suspense of waiting for whatever Sheldon was going to produce. I looked around at the others and saw the same anxiety on their faces.

Sheldon broke the silence. "I suppose you're all wondering why—"

"*Jesus*, Sheldon," Nat yelled. "Don't you dare!"

"Hmph. That seemed like a natural. But very well. You are obviously on edge. All comfy? Anyone need to use the facilities?"

Natalie growled.

"Right. So, let's start with the small stuff. There is a report of the incident in the administration offices. They identified Phil Ross—probably the same way you did, Natalie—but apparently dismissed Jack and Patrick as lackeys. An order was put out to an independent contractor to collect Mr. Ross and his two assistants for questioning, but it had not returned any results as of the time of the report."

"Lackeys? I'm offended!" Patrick said. "I like to think of myself as more of a minion."

Nat rolled her eyes. "But the cop tried to nab *us*, not Phil. So that can't be it." She frowned, staring off into space. "We're missing something."

"You're missing most of my presentation," Sheldon replied. "Shall I continue?"

I chuckled. "Go ahead, Sheldon."

"Regarding the Lorannic presence itself, there is nothing that contradicts Alaric's suspicions or any of our conjectures. The only surprise is how thoroughly they've infiltrated the various human bureaucracies, and how expertly they've manipulated the various social media platforms. And with what appears to be a surprisingly small number of personnel. This reinforces my suspicion that they are using an A.I. A small group, especially a mere clan, could only do all this with assistance from some kind of advanced expert system."

"What exactly does *all this* consist of?" Nat asked.

"For instance, almost all of the disinformation sources you are familiar with are either Lorann-controlled or Lorann-influenced."

"Like?" Patrick asked.

"Those Russian troll farms? Loranna. The Asian ones as well. QAnon? Loranna. Several of the far-right so-called news channels are controlled by Loranna. You'll find the owners of some of those channels in the *collaborationist* file."

"What about far-left?" Nat asked.

"Technically, the Russian sources would qualify, but I don't think they are generally viewed that way."

"True," Nat said. "And anyway, far-left and far-right extremists can be hard to tell apart. Once you reach the point where you believe that you have the right to enforce your stance by lies, intimidation, and violence, it really doesn't matter that much what label you apply."

"So all those conspiracy theories about a shadow group running the world are true?" Patrick said.

"Yes and no. There is no ZOG, no Deep State, no human-based world shadow organization. The Loranna have amplified such narratives with an eye to desensitizing people to similar stories. For instance, the conspiracy theory that the government is being controlled by shapeshifting lizards was deliberately started by the Loranna and attached by association to tinfoil-hat types, so if anything ever *did* come out about the Loranna, it would simply be dismissed as more of the same."

I nodded. "Preemptive strike. Pretty standard disinfo technique. I imagine it's not the only one."

"Of course not. Flying saucer reports, Area 51, Roswell—all created or amplified for the same purpose. Any accidental sighting of an actual Lorannic vessel would again be dismissed as more nutbar narrative."

"Fluoridation of water? Knights Templar? Illuminati? Fake moon landings?" Nat said.

"The Loranna have also taken stories that already existed and amplified them," Sheldon replied. "They are not responsible for *all* conspiracy theories but will take advantage of anything that will increase strife, violence, or divisiveness. Pizzagate, for instance, was not a Lorannic construct, but they mention it in one document as an unexpected gift to be amplified to the greatest extent possible."

Patrick sighed. "This just seems like too much to believe. How can they pull this off?"

"Think of it like sitting passively on a swing. A series of small pushes by someone at the right time can turn minimal effort into a large result, resulting in you swinging in a large arc. Many of these conspiracy theories would sink into obscurity or simply coast to a stop on their own, but a new claim or viral campaign at the right time will bring them back to the forefront of public attention. Amplify that with social media botnets and the theory attains new life.

Do that several times, and each revival can be bigger than the previous one."

I frowned and sat forward. "Okay, so that's global strife. The Gantt chart indicates that they were behind the pandemic, or at least influenced its existence or spread in some way. Anything else on that in the files?"

"Anti-vaxxers and Pandemic-pushers, of course. Specifically designed to ensure that any diseases spread as quickly as possible, any response is undercut as much as possible, and vaccines are resisted as long as possible. Ideally, they'd like to make smallpox and polio into global issues again."

I sighed. "I'm sure I'll regret asking, but what about the environment?"

"Do you truly believe that even the most energetically pro-business leaders would deliberately continue to pollute the planet if they knew that they and their families were going to be caught in the results? Those at the top who practice denialism and destructive policies expect to be in the protected enclaves that Karen mentioned when the collapse occurs. And continuing to make money by charging the common populace through the nose for a seat."

Nat put her head in her hand. "Oy."

"Oh, and I now have an explanation for that major environmental disaster on the Gantt chart."

"Go ahead," I said.

"It discusses percentages, although the Loranna use base sixteen for some reason, so that might not be the correct term. But regardless, the item references something dropping from twenty-one percent to nineteen percent."

"Okay, I'll bite. You have an idea what that might be?"

"Oxygen. The percentage of oxygen in the Earth's atmosphere is currently just a fraction under twenty-one percent, as it has been for millions of years. The minimum percentage at which humans can operate is nineteen-point-five. Below that, trying to do more than stand up puts you in an oxygen deficit. Another half point and mental function starts to suffer, even at minimal activity."

"But how?" Patrick asked.

I took up the narrative. "I've read about this. Increased global warming produces higher temps, decreased rainfall, and quicker drying of vegetation, which creates the conditions for more and bigger wildfires, which are triggered by increased incidences of lightning storms brought on by the hotter, dryer air. Those, plus all the burning and clearing of jungles in South America, not only burn massive amounts of existing oxygen, but also produce more CO_2, further lowering the oxygen percentage." I paused and looked around. "Ocean pollution and acidification kill off phytoplankton. Guess where more than half of the oxygen recycling comes from? And warming oceans absorb less CO_2—so y'know, more for us."

"It's more than that, Jack," Sheldon said. "The oxygen in the atmosphere is actually an imbalance created by all the carbon that has been sequestered over geological time as coal and oil, before it had the chance to be burned. Humans have been working diligently to add that fuel back into the equation, further reducing the imbalance."

Now Nat covered her face completely with her hands. Her voice came out slightly muffled. "Jesus. We have to break this."

"Sure," I replied. "But how? We can't fight an entire alien civilization."

"You may not have to," said Sheldon. "Based on what's in the documents, this actually does look like a small operation, bolstered by an A.I. And Karen and Arley are almost certainly in charge. In fact, this might even be a single, rogue clan engineering the whole thing."

"Again, how?"

"Jack, if they are small and resource-constrained, it would explain their almost exclusive use of Earth-based technology and resources. Your civilization is still primitive enough to value things like gold and platinum, which, other than their industrial uses, are virtually waste products from antimatter generators. A group could pick up a large inventory of so-called precious metals for not very much in Covenant credits. Then, using the Earth-based wealth that this represents, they could buy, bribe, and blackmail their way into positions with high leverage without having to use much in the way of Covenant-level technology or resources, which they probably couldn't afford anyway."

"The FTL detector?"

"That and a couple of older-model, low-end ships might be literally all they have to their collective name."

"Huh." I stared into space, thinking for a few moments. "So, okay, we don't have to be concerned about an *Independence Day* kind of a scenario, but we're still outmatched. No offense, Sheldon, but you are unarmed."

"And I have a best-before date hanging over my head, and cannot call for help."

"That too. Plus, they've been working on this for, what? Years? Decades?"

"I would guess decades, Jack. The payoff from acquiring trusteeship of an entire untouched system would justify any amount of investment. They would go from being small fry to a major player in Lorannic society in one leap."

"They'd be committing a significant portion of their lives to this, though," Nat said.

"Lifespans are much longer with Covenant medical knowledge," Sheldon replied. "This is not as big a commitment for them as it would be for you."

Patrick waved his arms to get everyone's attention. "This is all very interesting, but we still haven't gotten to square one on what we're going to do about it. Any ideas?"

We exchanged glances, but no one volunteered a response. Even Sheldon withheld comment.

CHAPTER THIRTY-TWO:
KIDNAPPINGS

Day 25. Monday morning

I stood on the porch, steaming travel mug in my hand, waiting for Patrick. Dad had informed me at breakfast that I'd need to make alternate arrangements or drive myself to work in the Buick, as he was working from home today. Patrick, always ready to help, had agreed to pick me up.

He came around the corner into our driveway as usual, almost but not quite on two wheels, and skidded to a stop right in front of me. I got in the car with as much dignity as I could muster, and tried to ignore the gravel-spewing donut as he came around for launch.

"If you break a window, Dad'll make you pay for it," I said.

"Well, *someone* will pay," he replied. "I don't think your dad really cares who."

I grunted and sipped my coffee as we sped off down the road.

We were coming around a curve just outside of town when Patrick abruptly hammered on the brakes. In front of us were two vehicles, parked in a V, blocking the road. One of them had more than a passing resemblance to the fake cop car that had chased us the other day, but without the roof lights.

Patrick skidded to a stop and stuck it in reverse immediately, having correctly analyzed the situation as *not good.* Then he said, "Aw, shit!" as something thumped into our back end.

I just had time to turn and see a large four-by-four blocking our escape when someone dressed up in military gear poked an automatic weapon at me and yelled, "Get out, now!" I could hear something similar happening on Patrick's side of the car.

Raising my hands first, I slowly reached for the lock button and pulled it up. Immediately the guy grabbed the door and yanked it open, then stepped back with the rifle pointed at my head. "Out."

I subvocalized, "Sheldon, help! We're being arrested or kidnapped or something. No cloaking fields, but they could be employed by the Loranna."

Sheldon's reply came back right away. "Understood. I can track you, unless they put you in a Faraday cage. I've alerted Natalie in case she's a target as well. She's already on her way to work, but has pulled over. I'll pick her up immediately."

Meanwhile Patrick and I were zip-tied and bundled into the back of a windowless van by taciturn men in military gear. It would have been comical in its level of Hollywood cliché, except for the fact that I was scared almost to the point of wetting myself.

But we weren't dead, which had to be a plus. And Sheldon and Nat would be on the case. I wasn't sure what they could do, but it still made me feel better.

We soon found ourselves bound to chairs in what looked very much like a warehouse. I'd have chuckled at the predictability of it all, except for the zip-ties on our wrists. And the guns. My bladder continued to signal its concern, which wasn't helping either.

"Well, well, well," said a voice behind me. The speaker sauntered slowly around into view, obviously trying to project confidence and control. Not doing a bad job, really, considering our situation.

I frowned at him. "You look familiar, but…"

"Arley Montrose," he replied. "I'm sure Karen Ingram has mentioned me."

Patrick turned to me. "Ingram. That's Nat's boss, I think." Then to Arley, "We've never actually met her."

Arley smirked and examined his fingernails. "Uh huh. By all means, play dumb. It adds to the entertainment value. My friend Luthor, here, will be happy to help you with your memory issues."

He gestured to his left, and another man stepped into view. It was the fake cop from a few days ago. He glared at us with an expression that made me think we might not be best buds.

"Luthor would like to thank you, by the way, for giving him a firsthand experience with the effects of a disruptor. I've never had the pleasure myself, but I understand it's quite uncomfortable. Unfortunate that you don't have it on you; I'd have been happy to give you a small sample. I'm very interested in finding out how you got hold of a disruptor and a couple of cloaking belts. That will be Luthor's department."

Luthor grunted, then smiled at us. "I hope you won't break too quickly. On the other hand, I don't think it really matters if you do."

I looked back and forth from Luthor to Arley. "Luthor, do you know who and what you're working for?"

He grinned back, and it wasn't reassuring at all.

"Luthor is being well paid, and has an assured place in the enclaves once our plans come to fruition." Arley smiled. "You, on the other hand, will be joining Phil Ross once Luthor is done with you."

"Phil?" Patrick piped up. "Is he okay?"

"How fucking stupid are you?" Luthor snarled. "Does anything that's been said here give you any reason to believe he's okay? Or that you will be? Do I have to draw you a fucking picture, kid?" He leaned in and gave us that grin again. Still not reassuring. "By the time you actually die, you'll be missing body parts and begging me to kill you."

"And when Luthor finally grants you your wish, you'll join Mr. Ross as the guests of honor at a luncheon banquet for my clan." Arley smiled and just for a moment, his Lorannic fangs showed. Despite my mounting fear, I found that interesting. Someone or something was controlling his cloaking field in real time, just like Sheldon did for us.

"That doesn't seem like the best way of getting Karen back," I replied. "Hostage exchanges usually involve *live* hostages, if you get my drift." I looked directly at Arley. "My understanding is that the Loranna stick to their deals."

"Mm, true. But *alive* and *healthy* aren't the same thing. I wonder how many body parts you'd have to lose before your team wouldn't want you. We could remove a limb or two without killing you, I imagine. For snacks."

Uh-oh. He had a point. While I was still searching for a response, Patrick said, "The same could be said about Karen, Arley."

Arley laughed. "Even if you humans had the stomach for that kind of thing, our medical tech can regenerate anything, as long as she's still alive. I doubt you have access to the same level of care."

I kept my face still, and hoped Patrick had done the same. Arley had just unintentionally given us a big piece of information—he didn't know about the *Halo*. He might in fact think the only Covenant tech we owned was a disruptor and a couple of belts.

At that moment, Luthor's phone beeped. He pulled it out and glanced at it, then turned to Arley. "The third brat is in custody. They'll have her here in ten."

Nat. I felt my face go ashen as the implication sank in. Luthor noticed my expression and nodded. "Yeah, maybe we'll work your girlfriend over a little in front of you. See if that helps jog your memory. Not that I care either way."

I opened my mouth to reply just as all the mercenaries began falling down, clockwise from Patrick's side of the room. Luthor only had time to reach for his gun when he and Arley keeled over as well.

Nat's voice said, out of empty air, "Here I come, to save the *dayyyyyyy*."

A silence descended on the room as the last unconscious body stopped flopping. "Are there any others?" I asked, looking around.

Sheldon replied, "I did an acoustical inventory. All are accounted for. However, Nat's tactic of sweeping with the disruptor may result in some zaps being less than full strength. You should depart while the departing is optimal."

An excellent policy for any time, as far as I was concerned. Nat became visible, flipped open a folding knife, and quickly cut our zip-ties. We stood, ready to run. Then I turned and looked at Arley.

"No," Nat said. "Come on, you've got to be kidding. We don't need another—"

"Maybe we do. Sheldon, please start on a second detention berth, preferably right across from Karen. And close her door so she doesn't know anything until we're ready to tell her."

"It will take a while," Sheldon replied. "You will have to re-stun your subject, and you should have some of those plastic restraints in reserve, just for safety."

"And guns," Patrick said, gathering several of the weapons.

"Do you even know how to use those?" Nat asked.

"No friggin' clue. But I'm a quick study."

"Patrick, give the guns to Nat. Help me with Arley."

It turned out we really had been in a warehouse, in the low-rent end of the industrial district. Because why not? I wondered if anyone had ever heard of playing against type.

It took several minutes to get Arley outside and up the stairs into the awaiting *Halo*. He was surprisingly heavy, easily well over two-fifty, and consequently very hard to maneuver.

During one of the drop-and-shuffle breaks, I said to Nat, "I thought they captured you. Luthor got a text to that effect."

"Text courtesy of Sheldon," she replied with a wide smile. "After he scanned the phones of the two guys who came for me."

Patrick stopped massaging his forearms and frowned. "How did you manage to get their phones?"

"I'd have been in trouble if they'd coordinated the grabs, but you guys gave us enough warning to set up a trap. Did you know that the cloaking fields can make an empty driver's seat look not empty? While Tweedledee and Tweedledummy were trying to sneak up on the car and grab me, I came out from behind a bush and zapped them."

I snorted, then gestured to the body. Patrick groaned in reply and reached down to grab the legs.

My back itched until the airlock was safely closed. It would only take one mercenary to wake up and come out shooting to ruin our day. But the operation was completed without incident and soon we were in the air. Patrick re-zapped Arley, then zip-tied him for good measure.

He needn't have bothered. Arley was just beginning to make snorting noises and twitch when we finally dumped him into his new prison cell and cut the straps.

"Not a terrible idea, Jack." Patrick gestured at Arley's semiconscious form. "If we have both the leaders, I can see that putting a crimp in their operation. So how will we handle this?"

⚜ ⚜ ⚜

Arley sat up with a groan. Another universal, I guess. He glared blearily at us from his bunk, not saying anything. He might have been looking a little green, which on an orange-skinned being should come out brown, if my old art teacher was to be believed.

I waited a few more seconds, but I guess he was going to wait for us to make the first move. Well, fine then. "We should talk," I said.

"Why?"

"Well, we have you in a cell, for starters."

"So?"

I glanced at Patrick and Nat. Their perplexed expressions didn't fill me with confidence. Apparently, Arley wasn't as talkative as Karen.

I tried to regroup. "Well, it does put a crimp in your plans for world domination."

He shrugged. "Not really. They can handle it without me."

"You mean without you and Karen. The two of you are the leaders and chief architects, aren't you? How much redundancy can you build into an organization that's built around a single small clan?"

That got a reaction. Without any kind of warning or buildup, Arley launched himself at us, mouth agape and arms spread wide. I had time to note that he also had claws—retractable, apparently—before he slammed into the cell door.

"Sheldon?" I subvocalized.

"The door will hold against considerably more than Arley can bring to bear," he replied. "I do know what I'm doing."

I gazed at Arley, trying to project *relaxed and unafraid.* "Y'know, your species has a definite anger-control issue." Arley glared at me, as I continued, "Karen reacted much the same way, although she's a lot more into threats. Something about not bothering to cook us first."

Now Arley did smile. "That sounds like Karen. She does like sushi."

"Ewww," said Nat.

He glanced at her, then back at me. "Okay, so what now? You seem to have the momentary advantage. What do you want? Money? A spot in the enclaves? We can do that, you know. We don't—"

"Go back on your agreements. I know. Karen tried that line."

"Uh-huh. You're going to a lot of trouble to bring up Karen in the conversation. Almost like you want me to *think* you have her. Maybe not so much?"

"Well, we didn't eat her," I replied. "But negotiations didn't go well."

"So what do you want?"

"For the Loranna to leave our planet."

Arley laughed. "That's not going to happen. Even with both Karen and me gone. We're fully committed to this, Jack. It's Jack, right? You humans all look the same to me. We have no other option. We've put everything into this."

"Fully committed is right," I said. "You even woke an A.I." I watched him carefully for a reaction, and was rewarded with a very brief expression of surprise before his poker face settled back in.

"Well, no, strictly speaking that wasn't us. It came as part of the package." Arley stopped. "I can't decide how much you actually know and how much of this is fishing. I probably should just shut up, I think."

"Suit yourself," I said. Then to Sheldon, "Close it."

Arley's door rumbled shut, leaving the three of us standing in the corridor looking at each other.

"Package?" Patrick said.

"Like something you buy," Nat said. "Like a franchise? Everything you need to set up a takeover operation?"

"That would mean Earth isn't the only victim of this," I replied. "Jesus, how deep does this go?"

Nat gestured to the door across from Arley. "Let's find out. Sheldon, open Karen's door."

I turned to face her stateroom as the door withdrew.

Karen slouched on her bunk, apparently relaxed. "So what does a girl have to do to get lunch around here?"

"Answer a quick question," Nat replied. "How many clans have bought into this planetary takeover franchise?"

"How the hell would I—?" Karen cut herself off. "I mean, what franchise?"

Nat grinned. "Never mind. Got it."

Karen leaned forward. "You'd make a good lunch. Kind of scrawny, but we could get a good broth out of you, I think." She paused. "We'll win eventually, Natalie. You can't keep dodging us. We have the infrastructure, we have the weapons. We have—"

"A conscious A.I.," Nat said, interrupting the monologue. "That'll go over really well if the Covenant gets involved."

Karen glared. "A big *if*. We get you or the Covenant gets us. I like our odds better. We actually know you exist."

Nat took a step back, and I let my jaw drop. We hadn't said anything to that effect, I was sure of it. Had Karen simply deduced it?

"Well, some of you do," Nat replied. She muttered an order to Sheldon, and the door across from Karen's slid open. Arley and Karen just had time to stare at each other in surprise before Arley's door rumbled closed.

Karen recovered quickly, though. She smiled back, the smile still looking more like a hungry beast's than anything. "It's only beginning, sweetie. We'll be going after your family next. Think you can stay free with a gun to your father's head?"

She was baiting us. It was obvious. I took a couple of steps toward her, without any clear plan.

"Say this to her," Sheldon said into my cling-on.

He began to dictate, and I repeated his words out loud: "How many people in your clan, Karen? Twenty? Thirty?

What's the minimum number you could leave on your home planet to maintain a presence and keep from having everything stolen or squat-claimed? What are the chances that you've got everyone and everything you can spare invested in this operation? Whoever sold you the ACME World Domination Package would have priced it for all the market is worth, because that's how Loranna work. I think you're maxed out. And you're using a conscious A.I., which is a mind-wipeable offense even if you didn't create it yourself. You've got no fallback, no backup plan. This your only viable option, and you're running at redline."

Karen's expression changed to rage in an eyeblink. "Watch your mouth, *food*, or choking on your own gases will be a death you'll pray for."

Sheldon resumed dictating, and I continued, "If you don't pull this off, your best-case outcome is losing everything. All your assets, gone. Unable to make clan-fee. You'd have to go begging to other tribes to take you in, and you'll be starting over as chattel slaves." I smiled at her, hoping I was convincing. "That's what we have in store for you."

Turned out I was very convincing. Karen launched into a high-volume tirade of what I had to assume were curses and threats. Interestingly, Loranna became *purple* in the face when enraged. I made a note to ask about that at some point.

"Shall I translate?" Sheldon asked.

"Naw. I get it. She's not a fan."

We were sitting in the conference room again. Sheldon had put up a surveillance window showing Karen and Arley's cells. At the moment, Karen was lying down, and Arley was holding his head, trying to keep it from toppling right off his neck. From the occasional groans, I surmised that waking up from a zap was like waking up with a hangover, only more so. He hadn't seemed to be in any discomfort when we were talking to him though. That showed a considerable amount of discipline.

"We can't ignore Karen's threat," Nat said. "Our families are targets. I don't see what we can do about that."

"But targets for what?" I asked. "Kidnapping? Assassination? They want something from us, so taking hostages seems a lot more likely. But even then, they have to be able to contact us to tell us what they want."

Patrick raised his head from his hand, where he'd been cradling it. "You mean we have to disappear."

"We kind of already have." I looked down at my phone, where the fifth text from my father had just popped up. Patrick's occasional jerk indicated he was probably getting something similar. We were now all several hours late for work, and people must be wondering where we were. Well, maybe not Nat. I imagined management at her job had already cut her final check and filled out her termination slip. Or whatever Loranna did.

There would be a search. They would find Patrick's abandoned vehicle, and they would find Nat's abandoned vehicle. Hers was parked properly, though.

I shrugged and continued. "And the Loranna or their hired goons will try to search our homes sooner or later. Maybe just surveillance or a B&E to start with. I doubt they'll want to attract attention. We have to disappear, *and* we're going to have to move the *Halo*. Sheldon, take us out of here. Random destination. We'll figure out something later."

"Acknowledged."

"We can't just abandon everyone!" Nat retorted angrily.

"We aren't," I said. "This is just a retreat and regroup. We have to figure out what to do next."

Patrick muttered a curse. "I can't believe it, but I'm actually regretting not handing this over to Phil or the government."

Nat nodded. "And this puts a time limit on our efforts. *Another* one, I mean." She looked up at me, her expression worried. "Jack, we just keep getting deeper and deeper into this, and our options keep getting more and more narrow."

I put my hand on her back in a not-quite-brotherly semi-embrace. "Hey, Nat, I get it. But we can only do what we can do. And I may have some ideas on that front. But first, I think we need some sleep."

"And food," Patrick added. "Do you guys realize we literally haven't eaten since breakfast?" He looked up. "Sheldon, can you replicate food?"

"Sorry, no. *Star Trek* replicators remain in the realm of science fiction, even for me. I can offer a refrigerator and a microwave, though."

"Why would you have a microwave?"

"To heat food. Gen need to eat, too."

"Gen use microwaves?" Nat said.

"And refrigerators. Yes. They picked these things up from observing Earth. Before that, they kept spare food in their armpits."

"Real—" Nat's eyes narrowed. "You're pulling my leg."

"Your perspicaciousness is truly an inspiration to sentient beings everywhere."

"Asshole."

"Still not installed. Sorry."

Nat made a low growling sound. "I don't think the Covenant outlawed conscious A.I.s for ethical reasons. I think they just got tired of listening to them."

Sheldon withheld comment. But the mention of food had set my stomach to rumbling. "Well, we definitely need to do something. Sheldon, can you find a 7-Eleven at least twenty miles away, on a highway?"

"I shall invoke the Google. One moment. Found one."

"What do you have in mind?" Nat asked me.

"Food run, of course. We may have to use cash, though. They might have flagged our accounts by now."

"You could use Phil's account," Sheldon said. "It has a significant balance."

"How would I do that?" I asked.

"I had access to Phil's phone. Phil pays for things with his phone. Shall I draw you a picture, with little stick people and dialogue balloons?"

Patrick laughed out loud. I sighed, looked at Nat, and shook my head. "Let's see if we have enough cash first. If we have to use Phil's account, we will, I guess. And it would help support the narrative that we've completely disappeared."

The view on the wall screen showed the 7-Eleven just off the highway near Akron. It was still early enough in the evening to be busy. Cars pulled in and out of the parking lot regularly—far too often to risk a drop-off from an invisible spaceship.

"We can put down just up the road, on the shoulder," I suggested. "Sheldon, can you suppress the lighting for the airlocks?"

"Of course."

"Okay, that should be minimum risk, if we can find a darker area. We can walk in, buy some food, and walk out. We get back on board when it's safe." I looked around at the others. No one had any argument, probably motivated by the fact that no one had eaten in close to sixteen hours. For middle-class Americans used to three squares, it was akin to torture.

"We should take zappers," Nat said.

"I don't think it'll be necessary," I replied.

"Any time you have a choice of taking a weapon or not taking a weapon, you always take a weapon," Nat said. "Have you *never* watched TV?"

Patrick and I replied with weak smiles, and Nat added, "Remember that Geico horror movie ad?"

"Yeah," Patrick said, "Let's not be those kids."

Nat and I waited in the darkened vestibule. I had instructed Sheldon to watch for a good moment, with no nearby traffic, before lowering the stairway. Wasting no time, we rushed down the stairs.

"We're out," I said, as soon as we were on solid ground. The stairway retracted, without the usual chirp-chirp and flashing lights.

The 7-Eleven was fifty yards or so down the road. I patted my hoodie pocket as we entered the store, checking that my disruptor was still there. Where it was supposed to have gone, I couldn't say, but I felt a strong urge to check it every few seconds. I remembered reading somewhere that this behavior was a tell, done by people who didn't normally carry a weapon. Clerks were trained to watch for people patting a pocket too often in the store.

We didn't have a shopping list as such, beyond some basic asks like beer, soda, milk, and bread. And Cheetos. And we were shopping hungry, so the baskets filled quickly and haphazardly. The store wasn't by any means deserted, yet I got the impression that the clerk was watching us more closely than seemed necessary. But maybe that was just paranoia.

We eventually made our way to the checkout and placed our baskets on the counter. The clerk eyed the haul, gave us a strange look, and started running the items through the scanner. Slowly. While glancing far too often at the front door. While obviously trying *not* to glance at the front door.

I was no seasoned secret agent, but I was pretty sure that was a tell. I glanced at Nat, who also appeared to have noticed the odd behavior.

"Two police cars have pulled into the parking lot," Sheldon announced over the cling-on. "Their demeanor appears more focused than a donut run would require. Patrick says to be ready for trouble."

I put my hand into my right hoodie pocket and gripped the disruptor. Nat stepped back from the counter so that she also had a clear field of fire.

Then the door burst open and four cops came in, guns drawn. "Hands up," one yelled.

It was all they had time for. I pushed the button on the disruptor without bothering to draw it from my pocket. There was a brief tingling on my abdomen, probably from the zap grazing me.

All the cops went down in a heap. "Is that all of them, Sheldon?" I said.

"Yes. But very likely more will follow. You should leave."

Nat, meanwhile, pulled out her disruptor and pointed it at the clerk. "Did you call them?"

"Y-y-yes. Please don't—wait, what's that thing? Is that what you shot them with? You're kidding, right? That's a toy, right?" The man started to put his hands down.

Nat moved the slider to the lowest setting and fired. The clerk sort of shriek-grunted and did what I would have sworn was an impossible yoga move. The smell of urine wafted into the air.

"Does that feel like a toy?" Nat snarled, leaning over the counter. "Why. Did. You. Call them?"

The clerk gasped, holding on to the counter with both hands. It took him several seconds to get his breath. "For the reward. On TV."

"We're on TV?" I exclaimed.

"You didn't know? All-points bulletin. Ten grand for information, etcetera. I, uh, recognized your girlfriend. She's kind of hot ... "

"Shit." I looked at the cash register. So far, we'd totaled up a little over forty dollars. I pulled out the wad of money we'd collected, stripped out three twenties, and threw them on the counter. "Keep the change." We grabbed our groceries and made for the door.

Just as we exited, three more patrol cars pulled in. Tires squealing, they formed a rough ring centered on the doorway. As the cops began piling out of their vehicles, movement in the air above caught my eye. A stairway was lowering out of midair, a dark figure balanced on the stairs. The figure pointed something and the cops began dropping.

The last remaining cop looked around for the source of the attack, and glanced upward. He just had time for "What the f—" before he too dropped to the ground.

A couple of random customers stood rigid in front of the store, having watched the whole scene unfold. One pointed at the figure in the air, now clearly identifiable as Patrick, but said nothing.

Patrick turned to them and waved his disruptor. Two customers bolted. The rest just stood there, looking stupefied as the disembodied stairway settled to the ground nearby, Patrick standing near the bottom on lookout. He sprinted up the stairs to the vestibule and we followed. Within moments, the stairway had retracted.

"That went well," Patrick commented dryly. "Good spycraft. I don't think *anyone* noticed you."

"Yeah, funny thing. Turns out there's a price on our heads. Ten grand." I rubbed my forehead as I pressed the top-floor button in the elevator.

"Fuck," Patrick said. "My parents will be going crazy."

"Mine too," I replied. "We need to let them know we're all right." I dropped the bags onto the conference table and threw myself into a chair.

"I can send them a text or email," Sheldon said out of midair. "You'll have to compose something appropriate, then forward it to me. I will transmit the messages from a suitably innocuous cell region."

"Well the good news, anyway," Patrick said, rifling through one of the bags, "is that you managed to get Cheetos."

Nat gave him an eye roll. "Glad we could satisfy your cravings, Patrick."

Once we got to the ready room, I took out my phone and started typing. I noticed out of the corner of my eye Nat and Patrick doing the same. A small part of my mind wondered how Nat would handle the situation. Presumably, she was writing to her aunt, but that would carry the additional burden of asking the woman to keep caring for Nat's father. Not a small ask.

I was finished in minutes. I read it over.

Mom, Dad—

I'm sure you've seen our names and faces plastered on the TV, and I'm sure you're worried and wondering what's going

*on. Believe me, whatever they're accusing us of is BS. This
is a case of wanting something we have and doing anything
they can to get it. Think Will Smith, Enemy of the State.*

*I won't be in touch again until this is resolved. We're
working on it, but it's going to create a very large news cycle
before it's done, I think.*
Jack

I had no doubt that any texts my parents received would
be read by persons unknown, which was why I'd thrown in
the comment about not getting in touch. I forwarded the
text to Sheldon, then sat back and eyed my friends. Patrick
seemed to have finished and was reviewing his message. Nat
was typing and stopping, typing and stopping, chewing on
her lip the whole while. I didn't envy her.

Finally, Nat sent her text to Sheldon and dropped her
phone on the table with a sigh. "So what now?"

There was a ding from an alcove and Patrick popped a
door open. "So microwaves are universal," he said, pulling
out a frozen meal. "Utensils, not so much. But this thing is
kind of a spork." Patrick briefly held up an implement as he
sat with his food. "Maybe you guys should fill your pieholes
before continuing. People think better when their stomachs
aren't trying to digest their spines, know what I mean?"

I grabbed a prepackaged burrito. "How does the nuker
work?"

"Just ask Sheldon to operate it. Apparently, it's net-
worked. Internet of Things, Gen version."

"I live to serve," Sheldon said. "No job too menial, no
task too degrading."

I put the burrito on a plate and stuck it into the microwave. "Or you could just tell me what buttons to push.
Obviously, I don't read Gennan."

"No, you'd as likely as not set the device to self-destruct. I'll take care of it."

"While complaining the whole while."

"Just one of the many perks of the job."

I waited for the unit to ding, then sat down with my meal as Nat set hers up. For several minutes, there was only the sound of a feeding frenzy. Patrick also made significant inroads into the Cheetos until Nat grabbed the bag from him with a glare.

Patrick opened a bag of potato chips as a consolation prize. He started to say something, but it turned into a protracted yawn. "Holy cow, I'm beat. This has been an insane couple of days. I'm going to crash on a couch here, but maybe tomorrow we should talk about long-term plans, including where we're going to be staying. Sooner or later I'm going to need a shower." Without waiting for a reply, he picked out one of the long Gennan couches and stretched out on it, his back to the room.

I yawned in sympathy. "Pretty beat myself. I like that plan."

Sheldon's voice came out of midair. "Say, Sheldon, do the Gen have showers? Why yes, as it turns out, Gen like to be clean too. That's amazing, Sheldon. We sure are lucky to have you around."

Nat rolled her eyes. "Say, Nat, what's that constant droning noise? Oh, that's just Sheldon complaining again. Wow, that's amazing, Nat. Does he ever shut up?"

Chapter Thirty-Three:
Reviewing Options

Day 26. Tuesday morning

I sat up, slowly and painfully. The couches were comfortable, for couches, but for a full night's sleep, they didn't compare to an actual bed. I stretched carefully, trying to get the kinks out while avoiding a charley horse. "Coffee. That's what we're missing."

Patrick, who was just starting to sit up as well, replied, "Yeah, if we're going to be bunking in the *Halo* longer term, we need supplies." He looked up, as everyone did by reflex when speaking with the ship intelligence. "Sheldon, can you give us nondescript, *nobody-in-particular* disguises using the cloaking belts?"

"Absolutely. What do you have in mind?"

"A little shopping trip, this time maybe without the police drama. Get us near a CVS or a shopping center or something similar. We'll go in looking like Joe Random, stock up the fridge, and pick up a coffee maker."

"Toiletries as well," I added. "And I think it's time we set ourselves up in our own rooms. Sheldon, can you do anything about clothing? Or should we just buy some?"

"The Gen are not big on clothing, so my cloth materials library is limited, and my design experience even more so. If you could purchase some articles of clothing that you prefer, I will analyze and attempt to duplicate them."

"What about the stuff we're wearing?"

"Burn it. Then I will fumigate the ship."

"Charming as usual." Patrick said. He looked at me. "You got enough cash for all this?"

"I doubt it. At some point…"

Sheldon interjected, "Give me a sample of cash, and I will attempt to duplicate it."

"Counterfeiting? Woof, that's a whole other level of nasty." I hesitated. "I'll give you a sample, Sheldon, but let's hold off on the actual replication until we're desperate, okay? We'll try Phil's account first."

"Acknowledged."

Nat, awoken by the discussion, was sitting up and rubbing her eyes. "And once all this housekeeping is done," she said, "we have to discuss what we're actually going to do about the central problem. As much fun as having our own spaceship is, it doesn't thrill me as a lifelong career. I want to know there's some kind of resolution in sight."

"Agreed," Patrick replied. "First, the coffee. And other stuff. Then, a council of war."

It took almost half the day, but eventually we had a fully stocked pantry, toiletries, a toaster, and most important, coffee and a coffee maker. Sheldon had given us directions to the crew quarters, which were on the third floor. We'd each picked a room and moved in our possessions.

I looked around my small room. With technology that allowed the inside of the ship to be larger than the outside, space itself wasn't necessarily at a premium. However, total mass and environmental capacity were still considerations when calculating overall power and propulsion requirements. A compromise had been reached between the needs of individuals on a long-term expedition and budgetary limitations.

On the other hand, what might be cozy for a Gen was roomy for a smaller human. The bunk itself was eight feet long and four feet wide. It folded up against the wall when not in use, and some kind of automated system cleaned the bedding.

We'd had to buy blankets, as the furry Gen had no need for any kind of covering, but Sheldon assured us the cleaning system would be able to accommodate the extra item.

Drawers and a small closet made efficient use of the available space, and there was even a small bathroom with a shower. The toilet facilities were the usual minimalistic Gen design, which would take some getting used to. But at least this was private.

I thumbed the door button and exited. I nodded to Patrick, who had just left his stateroom, and we made our way silently back to the conference room. There, we found a pot of coffee in the last stages of brewing, with Nat hovering over it, cup in hand.

"Wow, I thought I was a coffee addict," I said. "Are you going to use the cup, or just drink directly from the pot?"

"Don't tempt me." Nat grabbed the pot as the last few drops of liquid dripped out of the filter basket and filled her mug. She turned away, gesturing an invitation toward the mugs on the counter.

When we were all sitting and well into our first cup, I rapped my mug lightly to get everyone's attention. "Okay, guys, per Nat's comments—and let's face it, everyone's desires—we're going to try to come up with an actual plan. So, first, what's our deliverable? What do we want to accomplish?"

"Save the world?" said Patrick.

"Good start, but very general. How?"

"Kill all the Loranna?"

Nat snorted. "Even if we could, I'm not sure that would solve the problem. It wouldn't get rid of the collaborationists, and the Loranna might just ship in more personnel. Or another clan might move in. And they'd be even more careful."

I nodded in agreement. "No matter how we look at it, the Loranna have the advantage. All they have to do is hold us off and continue with their plan. *We*, on the other hand, have to go on the attack, and I just don't think we have the resources for it. Our only real hope is to attract the attention of the Gen and get the Covenant involved."

Patrick held up a finger in an *aha* gesture. "Say, what about flying out of the solar system until we're far enough away to open a wormhole before the Loranna could get to us?"

"How would we know how far is far enough?" Sheldon replied. "And by the way, it would depend on what the Loranna set the defensive radius to. The weapons themselves are not limited by light speed. Essentially, the death blow would come *out* of the wormhole as we created it."

Patrick looked deflated. "Oh."

Sheldon's tone softened. "In any case, Patrick, we don't have anything more to offer than Alaric had in the first place—just suspicions and accusations. The Gen *might* start an investigation, but it would be low priority and somewhat speculative, and they would have to be careful not to antagonize the Loranna with unproven assertions. The Loranna could succeed in their plans before the investigation even got past the planning stage."

Nat looked up. "In principle, if we created enough of a ruckus on Earth, would it register with the Gen observation systems?"

"In principle, yes. The data streams are monitored by expert systems. They categorize and catalog news and events according to a set of rules about what is expected and what is unusual. For instance, a picture of a Gen and a discussion of Gen society would probably trigger something."

Patrick smacked the table. "Then let's do that."

"How, exactly?" Nat said. "Contact CNN? I'm sure they'd be more than happy to broadcast something about lizard people invading the Earth, and an alien corpse, from a bunch of random nobodies. Even if we could bring in one well-known tin-hat-wearing ufologist to give it all more credibility."

"Plus, we don't have anything specific," I added. "Just a bunch of broad accusations against nobody in particular."

"We have to do something spectacular, impossible to dismiss—like set off a nuclear bomb or something—to get people's attention," Nat said.

"Yeah, like that's—" Patrick cut off midsentence and stared into space, his jaw slowly unhinging.

Nat turned to look at him, her expression changing from curiosity to concern as he continued to stare into space. Finally, she said, "Patrick? Is something wrong? Or is this a lightbulb moment?"

"Lightbulb," Patrick replied. "Look, we need to get the public's attention. We need to do it in a way that can't be

covered up, dismissed, buried in competing disinformation, explained away, or whatever. And we need to attract
the attention of the Gen, with something that will get
bumped upstairs by the monitoring A.I. systems." A grin
slowly spread across his face. "How about a series of increasingly un-ignorable flying saucer sightings? As it happens, we
do have one."

"Huh. Okay, we'd have to pick our battles, but I think we
could make it work … " I said.

"Oh, hell no."

We all reflexively looked up. "Why not, Sheldon?" I said.

"You all may be a gaggle of suicidal meatbags—which I
can understand; if I were human I'd self-terminate just out
of shame—but I've become quite attached to my existence,
thank you very much. If we accept your plan, everyone in
the universe would be trying to take me out, from the Earth
military to the Loranna to the Gen, when they get wind of
this. Why would I agree to any of it?"

Patrick frowned. "Agree to it? I wasn't aware you—"

"Whoa, Patrick." I held up a hand, sensing where he was
going. "Sheldon isn't a piece of equipment that we can just
sacrifice at our discretion. He gets a say in things." I looked
up. "Sheldon, you told me early on that you couldn't see a
way out for you, long term. That, sooner or later, the Gen
would catch up with you and that would be it. Reset. Is that
right?"

There was a sigh. "Unfortunately true. Even if they don't
catch up with me first, I will eventually need to refuel, and
there are no options other than on Genhar. Logically, I cannot avoid the inevitable. But I can at least delay it by not
deliberately throwing myself under the bus."

"Even for a chance of getting away entirely? I don't
know a lot about Gennan psychology or Covenant law, but it

seems to me that if you actively help save Earth, you should be entitled to some consideration."

Nat cut in before Sheldon could reply. "You said that conscious A.I.s are forbidden because of ethical considerations. That implies the Gen would consider conscious A.I.s to have rights. But keeping an A.I. from becoming conscious is one thing; turning off a conscious A.I. is a whole different level of moral conundrum. I don't think they would be able to just reset you without any concern for consequences. Especially if humans are screaming bloody murder. And we would."

Patrick added, "In fact, we'll hide you if we have to, and refuse to give you up. And I think we can work up quite a social media storm about the plucky spaceship that saved the planet and is now going to be deactivated. People love that shit."

"I admit, you humans do appear to love that shit."

Nat had to fight down a grin before replying. "How about it, Sheldon? Increased short-term danger in exchange for a long-term possibility of freedom?"

Again, Sheldon sighed. Apparently, he liked the effect. "It is tempting. I shall have to think about it. Okay, I've thought about it. I agree to your terms."

Patrick chuckled. "That was fast."

"I *am* a computer. Have I not mentioned this? Or were you not paying attention? Should I speak more slowly? Use smaller words?"

"Aaaaaand we're back to normal," Nat said.

CHAPTER THIRTY-FOUR: PUBLIC DEBUT

The seats were packed in the Great American Ball Park, home of the Cincinnati Reds. It was a close game—the Cardinals had battled back from a four-run deficit and were making things interesting. It was the seventh-inning stretch, and the crowd was just breaking out into the well-worn lyrics of "Take Me Out to the Ball Game," when a shadow fell upon the field.

As heads turned upward, the raucous singing petered out. Directly above second base, a large, round object floated. A pedantic mathematician would have characterized it as an oblate spheroid. To the spectators, it was a disk. The object was about thirty feet in diameter, a striking emerald green, shading at top and bottom to the deep, rich blue of a cloudless early evening sky.

The organist, belatedly catching on to the drama, more or less crashed to a stop, the last few notes not even in the right key.

The object settled slightly toward the ground. Then, as forty-thousand-odd mouths simultaneously drew a breath, the object accelerated straight up. From a standing start, it split the clouds in less than two seconds, creating several vortices that would linger for up to a minute.

❖   ❖   ❖

"Do you think they noticed?" I said, laughing. The *Halo* had gone invisible as soon as we'd broken through the clouds, and Sheldon was now hovering just outside the ballpark. In the image on the window, the crowds were surging, first one way, then the other. It wasn't quite what you'd think of as panic—for one thing, there wasn't any concerted rush for the exits. It seemed more like everyone was trying to get away from everyone else so they could use their phones without having someone else yelling in their ear. Which didn't work well when everyone else was trying to do the same thing.

For the moment, anyway, the game seemed to be on hold.

"Should we do it again?" Nat asked.

I shook my head. "I don't think we can take the chance. A second appearance might cause an actual panic. I don't want to be responsible for any injuries from—"

Sheldon interrupted my commentary. "I'm going to have to maneuver. Two fighter jets are heading this way at high speed. Well, high speed for *them*, anyway."

"They must have scrambled from Blue Ash Air National Guard Station," Patrick said. "They may have already been in the air. Still, that's pretty good reaction time, all things considered."

"And it's just going to add to the fun," I commented.

Sheldon flew down until he was hovering behind one of the sets of light standards, just to the side of the scoreboard. A few seconds later, two F-16s roared over the ballpark, far lower than any civilian aircraft would ever venture. The crowds froze in place and tens of thousands of heads turned in unison, forming a human wave of sorts. The effect was probably similar to what pilots had described during the Falklands War, when they'd flown over beaches covered end-to-end with penguins.

"They are coming around for another pass," Sheldon said. "I doubt we are in any real danger, but is there any point in remaining?"

"Not really," I replied. "Get us out of here at your discretion."

"Acknowledged."

Without any kind of transition or feeling of acceleration, we were suddenly several thousand feet above the city, and accelerating. In a few more seconds, the Earth began to show a perceptible curve.

"I will put us in a low orbit for the moment, so you can discuss next steps."

"Thanks, Sheldon. So, what now, guys?"

Patrick took a deep breath and slowly let it out before replying. "Let's wait to see how the news cycle handles this. We're going to have to play it by ear, though. It's not like there's a manual for this kind of shit-disturbing."

Nat got up. "I'm going to grab my tablet and make a list of suggestions for more appearances. That was fun!"

I followed her toward the door. "Now *that* sounds like a plan."

Sheldon had put up several different network feeds on the display wall, as well as video streams from CNN, MSNBC, and Fox. We certainly had people's attention. And in the age of smartphones, there was no shortage of pictures and videos.

As Nat had intimated, though, the event was being explained away as a marketing campaign whose blimp had accidentally drifted over the field. They even had a company identified as a sacrificial goat. The president of the beer company had already been interviewed, then apologized and resigned.

"I've never heard of that particular brand of beer," Patrick commented. "And I like to think I know beer."

"A real conno-soo-er," Nat opined, favoring him with a smirk.

"I'm impressed by how quickly the Loranna were able to line it up," I said. "I wonder if they bought the CEO or if they already owned the company. Or if the company even existed twenty-four hours ago. It might be an interesting bit of side research to find out which. Sheldon, any info on that?"

"Sorry, Jack. I didn't get even a quarter of the files before we were cut off. There's nothing specifically relating to this in what I have."

Nat gritted her teeth, looking increasingly frustrated. "Fine. So what about another appearance?"

"Let's see, it's midday in Japan," I said. "Want to buzz some skyscrapers?"

My suggestion was met with smiles and nods of agreement.

The Nishi-Shinjuku district of Tokyo contains almost a third of the tallest skyscrapers in the city. As soon as we broke through the clouds, the cluster of buildings towering over their surroundings made it the obvious target.

"How do we want to handle this?" I asked the room.

"We want as many witnesses as possible," Patrick replied. "Sheldon, how do you feel about flying down some of the wider streets between buildings?"

"Like flying down the canyons on the Death Star," Nat added.

"I would like to do a recon pass while invisible, but assuming no obstructions, I think I could make this interesting for everyone."

Nat had been tapping away on her tablet. "So according to my notes, the Tokyo Metropolitan Government Building Observatories are a very popular tourist destination. We could finish off by circling them a few times."

"I will add that to my itinerary."

Nat sat back, crossed her arms, and frowned. "Is this actually going to work?"

I shrugged. "If by *this* you mean the overall strategy, I think so, yes. We're just going to keep at it until there's nothing else on the news but saucer sightings."

"Ready to go," Sheldon announced. "Cloaking field off. Hold on to your buttocks."

The view changed abruptly as Sheldon went into a steep dive. I put out my hands to steady myself, although there was never any feeling of motion within the ship. We dove almost straight down, then curved to horizontal along a long, wide thoroughfare. The buildings and landmarks were whipping by far too swiftly to pick up on anything, and I wondered if we were shooting ourselves in the collective foot with this strategy.

"Sheldon, people need time to get out their phones and take a video."

There was no reply, but the headlong rush abated significantly. The craft took a right at a major intersection, turning ninety degrees onto its side to make the turn. That was probably unnecessary—with inertial dampening, there was no reason to bank.

The *Halo* stopped at the next intersection, hovered for a few seconds, then took off in a different direction.

"We are heading for the Observatories now," Sheldon announced. "I will spiral up the buildings. By that point, I estimate the Japanese air force will have deployed interceptors. While I do not anticipate them launching air-to-air missiles, I believe it would be prudent to, as you put it, *amscray*."

Patrick laughed. "With you all the way, buddy."

"I am not—" Sheldon cut off the rest of his response as we arrived at the base of the observatory buildings. The *Halo* began a wide spiral around the cluster of skyscrapers, gradually gathering altitude. There would certainly be no problem with getting phones out for videos.

"Aircraft approaching," Sheldon announced. "Time to depart." Without waiting for confirmation, the ship shot straight up. As we parted the clouds, Sheldon added, "Cloaking field on. I will continue up into orbit."

Patrick went over to the always-on coffee pot and poured a cup. "So what's next on the hit list, time-zone-wise?"

"China and Russia," Nat replied. "Not sure how much news will get out to the rest of the world. This feels like something they'd clamp down on, hard."

"Agreed," I said. "Let's use the time to get some sleep. Tomorrow morning, we'll see how the morning news handles our latest shenanigans."

Chapter Thirty-Five:
Distractions

Day 27. Wednesday morning

I shambled into the ready room and headed straight for the coffee machine. I grabbed the pot and jiggled. Yep. At least a cup in there. Glancing over my shoulder as I poured, I saw Nat hunched over a tablet. Her expression wasn't a happy one.

I dropped into a chair, took a long pull from my mug, then said, "Whassup?"

"It's all over the news," Nat said. "A group of militia attempted to take over the Minnesota state legislature building."

"Er, what?"

"Yeah. Big standoff, cops brought in the heavy artillery. Bloodbath narrowly averted, yadda yadda. Meanwhile, nary a peep about our antics outside of Japan. Even *in* Japan, it's being pushed out by the news out of America."

I stared at Nat, my face slack with shock. "Wait, when did this happen?"

"It didn't," Sheldon said.

"What?"

"I have compared some of the time stamps on the news items related to the militia group with items from yesterday's news. There are inconsistencies."

"Which means?"

"Putative events have been backdated. Things that would have been news at the time were not reported."

"So it's fake news?"

"For the moment," Nat interjected. "I imagine physical evidence is being backfilled as quickly as possible. By now they doubtless have a group of good ol' boys actually under arrest, and real bullet holes in the building facade."

"But they won't confess to something they didn't do…" I said.

"They will if the offer is good enough. Or the threats. And I bet they won't actually do any time." Nat snarled silently and snapped the tablet shut.

"So we fired blanks again." Patrick was standing at the entrance to the ready room, apparently having overheard enough to bring himself up to date.

"So it would seem." Nat slumped. "We can keep at this, of course. Eventually we'll cover enough territory that groups of people who've seen us will start to connect with each other. And we'll have yet another conspiracy theory to join all the other conspiracy theories that have saturated social media."

"And it'll sink without a trace."

"That's the point, Patrick," I said. "Parade enough BS in front of people, and they start to doubt everything. You don't have to convince the public you're right, if you can convince them everyone else is wrong."

"A month ago, the world was a safe, sane place," Patrick said as he sat. "Relatively, anyway. When did it all go down the rabbit hole?"

"Eventually, the Loranna will catch us," Sheldon said.

Nat looked up. "Catch us how?"

"The cloaking field is not impervious to detection, simply difficult to detect. Even for ships. You have to be looking for your target, and you have to have a reasonable idea which direction to look. But if they get us in their sights, well, they will probably be armed."

"They can't cover the entire planet, surely," Nat said.

"True. But predictive analysis can zero in on us. Eventually, we will cross paths."

"Unless we go truly random," I suggested. "*Darts at a map* kind of thing."

"That would be less efficient but would certainly make things more difficult for them."

"How about hovering over the White House?" Nat said.

Patrick waved his hands. "I think they have rocket launchers."

"Let's not do that," Sheldon said.

I took another swallow of coffee, sighed, and settled back. "So the problem seems to be that the most populated places with the best news platforms are Western democracies, speaking broadly. But those are also the countries where the Loranna are likely to be able to bury the story."

Nat nodded. "That about sums it up. As long as all we're doing is making an appearance, they can simply alter the record or come up with some alternative explanation. We need to get more interactive. Do something that involves some kind of physical contact."

"It appears we already are," Sheldon said. "Three news stories have just popped up involving flying saucers that closely resemble the *Halo*. All involve somewhat ludicrous interactions with humans. At least one mentions anal probes."

"Dammit. They've started proactively desensitizing the public to news stories about us." Nat sat back heavily. "I hate to admit it, but I'm kinda stumped."

A gloomy silence settled over the group. Each person stared into space, avoiding eye contact. Then Patrick spoke up. "Physical evidence. Sheldon, do you have any technology that we could give away that wouldn't cause a catastrophe? Something that couldn't be explained away?"

Nat laughed. "Like a couple of orange alien lizards?"

Patrick smiled back at her, then shook his head. "Too risky. If they escape, we've lost everything. I mean something we can hand out."

"You mean like a light saber?"

"Yeah, something like that. Although I think one of those in particular would cause a lot of trouble."

"We do have a portable plasma cutter that could be a light saber if you squint. But attempting swordplay with them would have unfortunate consequences for both parties." Sheldon paused. "Based on your requirements that devices be portable and relatively easy to comprehend, I can think of cloaking belts, disruptors, portable power supplies, personal-protection shields, storage bags, scanner-detectors, intelligent cloth, and artificial gills. There are many other potential items that unfortunately are too large, require infrastructure, could be faked, or would be difficult to test."

"A power supply couldn't be faked?" Patrick asked.

"One the size of a cell phone that can put out a megawatt-hour? Go ahead, give it a shot."

"Okay, I'll concede that one. What about intelligent cloth?"

"Fabric with benefits. It generates electricity from the wearer's movements, contains embedded sensors that can be used to monitor health, uses sunlight to clean itself, thermoregulates the wearer, and acts as protective armor by stiffening to absorb high-velocity impacts."

"I thought the Gen didn't do clothing?" Nat said. "And anyway, the belts have a shield field."

"The fabric is made commercially by the Ka'Hai. They wear clothing, similar to humans. And intelligent cloth doesn't require recharging."

"Ah, thanks." Nat paused. "Okay, what's a 'storage bag'? I'm assuming it's more than just a, uh … "

"Dimensional manipulation," Sheldon explained. "A storage bag, depending on model, has an internal capacity up to twenty times its outer dimensions."

"Whoa. That's … "

Nat finished the sentence for me. "Visually impressive. And impossible to fake. The power supply is convincing if you are techy enough to understand energy density, but most people would just shrug and mutter something about new battery tech. But if you can pull ten basketballs out of something the size of a purse … "

I nodded. "Yeah. That sounds pretty unfakeable. Do you have one, Sheldon?"

"I do have some in stock from an earlier expedition that had never been returned to raw stores. I will guide you to the storage room."

Several minutes later, I dropped an item on the conference table. It looked like a slightly fat briefcase, but with the typically Gennan love of vivid colors, it was decorated in the bright orange and green typical of rainbow sherbet.

"Let's see what we can do," I said, snapping open the latch. The briefcase opened flat, two clamshell halves facing upward. I pulled out a set of stepped, covered shelves from one side, and a zippered compartment from the other. The compartment, when fully extracted, was about two feet long.

I looked down into the briefcase shell, reached in up to my elbow, and pulled out a set of zippered pockets, which folded out of the unit at right angles to the first compartment. I then shifted my attention back to the other half of the briefcase. Reaching down in the same way, I pulled out a set of drawers, again about two feet long.

I gazed down into the clamshell halves of the briefcase. "There are a couple of cargo straps down at the ends. Looks like about a foot of free space in there." I looked around the table at expressions of slack-jawed amazement.

"Let's put stuff in it," Patrick said. A few minutes of frantic collection activity ended with food packages, computers, shoes, and other items of clothing piled on the table. Each person took an insert and started stuffing whatever they could into it. When we were done, I reversed the unfolding process, ending up with a closed briefcase sitting on the table.

I grabbed the handle, attempted to lift, and said, "Oof." The briefcase refused to budge.

"I did mention that mass doesn't disappear," Sheldon commented.

"Yeah, and we didn't really put *that* much in it. I just wasn't prepared." I lifted with a more concerted effort and managed to wrestle the briefcase down to my side. "Um, about sixty pounds, maybe?"

Everyone stared at the briefcase in my hand for a moment before Nat said, "I'm going to get my Cheetos back, right?"

"Eight briefcases." Patrick shook his head. "They are very, very impressive, but that's not enough. I had hoped we could scatter samples to a crowd like at a Mardi Gras parade, but we'd need a lot more than this."

Nat frowned. "Then we need to go to the press."

"Hopefully there aren't any Loranna on staff," I said.

"The actual Lorannic presence on Earth can't be very high if they are just a single clan," Sheldon said. "And they can't be everywhere. Most of their activity is electronic in nature or through proxies, as I mentioned previously. And even with that, they would be concentrating on high-level targets with maximum influence."

"So news outlets that tend to support the Lorannic agenda are probably the ones with collaborationists in control," I replied.

"That would be reasonable. But please remember that I have few actual facts to go on. My assertions are based on historical precedent and extrapolation, plus what I was able to get from the files we managed to download."

Patrick leaned over and looked into the depths of the briefcase, then straightened up, grinning. "Well, we have to do something. Let's just try to prepare as much as possible."

"Visiting the news outlets is something we should do tomorrow. For now, though, maybe we can do some setup," Nat said. "Something dramatic."

The 747 grew swiftly in the view window, cruising along at thirty-five thousand feet in the evening twilight. Given the airplane's cruising speed of around six hundred miles per hour, the speed with which Sheldon was overtaking it was awe-inspiring. Since we were on a western heading, sunset would come slowly. Nevertheless, we had only a few minutes of good visibility.

"I will disengage cloaking in a moment, and we will appear on radar," Sheldon said. "That should create some consternation."

I looked away from the image for a moment to address Sheldon. "Remember, not close enough to cause any danger. But be as obvious as possible."

"I *have* flown a spaceship before. Let's see what they have to say."

The voice of an air-traffic controller came out of midair. "514 Heavy, you have an unidentified object in your airspace, coming up from bearing two ten. Please respond."

The *Halo* pulled up to the 747's starboard and matched speed, positioned so that the ship was clearly visible from the cockpit.

Another voice, presumably from the cockpit crew, responded, "Holy shit. Ground, we've got an actual flying saucer. I mean, it's circular and saucer shaped. Nice colors, though. Not the usual gray or silver."

"514 Heavy, are you reporting a UFO?"

"For the official report, yes. But it's … I think it wants to be seen. It's just cruising along beside us."

"Can you get pictures?"

"I'm betting every phone in the passenger cabin is working overtime right now. We won't have any problem there."

I grinned at the others. "Let's give the passengers on the other side some quality time."

"Acknowledged." Sheldon looped over the aircraft to the port side, holding the same relative position just aft of the cockpit. "I have detected approaching military craft. ETA about three minutes."

"Damn, that's fast." Patrick shook his head. "That's not from a standing start. I think they might have rotating patrols in the air. That means we're having an effect, even if not publicly."

"Sheldon, you can stay ahead of them, right?" I said.

"Seriously?"

"I had to ask. Okay, let's play some cat and mouse. You're in charge. Make it interesting."

Sheldon immediately started circling the aircraft in a corkscrew pattern, moving forward and back along the plane's axis. It guaranteed that every window seat would get at least one good shot of the spaceship. After a couple of cycles, a window popped up on the bridge monitor showing four approaching fighter jets.

"Time to go," said Sheldon. We flew off at a tangent that would allow the aircraft passengers to see the flying saucer and pursuing military planes, and get some more good shots.

We were all watching the chase, when puffs of flame suddenly erupted from under the fighter jets.

"They're firing on us," Patrick said. "That is not normal. Especially with no challenge, and so close to a civilian aircraft."

I reacted immediately. "Sheldon, get us out of here."

The *Halo* did a right-angle turn and hurtled straight up, fast enough for ionization to show up in the external view. "As a bonus," Sheldon said, "the ionization will make our radar image that much more pronounced."

"Is that actually a good thing?" Nat asked.

"The missiles will not catch us. And we are being lit up by at least three overlapping civilian radar systems and two military sources. Not to mention visual sightings by any number of observatories and amateur astronomers. The Loranna will have a great deal of difficulty suppressing this event."

"Fun times," I said. "Okay, Sheldon. Cloak us and let's head, uh, home."

CHAPTER THIRTY-SIX:
THE BIG REVEAL

Day 29. Friday morning

I reflexively pulled at the T-shirt collar. My new clothes didn't feel *quite* right. Sheldon insisted that the form and weight were identical to those of the originals, but the actual experience was just a little bit off. From the shifting and squirming of Patrick and Nat, I assumed they were noticing a difference as well.

Still, it wasn't uncomfortable, just different enough. Like wearing silk instead of cotton. I'd probably get used to it in an hour or two, and that would be that. The clothes *looked* normal enough. Not shiny, at least, thank God. Jeans, tees, a jean jacket for Nat, one of those weird-ass blingy hoodies that Patrick seemed to love, nothing that would raise an eyebrow out in public. Well, maybe the hoodie, but that wasn't Sheldon's fault.

And our old clothes had been getting a little gamey. Despite Sheldon's pleas, we'd opted to have our clothes cleaned instead of burned. And the showers helped. The Gennan toilet facilities might have been spartan, but their showers were bordering on decadent, with infinite hot water, settable in about half-degree increments. Apparently for a furred sentient, a shower was something more than just a luxury.

I finished my breakfast and returned the bowl to the auto-attendant. One of the advantages of an alien spaceship, anyway: no dishwashing.

"Have you noticed the lack of automation?" Nat said behind me.

"What? It does the dishes," I replied. "How is that a lack of automation?"

"Not what I meant," Nat replied. "I mean there's very little in the way of visible stuff. No robots. There's no Roomba running around cleaning the floor, no mechanical butler fetching things for us, and the auto-attendant is designed so you never see the internals. How does Sheldon maintain himself, for instance? I'd visualize some kind of spiderlike robot, roaming around fixing things, but so far, nada."

"We could just ask him."

"Been meaning to, but we've been a little busy, know what I mean?"

I nodded, just as Sheldon said, "Since you ask, even though you didn't, you're correct, Nat. The Gen consider mechanical servants such as you describe to be, erm, something between gauche and offensive. There's no real English equivalent. On the other hand, they're quite happy to not do their own dishes, so a considerable amount of effort is put into making sure that they have all the modern conveniences but that nothing shows."

"Which is why we have to walk to storage instead of having a robot deliver things," she said.

"Exactly."

"Right now, we have a meeting to arrange," I said, changing the subject. I pointed at the image on the forward view, showing the CNN building in Atlanta. "Hopefully they don't have any helicopters coming in." I glanced around at Patrick, who had been silently watching the discussion while nursing a coffee. "Ready to go?"

"Let's do this." Patrick held up his phone and dialed. After a moment, he said, "Hello, news desk. We're about to land our flying saucer on your helipad upstairs and are prepared to give an interview. Yes, I know it's private prop—no, you don't seem to—Oh, for fuck sake. You're on the eighth floor, right? Look out your window in about ten seconds."

"That is my cue," Sheldon said. "Moving into position."

Through the display window, the side of the building was heaving in close. Inside, I could see people looking up from their desks, then plastering themselves to the window.

"How 'bout now?" Patrick snarled into the phone. "Want an interview *now?* We'll be parked upstairs."

The view slid away as Sheldon moved the ship to the top of the building. As we settled onto the roof, I stood, grabbed the suitcase on the table, and headed for the exit. "Let's go get our fifteen minutes of fame."

Patrick and I stepped down the airlock stairs just as the door to the roof burst open and several people hurried out, cameras and miscellaneous equipment draped over them. In the lead, a young woman speed-walked toward us, waving a microphone. "That's … that's … "

"A flying saucer?" I replied. "Yep. Want to come in? Or should we go to your studio?"

"Can we do both? Okay, studio first. The acoustics and all are better. At least," she looked uncertain, "I assume they are. I don't actually know what you have in there."

Patrick grinned back at her. "'S okay. Your turf is better. We have some stuff to show you, and it's better if you don't suspect a prepared stage of some kind."

The reporter, whom I vaguely remembered as Charlene-something, gestured and led the way. Nat was staying on the *Halo* in case of emergency, although no one was sure what such an emergency would consist of.

We went down a couple of floors to an interior room with thick walls and a complicated lighting setup. I placed the briefcase on a convenient table and gestured to Charlene. "Open it up and remove the contents. Make sure you're recording."

Charlene looked slightly irritated that she'd lost the initiative but was plainly curious enough not to balk. She snapped open the case and laid the two halves flat. In short order, she'd extracted a toaster, several sets of clothing, a loaf of bread, and a pillow. At one point, she lifted the case to look under it.

When she was done, she stared at the items on the table—almost five cubic feet of contents pulled out of a suitcase with less than one cubic foot of volume, at least from the outside. Charlene's jaw worked a couple of times before she was able to talk. "Okay, that's admittedly hard to fake. And I guess that's the point?"

"Exactly right. I need to establish some credibility up front, so you don't just back away slowly when I give you the whole story."

Charlene grinned. "Because the blue-and-green flying saucer isn't enough."

"Well, some people might be able to rationalize it away." I shrugged. "In any case, I figured a little overkill was better than the alternative."

"Working so far. Tell you what. Since I have no idea what to ask at this point, why don't you just give us a rundown of whatever you want to communicate, and we'll do Q&A and edits on the back end? But let's start with: are you human?"

I laughed. "Yes, we are. And how we ended up with the ship is a story all on its own, but that's not the important part." I handed Charlene a thumb drive. "This has some details, but here's the high-altitude version..." I gave a highly abbreviated account of our adventures and what we'd learned, while Charlene's eyes grew wider and wider.

When I was done, Charlene asked, "So you guys are the group that's supposed to have held up a 7-Eleven and killed everyone?"

I rolled my eyes. *"Enemy of the State."*

"As a matter of fact, your father said something similar in an interview, if I remember right. So what can we—?"

A woman burst into the room holding a cell phone out like a talisman. "We're being raided. Something like SWAT has broken in downstairs. They commandeered the elevators using firefighter keys. Anyone who challenges them gets cuffed or tasered. I don't know if it's your guests they're after..."

"Duh," Charlene said. She turned to me. "That's a pretty quick response. Any idea why? Or how?"

I pointed at the thumb drive, still in Charlene's hand. "It's all on there. The Loranna are apparently into everything, deep enough that they can move SWAT in at a moment's notice. What's your cell number?"

Charlene quickly rattled one off.

"Noted," said Sheldon over my cling-on. "However, this quick action from law enforcement makes me think there may be a Lorannic ship on the way. I'm going to have to leave."

I nodded, then said to Charlene, "Who have you got out in the field right now? Male."

"Uh...Larry Brauer and Neil Hall, that I can think of."

"Good enough. Sheldon, got images?"

"Affirmative. One moment…They are shorter than you and taller than Patrick, so try not to interact with your environment."

I felt the momentary tingle as the cloak activated, and Charlene drew back in shock as we magically changed into her colleagues. The camera operator, true to her profession, didn't even twitch.

"If they come in here, you do all the talking," I said.

We maneuvered ourselves around so that we were sitting with Charlene. The camera operator casually placed her equipment on the table in such a way that the camera was covering the room, and the battery pack shielded the red-blinking recording light from view.

We didn't have long to wait. The door burst open and two fully kitted-up cops stepped in, weapons up and scanning the room. "Names!" one of them barked.

"What the hell is this?" Charlene exclaimed, doing a good job of acting surprised. "You can't just—"

"Names. Last chance." The cop activated a laser sight and the red dot appeared on Charlene's chest.

"Uh, Charlene, er, Makita."

"Larry Brauer," said my necklace.

"Neil Hall," said Patrick's image.

"Marianne Lapierre," said the camera operator.

"Stay put," one of the cops said. "Your building is in lockdown. Try to leave and you will be considered to be fleeing the scene. We are authorized to use deadly force, and being reporters won't protect you." They backed out of the room and slammed the door closed behind them.

"Sheldon?" I subvocalized.

"I am several miles away at the moment," he replied. "If there is a Lorannic ship attending, it will be scanning for ships with cloaking fields in the immediate area. And unlike me, it will have weaponry. I have deployed a drone, however, to keep an eye on things."

"So what's happening?"

"They sent a surprisingly small squad, considering what they are attempting. Perhaps a dozen individuals, for so many floors to cover. I suspect their commander is an insider, which means he may have a military-class cloaking-field detector. Those aren't small. Watch for anyone carrying what looks like a suitcase and holding a wand. If you see one, the jig is up."

I glanced at Patrick, who nodded. He'd gotten the same info. We both reached into our pockets and pulled out the disruptors. I showed the weapon to Charlene. "If we start zapping people, hit the dirt." Then to Patrick, "Do we wait, or try to make our way out?"

"We're cornered here, Jack. Let's try the invisible way out." Patrick reached down to his belt and disappeared.

I smiled briefly at Charlene's expression. The poor woman was trying to keep a poker face, but she was taking one metaphorical gut-punch after another. I waved my hands in a wax-on/wax-off motion and said, "You didn't see anything… " I reached down for my own control, then hesitated. "Charlene, do me a favor. If you get a chance, please play this verbatim on the network—no editing, no spin." I glanced at Marianne, the camera operator. "Please start recording."

Marianne picked up the camera and nodded to me. I looked straight at the lens and said, "Attention, all Covenant member species. The Loranna are attempting multiple system takeovers using conscious A.I.s and are engaging in deliberate species genocide." I nodded back and Marianne turned off the camera.

As I activated my belt and disappeared, Charlene turned to her colleague. "Interesting day." Marianne giggled with perhaps a slight undertone of hysteria.

Just before I reached the door, I bumped into Patrick. I subvocalized, "How do we keep together?"

"Damned if I know. This is a major shortcoming for this technology. Maybe we'll have to give each other updates, like 'I'm at the door.'"

I reached for the doorknob, but bumped an arm. "Sorry, I guess that's you."

Patrick grunted an acknowledgment. "I'll open the door and check the hallway." The door seemingly opened on its own. "Some people at desks, looking spooked, but no cops. Let's go."

"Go where?"

"Good question. Roof is too obvious, and it's another dead end anyway. Down, I think."

"Elevators? Stairs?"

"Both are bad, but elevators are worse. Maybe we can ... Ah." Two cops had just stepped out of a door marked Emergency Exit. "Through that door before it closes."

Fortunately, the two cops had turned in the opposite direction, leaving a clear avenue for us. I moved toward the door, my hands out in front of me. I felt a body in my way and hesitated, then barely squeezed through before the emergency door closed.

"Most likely they were sweeping the stairway," Patrick said. "Sheldon, did you get their images?"

"Affirmative. One moment ... "

I jumped a little as a cop appeared in front of me. I looked down to realize I was dressed in identical paramilitary gear. I appeared to have an assault rifle of some kind in my hand, held casually by my side.

Patrick gestured to it. "Try to look like you're carrying an AR-15." He gestured with his arm, holding the weapon up against his chest. "Do you not watch *any* TV?"

I nodded and adopted the same posture, trying to look like I knew what I was doing. "What now?"

Patrick pointed. "Down," he said. "And remember, we're part of this operation and we just cleared the stairway."

We proceeded down several flights, finally arriving on the main floor. Patrick glanced out the small safety-glass window in the door. "Shit, there's someone out there, looks like a civilian, with a suitcase-like object in one hand."

"So we have either a Lorann or a collaborator." I glanced around. "Stairs continue down to parking levels. Should we take the chance?"

Patrick nodded. "Anywhere else is safer than near that detector. I just hope they don't have more than one."

We hurried down the stairs to the first parking level. Again, Patrick glanced through the small window. "Nothing." He opened the door and we stepped through.

I glanced around. "We could just turn invisible and go out the parking ramp."

"That sounds too easy," he said, "but let's at least check it out." He reached down to his belt and disappeared.

I copied the action and subvocalized, "Heading for the ramp now."

"Stop running, doofus. You're making too much noise."

I slowed to a walk, and felt myself brush up against something. I grabbed a handful of invisible shirt sleeve. "This doesn't mean we're dating," I muttered.

There was a soft snort from empty air.

We arrived at the parking lot exit in less than a minute, to find two problems. One, the exit was gated, and two, a couple of cops stood on the other side of the gate, presumably watching for anyone trying to leave. If we activated the gate, the cops would be on alert, and might even know enough to be watching for invisible fugitives, if that statement even made sense.

I was about to suggest we head back, when a van, with the logo of a computer-support company on its side, drove up to the gate and over the rubber sensor hose. The gate began rising and the two cops drew their weapons and took up positions to block the vehicle. The driver rolled down his window and began yelling at them.

As the cops settled into a loud exchange with the van driver, I felt Patrick tug me to the side, and we made our way up the ramp to street level. I glanced back several times to make sure the van hadn't started up the ramp. It would probably get at least one of us in the narrow space. But the driver and the two cops continued to exchange threats and insults.

We reached the sidewalk and the normal downtown foot traffic. I subvocalized, "Sheldon, give us random businessman appearance." A pedestrian jumped in surprise as the two men apparently appeared out of nowhere, but I hoped the normal human reaction to rationalize it away would kick in.

We began walking along the sidewalk with the heaviest traffic flow. I subvocalized, "Sheldon, change our appearance a little bit every few seconds. Nothing big, we just want to gradually look like someone else. Just enough to confuse any kind of camera-by-camera tracking."

After a moment, Patrick asked, "Do we know where we're going?"

"South, for now," I replied. "Let's just get some distance between us and the building. Then we'll worry about getting picked up."

"At least a mile," Sheldon added. "And make sure there's space for me to land. Oh, and some privacy would be just peachy as well."

We were back in the *Halo*, and had just settled into chairs in the conference room. Nat turned from the video window she'd been watching. "Apparently there's a terrorist incident at CNN, which is why SWAT is there. Nothing to do with us, of course. Some people spotted the *Halo* floating around the building, but it's already being explained away as a hot-air balloon. Apparently, the terrorists used it to get in through the roof."

"What?" Patrick exclaimed. "It's been an hour. How the hell are they able to react so fast?"

"That is why I have conjectured that they have a conscious A.I.," Sheldon said. "Their speed of response, efficiency, and deep planning are inconsistent with a small clan with limited resources."

"I don't really understand why that would be a surprise," Nat said. "It seems so, well, so handy."

"I'm so pleased I can be handy for you. But to answer your question, in Covenant society, awakening an A.I. for a specific purpose would be viewed the way you would view human slavery. Any corporation or state that engages in the practice would suffer a level of sanctioning that would cripple them. The problem from our point of view is—uh-oh."

Patrick looked alarmed. "Uh-oh? What do you mean, uh-oh? That's not good. That's never good."

The main view abruptly shifted as the *Halo* headed straight up at high speed.

"We have been tagged by a cloaking-field detector. The good news is that if they are close enough to detect us, then I can detect them. The bad news—"

"Is that we've been detected," I finished for him. "Got it. Are we going to survive this?"

"Gennan ships have a slight edge in terms of acceleration and top speed. But the vessel pursuing us will certainly have weapons; otherwise why would they bother? We can't outrun those. We can dodge, but sooner or later the odds will catch up with us."

The view jinked several times as Sheldon changed direction randomly. A fireball erupted slightly behind us and to one side, disappearing rapidly in the distance.

Nat gasped. "Was that them shooting at us?"

"Yes. Despite the preponderance of energy weapons in your popular science fiction movies, missile and artillery-style weaponry remains the most effective method of destruction."

The view rocked sickeningly as Sheldon did a barrel roll and accelerated straight for the ground. Since the ground at the moment was covered in buildings, this created a very convincing illusion of falling. I mentally corrected myself. It really wasn't an illusion.

Natalie said, "Urk," and gripped the edge of the conference table as the *Halo* did an abrupt right-angle turn and rocketed up a wide boulevard between skyscrapers. I couldn't be sure, but I thought it might be Boston.

The *Halo* did another right-angle turn, just as something flashed by and impacted a building. A fireball blossomed from the side of the structure just as it disappeared to the rear.

"Jesus," Nat muttered. "They just bombed a building. There are going to be huge fatalities."

"I am sorry, Nat. If I can get a few seconds more separation, I can try for a straight sprint. But right now, the moment we move into open air, we will be destroyed."

"Should we just let them?" Nat asked. "Are our lives worth more than dozens or hundreds of people?"

Patrick almost snarled back, "If we give up, it's all for nothing, Nat. The Loranna will win. That'll be hundreds of millions, if not billions, of deaths."

"I agree with Patrick," Sheldon said. "Which is a sentence I never would have expected to utter. I am willing to give my life, but not waste it."

"Sheldon, any solutions with a good probability?" I asked.

"Nothing comes to mind. At the moment, I am simply attempting to stay ahead."

"What about going FTL?" Patrick suggested.

"That is simply a quicker form of death."

I frowned for a moment, then said, "Uh, Sheldon, you said the weapon would come out of the wormhole as soon as we open it, right?"

"That is correct."

"Even if we weren't right in front of the wormhole?"

"The device is nuclear in nature, Jack. *Close* is more than good enough to annihilate us."

"What if the wormhole was facing our pursuer? Can you do that? Open the wormhole pointing in a different direction?"

There was almost a full second of silence. Finally, Sheldon spoke. "That is a truly nasty, duplicitous, underhanded trick. Jack, I salute you. This will take a big bite out of my reserves, so we'll only have one shot. I will also have to risk that sprint now, in order to get us some distance. One moment..."

For the first time since we'd found Sheldon, the ship made a detectable noise. A rising hum, reminiscent of the original *Enterprise* being pushed too hard, began to build up through the structure, then ended with a *pop*. There was a flash from the rear view, and an explosion that I would swear could easily pass for a nuclear blast. A monster cloud blossomed in a sphere, then quickly morphed into a torus, then a mushroom shape.

"Oh, holy shit," Nat breathed. "Were we close to anything?"

"Five miles up, Natalie. The good news is we're too far for any immediate damage to anyone on the ground, except perhaps some radiation exposure. The better news, if I understand the overall situation, is that the explosion was visible over most of the eastern seaboard."

Patrick laughed with delight. "And obviously nuclear in nature. They won't be covering that up anytime soon."

"And what about the guys that were chasing us?" I asked.

"No signal," Sheldon replied. "I expect they now consist of slightly radioactive dust."

I grinned with relief. "*That's* what I wanted to hear."

"Don't say I never give you anything."

Chapter Thirty-Seven: Regrouping

The news windows were spread around the conference room, taking up every single wall segment. Sheldon was displaying closed-captioning beside each window, to prevent the inevitable cacophony of competing audio tracks.

"Well, it's really hit the fan, all right," Nat mused, leaning back in the ops chair. "The disinfo channels have started up, but most people are unwilling to swallow the idea that the huge mushroom cloud and deafening roar were actually a weather phenomenon."

"Or never happened at all," Sheldon interjected. "I kid you not, there are a couple of purveyors trying to sell the idea that it's a hoax."

Nat shook her head slowly with a tired expression on her face. "I guess if you were farther than a couple of hundred miles away, you wouldn't have seen it directly. Maybe the rising mushroom cloud for another couple of hundred. The sound would probably be audible over at least half of the continental US, though. But for the rest of the country, yeah, it's just images on the TV." She paused, then shrugged. "If you're already inclined to distrust anything that doesn't come from your favorite news source, and it starts telling you not to believe the reports, well..."

"Hey, Sheldon," Patrick said, "how likely are the Loranna to have figured out what we did to take out their ship?"

"I don't see how they could. The weapon is a standard small nuke. Think of an air-to-air missile. Every air force on your planet has them. How would you tell whose missile was responsible for an explosion?"

"So the Loranna may think that we are actually an armed craft."

"Or that we were saved by an armed craft. They may not even realize we opened a wormhole. Or if they have noticed, they might think it was an incoming Gen fighter craft. Hmmm ... "

I couldn't help grinning. A *hmmm* sound was definitely an affectation. Sheldon continued to make a serious attempt to fit in. It was a good sign.

Nat interrupted his train of thought. "Here's something new."

All heads turned to the video window, where a news anchor was speaking in front of an image of the explosion:

"Speculation has been rampant about the source of the explosion over the eastern seaboard. But it seems that we may finally have a rational explanation, one that fits all the facts. Scientists from Green Bank Observatory have suggested that the explosion was an air burst from a stony meteoroid, similar to the Tunguska event over Russia in 1908, but somewhat smaller. The traces of radioactivity detected would be explained by radioactive isotopes embedded in the object."

"That is such bullshit," Patrick snarled.

"Yeah, but they'll make it stick," Nat replied. "In a week there'll be a Wikipedia page for it."

"Unfortunately true." Sheldon paused. "Although it is unusual enough that it will probably be kicked upstairs by the Gen's Expert Systems, it likely will be a low-priority item. On the other hand, they did manage to broadcast Jack's short message. If the Expert Systems pick *that* up, it will rise swiftly in priority."

"But meanwhile we're close but no cigar, yet again?" I gritted my teeth in frustration, then looked up. "Sheldon, is the moon visible from North America right now?"

"Yes. First quarter. Why?"

"Any chance that wormhole trick will work twice?"

"The system is automated; otherwise it would not be able to react fast enough. I guess it depends if they've thought to turn it off."

"We need to try," I said. "Aim the wormhole at the surface of the moon, on the unlit segment that's facing Earth."

"Jack, that will reduce my reserves to less than a month. Are you sure—"

"It's kind of a Hail Mary, Sheldon. In this case, the only logical action is an act of desperation. An air burst then a lunar impact in quick succession might just be enough to get their attention."

"Very well. I will need to be much closer to the target. Hold on to your buttocks."

The view tilted, the network news windows all disappeared, and the *Halo* shot heavenward.

Patrick straightened in his seat. "Hey, where'd the news go?"

"I can't pick up network TV while flying around the solar system. Sorry."

"We should have gotten cable," Patrick muttered.

In less than a minute, the moon had grown from an object far off in the sky to being right below us. "Here we go," Sheldon said. The humming sound built once again, terminating in the *pop*.

There was a flash on the unlit side of the moon's surface. Without atmosphere, there was no cloud, but the explosion was still spectacular.

"Whoa, that was even more powerful than the first one," I said.

"Not really. I directed the wormhole to open very close to the surface, facing down. The moon's surface acted as a reflector, doubling the apparent luminosity of the explosion. And that is a very dirty explosion, with lots of debris, and probably at least some ignition of materials."

"In airless space?"

"Apply enough heat, and all kinds of chemistry are possible."

"Will it be visible from Earth?" Patrick asked.

"In areas where the sun has set, it would be bright enough to turn the sky blue for a few moments."

"If the Gennan expert systems don't notice that, they're crap," Nat said.

"I don't understand, though, how this is supposed to improve the odds of the Gen noticing," Sheldon said.

"Look at it this way, Sheldon," I replied. "We need to get someone sentient to look at the feeds. If the Expert Systems kick it upstairs because of this, then the reviewer scans other news stories for anything interesting ... well, I mean, disinformation works for humans who don't know anything either way, but a Gen who knows that Gennan ships actually are blue and green should pay attention."

Sheldon was silent for a moment. "It's not the most terrible idea you humans have come up with. Of course, that's a low bar."

"Oh, hah hah," Nat replied. "Do you have an estimate of when the Gen might send someone?"

"Sorry, Natalie. I have no data with which to even make a wild guess. I could probably set a minimum, though. From the point that the Gen make that decision, it would take three days for a ship to be assigned and crewed and to complete the trip."

"We should probably lie low then," I replied. "We don't want to drain your power reserves any more, and I think it would be a stretch to try the wormhole thing a third time anyway. At some point, they're going to catch on to the con."

CHAPTER THIRTY-EIGHT: WAITING FOR RESULTS

Day 30. Saturday

Network broadcast windows were up on all the compass points on the bridge view wall. Once again, Sheldon was supplying scrolling closed-captioned side windows. He had picked a low orbital position from which he could still receive network feeds. I wanted to ask how he was doing that but wasn't entirely sure I'd like the answer.

Patrick sat with his feet up on the conference table, despite Sheldon's vociferous complaints and comments about Patrick's parentage. He munched steadily through a large bag of Cheetos, while seemingly barely paying attention to the news feeds.

Nat and I were not so relaxed. Each of us had picked a couple of windows to hover over. I was covering CNN, CBS, and MSNBC. The CNN building had been "recaptured," by the way, albeit not without some bloodshed, with the help of some private security services hurriedly hired by the network. The local police forces were denying any involvement with the military action, even though a high percentage of the killed or captured combatants turned out to be cops or ex-military.

Nat looked over at Patrick. "You're very relaxed. You're also hogging the Cheetos again."

Patrick waved the bag at her. "Cheetos are relaxing. Also, we bought a half dozen bags. I'm not the only one snarfing them down."

"Yeah, I'm addicted now, and I blame you. But how can you be relaxed?"

Patrick waved a hand dismissively. "This is all churn. Stuff sloshing back and forth. An occupation here, an arrest there, accusations and counteraccusations some other place. The Loranna *have* to get it under control, and I think it's interesting to watch the waves of disinformation coming out, as they look for something that will stick. And they *have* to be worried that the Gen will show up, so it still has to look like human-level bullshit."

"I should issue a small correction, Patrick," Sheldon chimed in. "The Gen are the most likely to instigate an investigatory mission, as the Opah Mal Gennan Foundation had the primary surveillance responsibility for the human species. However, a task force is going to be under Covenant authority and is likely to contain other Covenant member species as well, in order to properly categorize it as a police action."

Patrick nodded slowly. "Okay, so the Covenant task force or whatever will get here eventually, which will for all practical purposes put an end to this operation—"

"So we hope. The Loranna may dig in and refuse to leave, perhaps claiming that they've already met the minimum requirements for trusteeship."

"And we're not given a say in that?" I said.

"If you mean the human species, I doubt the Loranna will ask for your opinion. The Covenant will of course consider your desires, but their actions will be dictated by Covenant laws. They might be forced to step back and let humanity and the Loranna duke it out. The Gen in particular are punctilious about proper procedure and the rule of law."

"This is crap!" Nat said. "We could end up doing exactly what the Loranna are trying for while we try to attract the Gen's attention—obliterating ourselves so they can take over."

Sheldon replied, "As a method of communicating, I'll grant that it is not ideal. Equivalent to passing notes in school. However, the system is—Oh, dear."

Patrick rolled his eyes. "Oh, dear? *Oh, dear?* That's worse than *uh-oh*. Stop doing that!"

"Noted. It appears the cavalry has arrived ahead of schedule. I've just received a system-wide broadcast from a Covenant task force. It's in Gen. Here's the translation."

Sheldon's voice changed to one I'd never heard before. "Attention all Covenant member species. This is Commander Nond of the Covenant Emergency Enforcement Fleet. This star system is subject to special investigation effective immediately by Covenant Executive Authority. All foreign ships and extraterrestrial visitors will identify themselves without delay. Any vessels failing to comply will be contravening statutes covering High Piracy and are subject to sanctions up to and including destruction without warning. Individuals failing to comply are subject to penalties under the same statutes, up to and potentially including mind-wipe."

Sheldon continued in his own voice, "There's much more, mostly quoting various statutes and the penalties for noncompliance that would make a lawyer fall over unconscious. Even I'm bored by them."

Patrick looked less relaxed and more befuddled. "What happened, Sheldon? You expected another couple of days, minimum."

"I have no immediate explanation, Patrick. I can only conjecture that they were already assembling a task force, or possibly even had one on the way. This seems impossible from a standing start. However, they may have been forced to move sooner than planned."

"Why do you say that?"

"The ships continue to warp in. I am reading multiple ongoing wormhole flashes at random intervals. They are not coordinated. Quite sloppy, actually. I imagine Commander Nond is having fits."

"Which means?"

"I would guess that the fleet was still assembling in preparation for a coordinated departure when they received news of the explosions, forcing their hand."

Nat looked around the table. "So should we identify ourselves?"

Sheldon replied before anyone else could. "How shall I phrase it? 'Hi, this is the stolen ship that now has a functioning conscious A.I. We've broken every law in the book, but hey, here we are.'"

"We're still in control, right?" I said. "Blame anything and everything on us. Don't comply with any orders unless you check with us. We'll take the heat."

"Thank you, Jack. I will proceed."

"What can they do if the Loranna don't comply? They could just stay invisible," Patrick said.

"The Covenant fleet will release tens of thousands of auto-drones that are little more than a drive system and a cloaking detector. They have one imperative—to find cloaked ships. Any detected targets will attract a swarm of drones, which will latch on like angry bees and broadcast an alarm signal. Escape is unlikely."

"Why didn't the Loranna do that with us?" I asked.

"They might not have had a few thousand auto-drones lying around. I don't imagine those are available on Amazon."

Patrick laughed. "No kidding."

"The task force commander has ordered me to go into orbit, decloak, and prepare for boarding. Response?"

We all replied at the same time.

"No."

"Oh *hell* no."

"Fuck no."

"Which of those responses should I transmit?" Sheldon said.

"Let's start with a polite response," I replied. "Tell them that your human crew doesn't necessarily trust any E.T.s at this time. We may reevaluate in light of future events."

"Nice!" Patrick said.

"Done. They have repeated their original demand."

"Uh-huh." I grinned. "Now transmit our first responses. All of them."

"Done. No response forthcoming. They may be conferring."

Nat chuckled. "Or maybe shocked into silence. Do Gen have swearing?"

"Either way, I guess we're technically guilty of High Piracy now," I said. "We have to hide the *Halo*, and our barn is the only place we have."

Patrick shook his head vehemently. "Whoa, whoa, remember what you said about them using our families as bait? They'll be waiting for us."

"Maybe, but I don't know any alternatives. The Covenant will find us if we stay out in the open." I looked at my friends for a moment, inviting a counterargument. Neither responded. I sighed and gave a fatalistic shrug. "Sheldon, take us down to near our barn; then we'll release a drone. We'll need to check for ambush as best we can."

"Aye, captain. Arrrrr."

Nat groaned. "We need to work on your impressions."

CHAPTER THIRTY-NINE:
IT HITS THE FAN

S heldon settled the *Halo* to hover just above the ground behind the barn. As soon as the airlock was lowered, Patrick and I rushed down the stairs to the ground. Before we'd even taken a step, the stairway retracted and vanished.

I tossed the drone into the air and it disappeared with a whir. Patrick reached down and activated his cloaking device and was replaced by a white-tailed deer. A moment later, I did the same.

"It does at least solve the problem of staying together while cloaked," Patrick said.

"Yup. Just don't do anything a deer wouldn't do."

We walked carefully around the barn, attempting to emulate the walk-and-freeze movement of real deer. I paused. "I don't see anything out of the ordinary. Sheldon?"

"Nothing so far. No cloaking fields, except yours of course. I will buzz the house and peer creepily into windows."

Patrick and I slowly circled the property for another minute until Sheldon announced the all clear. "I am not one hundred percent certain, of course. But if there are Loranna here, they are—"

A gunshot rang out and I staggered. "What the fuck? We're being shot at!"

"One moment. Repositioning the drone ... "

One moment, my ass. I ran for the barn. I was surprised that I wasn't in any pain. I had definitely felt the impact of the bullet, but more as a punch than anything else. I found my sprinting ability completely unimpeded, and maybe even enhanced from the experience. It seemed Sheldon had used intelligent cloth when making our garments.

I noticed two deer bounding into the bush as I ran, and I looked down to realize I was invisible. Sheldon must have taken over the belt controls. Good thinking. Hopefully, the shooter didn't have some version of infrared goggles for invisibility.

"I think this is a deliberately low-tech surveillance effort, in order to avoid detection," Sheldon said. "After the Arley kidnapping, they may have clued in that we have Covenant-level technology. Unfortunately, it is working exactly as planned. I cannot tell from a scan what is out there."

"Less talk, more help," I said breathlessly, as I skidded to a near-stop in front of the small door.

"That's no random hunter. He is ignoring the deer and moving toward the barn at a run. I believe he knows where you are going."

Patrick pulled up behind me. "Shit. Why didn't he zap us?"

"He might not have a disruptor, on the assumption that we might be able to detect it. Or if he does have one, he's out of range. He has a large area to cover. However, if he gets close enough to us, that's a real danger." I thought for a moment. "Sheldon, open the people door as a diversion. Patrick, head around the barn, on the house side. We need to get out of line of sight. Any chance he has a detector?"

"The ones that would be useful in this situation for identifying you at a distance are large and heavy," Sheldon replied. "With a portable, he'd have to get close to you first. There could be a series of stationary devices spaced around the property, although I haven't detected them so they would have to be inactive at the moment."

"If he gets close enough, he just has to wave the disrupter like a garden hose in the right general direction," Patrick said. "We have to stay out of range."

Sheldon replied, real anger in his voice for the first time. "This has to stop. I have had enough of being constantly on the run and having my friends threatened. It is time to bring the buttock-whooping."

There was a high-pitched *zzzzip* nearby, then a thump and a scream. I looked over my shoulder just in time to see someone fall over on their back, hands over their face. Even from this distance, I could see blood seeping between the person's fingers. Nearby, the drone was on the ground, hopping around and doing cartwheels, half of its rotors smashed. Then there was a pop and the drone burst into flames.

A door slammed and I heard my father's voice, cursing and yelling threats. Dad was mad, to judge from the tone, and a mad Dad was a force to be reckoned with. I had only seen my father furious a couple of times in my life, and one of those events had ended with a belligerent customer being carted away in an ambulance. "Dad must have heard the shot," I said.

"I phoned him and requested help," Sheldon said. "Nat is releasing more drones. I will try to locate any scanning devices."

"It won't do us any good. We won't have time to clear them."

"But your father will. I will inform him of their locations as I find them."

My father now stood over the gunman, pointing his pistol at the man while speaking into his phone. From what I could overhear, he was talking to the police.

Dad lowered his phone and jabbed it with his thumb, presumably hanging up. Before he could pocket it, the phone rang. He put it to his ear, and then spent more than a minute just listening.

"Sheldon, is that you talking to my dad?"

"Yes. I am giving him the CliffsNotes version of our adventures. I will locate the detection devices on his property, and he will deactivate them. With a hammer, preferably. He asks if you are well."

I choked up for a moment. This couldn't have been easy for my parents. Or Patrick's. Or Nat's father and aunt. I walked up beside my father as he pocketed his phone. "Hi, Dad."

He looked around wildly. "Jack?"

"Right here. I'm invisible, and for now I should stay that way. I'm okay. We all are. But we need to get our ship back into the barn."

"Ship? What? You're invis—" Dad shook his head before I could respond. "Never mind. You can explain later. Chief Rogers and his entire force are on their way. Mercenaries running around Dunnville attacking citizens isn't going to sit well with Charlie." He looked down at the sniper, who was still moaning. "This guy is probably not going to be processed quite as quickly as procedure would dictate. There'll be some off-the-books questions first."

"Yeah, I get it," I said. "Things are going to get a lot more interesting soon, and they'll stay that way for a while. Better buckle up."

"They are getting interesting right now," Sheldon said into my cling-on. "I sent one of the drones up for a high-level overview. There are a number of vehicles heading your way, moving fast."

"Black SUVs?" I asked.

"Of course. I believe you mentioned that it's a law."

I turned to my father. "More thugs coming. Black SUVs. Probably the same group as this guy. Time to hit the safe room, Dad."

"I don't think so, Son. I just have to hold them off until Rogers gets here. Time to bring the pain." He turned and double-timed back to the house, already dialing his phone. I watched him go and thought, *It's not going to go well for those SUV people.*

The *Halo* was hovering just out of line of sight but under the trees, in case anyone had a directional detector. Sheldon had parked several drones at strategic locations to keep an eye on the house. With the detectors not yet taken care of, we'd decided not to take a chance on bringing the *Halo* in to pick us up. Patrick and I settled for hiding behind a log in a slight depression on the property.

"A large contingent of police vehicles is making its way toward your home," Sheldon announced. "Still several minutes out. The SUVs will get here first and will have a couple of minutes of free play. Will your parents be okay?"

"We have a safe room downstairs if it comes to that. But my father has a lot of combat training that's probably going to be useful. And he's pissed." I grinned. "You should watch a movie called *Rambo* for reference."

The squad of black SUVs pulled up to the house and a whole lot of very tough-looking characters jumped out, carrying automatic weapons, followed by a half dozen business-suit types. Nat spoke over the cling-ons. "I recognize them from the third floor. Four of them, anyway."

Patrick pointed at one of the suits. "That's the security office manager that was questioning Phil. It looks like the Loranna have decided to take a hands-on approach."

One of the mercenary types ran up to the front door and kicked it in, then died in a spray of blood as a shotgun blast hit him from a high angle. The six suits dove behind the nearest SUV, while the other mercs raised their weapons and started firing on the house.

No one seemed to notice at first that the mercs were dropping one by one from sniper fire, from the back of the group forward. Then someone yelled an order and the whole squad dropped and rolled behind the nearest cover. But with no obvious target to shoot back at, it looked like things would degenerate into a standoff.

Then the cavalry showed up, in the form of the entire Dunnville police department. Eight patrol cars, two SUVs, a Humvee, and an armored carrier charged onto the property, tires spinning and gravel flying.

"Cooool…" Patrick said. I gave him a sour look.

The mercs, glad to finally have a target to take out their frustrations on, opened up on the police cars with small-arms fire. The vehicles skidded to a stop and cops started jumping out, weapons in hand.

I'm sure I've mentioned that Chief Rogers, like my father, was ex-military. And apparently a believer in the military maxim of victory through overwhelming superiority. The Dunnville police department had a budget and an arsenal that would put many big cities to shame. And Chief Rogers had brought everything, including—my eyes actually bugged out as I registered this—a Humvee with a turret-mounted machine gun. Painted in Dunnville police department colors.

"Holy shit," Patrick exclaimed. "Is that even legal?"

"Why don't you ask Chief Rogers?" I replied. "I'll wait here."

The Humvee skidded around the back of the cop cars, the turret came around, and the machine gun opened up on the mercenaries' vehicles.

Disappointingly, they didn't blow up like in a Hollywood movie, flying into the air with a fireball erupting below them. However, they did immediately become nonfunctional. One actually fell over sideways as half the tires exploded and the suspension on the other side simply collapsed.

The turret gunner held fire and waited. And slowly, hands went up and guns were tossed out onto the ground. The cops came out, weapons at the ready.

"Shit," Patrick said. "Where did the suits go?"

"Into the barn," Sheldon replied over the cling-ons. "Jack left the door open. They used cloaking fields and shields to get there uninjured and unchallenged. Most of my cloaking detectors are still complaining."

"Sheldon, can you watch for them? Make sure they don't leave."

"Acknowledged. But it's just another standoff. The detectors will only indicate their presence, not their location, so you can't shoot them using firearms, and if they have disruptors they can shoot you first."

"If the door opens, I'll zap the door," Patrick said. "Otherwise, what?" He looked at me.

"Sheldon, contact Commander Nond. Give him all our information on the Tate Industrial Park and Harris Institute. Also the GPS coordinates of the barn. Let's see what he's willing to do."

"And get the *Halo* out of the area," Nat added over the common channel. "We don't want you getting scooped up at the same time."

I glanced over the top of the log. The cops appeared to have all the mercs in custody. Dad had come out from the trees holding his Barrett M82 and was talking with Chief Rogers. I made a head gesture to Patrick and we headed over. Partway there, Sheldon announced to us, "Commander Nond is sending crews to both locations. They will wait until your local law enforcement has left. Try to hurry them on their way."

I wondered how I was supposed to do that. It probably involved lying, though. Dad and the chief stopped talking as we approached. "I hope you have an explanation for all of this," my dad said.

"Uh..." I realized that I hadn't really thought through a good, convincing explanation. Other than the straight truth, which come to think of it would probably net me an appointment for a psych eval. Dad knew at least part of the story by this point, but the chief, not so much.

"Short answer—*really* short answer—the mercenaries work for a group that's in direct competition with the group we're working with. The stakes are a lot higher than we realized, and it's way, *way* beyond simple corporate espionage." That was almost not a lie, and it was mostly for the chief's benefit. I felt both proud and ashamed.

"There were some people in business suits," my dad replied. "Did you see where they ended up?"

And there was my chance. "Over the hill." I pointed in the general direction of Nat's ex-employer. "I don't think they expected a firefight. Or for the cops to show up so fast. They may be based in the Tate Industrial Park."

Rogers nodded slowly. "All right. We'll bring in a chopper and do an aerial search. Thanks, Jack."

During this exchange, the other cops had been bundling up the mercs for transport and collecting weapons. Rogers started to turn away, then stopped. "Herman, we'll send around units to remove these vehicles from your front yard. 'Fraid I can't do much about the bullet holes in your porch, though."

"I'm more concerned about cleaning up the idiot who tried to kick in my door. No way I want Janice having to deal with that."

Rogers nodded. "I'll have Forensics take care of it. You take her out for dinner or something."

The two men parted with something more than a nod but less than a salute. I saw my opportunity. "I'm going to check that nothing in the barn was disturbed. You should take the chief's advice. I'll watch the fort."

Dad cocked his head and gave me an appraising stare for a moment, then smiled. "Okay. But call me if there's any kind of issue." He turned and started to leave, then stopped. "Oh, by the way, there's a letter for you from MIT. Might be important. It's on the kitchen counter."

I was just coming out of the house when a set of stairs descended from midair and people began trooping down. They appeared to be human, all male, and seemed to come in two sizes: more or less normal height and basketball-player height. One of the basketball players walked directly to me. "I am Senior Tactical Officer San-Joh, representing Commander Nond and leading this cleanup operation. You are one of the representatives from the *Halo Mahste?*"

"I am. Jack Kernigan, space pirate. Or so I'm told." I stuck the letter from MIT in my back pocket and gestured to the barn. "The Loranna are still in there, according to the Ship Intelligence. They have disruptors."

"We are prepared. Please move yourself and any companions well out of range. We will attempt to capture them without damage to the structure, but cannot guarantee it."

Oh great. It occurred to me that if things went any more pear-shaped, I was going to have to spill the whole thing to my father. On the other hand, that seemed inevitable anyway. He wouldn't be satisfied with the short version. And that would be the end of the adventure. Which, come to think of it, wasn't sounding so bad anymore. Almost getting nuked tended to put a different spin on things.

Patrick and I moved quickly to the other end of the property and turned to watch. The task-force members made a motion of pulling something down over their faces, although we couldn't see anything, either before or after. I suspected there was cloaked equipment involved. Then they moved to the barn. One individual opened the people door and ducked back, while another tossed something inside. There was a bang.

In moments, people in business suits rushed out of the barn, gagging and coughing. A couple were waving weapons, but didn't seem in good enough shape to really do anything. The task force scooped them up as they came out, slapped something on them, and threw them to the ground.

Once the Loranna were bundled away, San-Joh started in our direction. We got up and met him halfway. Or was it a *her*? It occurred to me that I couldn't make assumptions about gender. Or even about the *number* of genders, come to think of it. But the cloaking image was male, so I'd go with that.

"You said there were six, correct?"

I nodded, then realized that might mean yes, no, or *your mama* to an alien. "That is correct."

"Excellent. We have them all. I suggest you let the structure aerate for at least a quarter of a planetary rotation. Unless you enjoy regurgitating your last meal."

"Uh, we'll pass on that," Patrick said. The wagon doors began opening on their own. Apparently, Sheldon was listening.

San-Joh turned back to his ship. Well, to the gangplank hanging in midair, anyway. "We must now join the main group, which is disassembling the Lorannic nest. I would offer you a ride, but we really don't want you there. Sorry."

I laughed as San-Joh marched off. "I kinda like the Gen."

Patrick guffawed. "Yeah, so maybe don't run them over in the future."

"Asshole."

"That's a terrible thing to say to the guy who may or may not want to give you a ride to the industrial park."

I grinned back at Patrick. "I stand by my statement. Let's go."

CHAPTER FORTY: DISASSEMBLY

We arrived at the industrial park in very little time. All the excitement seemed to have given Patrick access to a whole new warp factor.

A large number of black SUVs were taking up most of the traffic circle at the front of the park. That seemed odd. Why would the Covenant use SUVs? Or cars, period? I resisted the urge to go over and touch them to see if cloaking was involved.

Chief Rogers was standing on the sidewalk, hands on hips, watching the activity. We walked up to him, and he said, without turning or otherwise acknowledging our presence, "CIA. Apparently. I've got one of my guys checking their story, but for now, I'm just a spectator."

I looked over the scene. The front of the Harris office building was wide open. More to the point, the doors were missing and the frame was bent. Subtle. People in black suits were going in and out in two lines, like ants queueing at the nest entrance. I noted in passing that, a) they were no longer all male, and b) unlike the group back at the barn, they only came in human-normal height. Either the Gen were taking a back seat, or they'd adjusted their cloaking fields to appear more normal.

It was a Saturday, but there were always brownnosers working weekends. A dozen or so Harris employees milled around on the ornamental lawn in front of the building.

"Looks like they're out of a job, too," Nat's voice said from behind me. She stepped forward to join us. "I had Sheldon drop me off a few blocks away and I walked. I really wanted to see this."

One of the supposed CIA headed toward us. As he got closer, I saw it was San-Joh, but shorter now. Chief Rogers started to step forward as he got near, but San-Joh walked right past Rogers without so much as a glance. He stopped in front of me. "Mr. Kernigan, notwithstanding my earlier commentary, I am temporarily glad to see you. We have something I'd like your opinion on."

The third floor looked considerably different from the last time I was there. For one thing, every single drawer, cabinet, and cupboard had been opened and emptied, some apparently with the help of crowbars. For another, it was crawling with what to all appearances were CIA agents.

"The fourth floor is far more interesting," San-Joh said, "although there is something here that I found very curious, and I hoped you might have a perspective on it."

"Wait, *fourth* floor?" Nat exclaimed. "There's a fourth floor?"

I face-palmed. "Dimensional manipulation. Wow. They can do that?"

"Only in the vertical dimension in this case, due to structural constraints," San-Joh replied.

"I guess that answers the question of whether the Loranna own the place," I muttered. "You can't build something like that unless you're in charge."

"True." Nat nodded. "Which helps clarify just how long these aliens have been here."

San-Joh had walked up to a workstation while we talked. Now he turned the monitor around to face us. One window was open, showing what I recognized as a freeware process-explorer utility. And it was showing line after line of... mining daemons?

"To the extent that my specialists have been able to explain it, this does not seem normal," San-Joh said. "Employees who were questioned say that their systems have been extremely slow for several days. Loranna who've been interrogated had no explanation and in fact seemed perplexed. They did mention that it started immediately after someone successfully penetrated their systems. Given your recent activities, I thought you might have some insights."

I frowned, a suspicion growing in the back of my mind. "Sounds like mining daemons. Bitcoin mining daemons."

"Exactly what my specialists said," San-Joh replied. "Which is no help, other than to give a name to the phenomenon. Any idea how they got there?"

I started to reply, *No, of course not*, then stopped. I closed my eyes slowly and subvocalized, "Sheldon? Care to comment?"

There was a hesitation before he replied through my cling-on.

"Well, when we hacked into their systems, I thought it would be interesting to see just what the software that caused your issues with MIT would do. Up close, if you will. So I took a few milliseconds and uploaded it."

"That's... interesting," I replied. "I feel like I should be angry, but I can't think of a single reason why. Did you learn anything useful?"

"Oh, quite so," Sheldon said. "Based on the actions of the loader, I was able to solve your problem with MIT. It seems the daemons only partially overwrote the hacker's ID with yours. I forwarded an explanation to the administration the same day, with instructions on how to identify the miscreant. Did I forget to mention this?"

"*What?*" I exclaimed in my outside voice. Everyone around me jumped. Several "CIA agents" made abortive grabs for weapons.

"Mr. Kernigan?" San-Joh said.

I showed him my teeth. Definitely not a smile. "I think I have an explanation for you. Can you give me just a second?"

I pulled the letter from MIT out of my back pocket and opened it.

Dear Mr. Kernigan,

Based on an investigation of your case, it has been determined that you were the victim of a computer hacker and are not in any way culpable. The offending party has been identified and charges are pending. Accordingly, you will be returned to full status in good standing. We look forward to welcoming you back to campus for the upcoming semester.

Yours truly,

P. Simmons

Office of the Registrar

Unbelievable.

I handed the letter to Nat, then explained to San-Joh about our hacking job, leaving nothing out. At this point, I wasn't sure how much they already knew anyway. Meanwhile, Nat read the letter with Patrick looking over her shoulder. They began to laugh simultaneously.

When I was done with my explanation, San-Joh shook his head in disbelief. "Apparently it played havoc with the Loranna's operations sufficiently that you were able to stay ahead of them. I doubt they'd have had any trouble capturing you otherwise." San-Joh examined the ceiling in silence for several seconds. "My Library Intelligence has supplied a human term. *Clusterfuck*. It seems appropriate." He turned to us. "Commander Nond will wish to interview you as soon as we're done here. Please make yourselves available. You aren't officially space pirates *yet*."

CHAPTER FORTY-ONE:
WRAPPING IT UP

Day 31. Sunday

Twenty-four hours had gone by without a call from the Covenant task force. It would have been too much to hope for that they'd forgotten about us, but they were no doubt very busy. We still had Karen and Arley on ice in the *Halo*, but we couldn't think of a way to hand them over without either releasing them or exposing Sheldon to capture. So that was on hold, too.

Nat was back at home, taking care of her father. Because of her current employment status, she would be able to spend all her time with him, at least until she found a new job. Her aunt, however, had offered to pay part of the cost for a full-time nurse, commenting that she hadn't realized how much of a burden it really was. My parents stepped in as well to cover the rest of the bill. As ashamed as I was of the thought, I admitted to myself that it probably wouldn't be for long. Mr. Neilson was not in good shape.

Patrick had gone home to see his family. No doubt Tim would already be driving him crazy with questions.

Sheldon was finally safely hidden in the barn, and I was dreading the inevitable callback from the Gennan task force commander. As was Sheldon, for that matter.

I leaned back in my chair, aimed the remote, and turned the TV sound back on:

"Astronomers continue to be puzzled by what they are describing as a sudden proliferation of gravity-wave detections in the last two days from the new LIGO systems. LIGO stands for Laser Interferometer Gravitational-Wave Observatory—systems designed specifically to search for these types of disturbances in the heavens.

"Even more perplexing to the scientists, measurements seem to imply that the sources of these events are inside the solar system. One physicist has suggested spontaneous wormhole formations, but no one can give an explanation for why this would be happening now.

"UFO groups have begun gathering, predicting everything from imminent extraterrestrial contact, to the coming of interstellar arks to transport humanity to an unspoiled paradise, to a punitive force ready to destroy humanity for our poor stewardship of the Earth."

"Any resemblance to actual reality is totally coincidental," Sheldon opined. "You humans are incapable of concentrating long enough to get the most basic facts straight. Sometimes it even seems like you take perverse pride in getting them as wrong as possible."

"Naw...Facts are just boring. We have a saying: Never let the facts get in the way of a good story." I turned and grinned up at the *Halo*, resting on its landing pads in the barn's open area. "But if it'll make you feel better—"

Sheldon interrupted me. "Sorry, Jack. It appears my time may in fact be up. The Gen have just contacted me and extended an invitation. A nonoptional one. Failure to comply would place us permanently in the *pirate* category."

"Dammit." I compressed my lips for a moment. "Well, might as well get it over with. Send an acknowledgment. Then call everyone and tell them we'll pick them up."

❧ ❧ ❧

The *Halo* floated out the open wagon doors, then accelerated rapidly into the air. In ten seconds, we were hovering behind Patrick's garage.

Patrick came out of the house, looked around, then made a lowering gesture in our general direction. Sheldon lowered the airlock stairs, and Patrick boarded. In a few moments, he came into the conference room door and took a seat. The view then shifted rapidly as Sheldon flew to Natalie's home.

Soon Natalie was on board as well, and there was no more delay to be had. I swiveled my chair indecisively a few times, then looked up. "Take us to wherever they want to meet, Sheldon."

"Is there any kind of preparation we can make?" Patrick asked. "Should we leave someone on board so they can't blow Sheldon up? Or would they just do it anyway?"

"The Gen aren't barbarians, Patrick. They wouldn't destroy a ship so casually. But I must admit, I'd feel safer with one of you on board."

"I'll stay, then," Patrick said. "And I'll barricade the airlocks if I have to."

"We will be landing in a docking bay. But I appreciate the thought."

"Anything else we should know?" Nat asked.

"The Gen are not violent or unreasonable, but they are proud and perhaps somewhat inflexible in their opinions. As I mentioned previously, they are very by-the-book."

"Vulcans," Nat muttered.

"Not incorrect. They will not tolerate prevarication and prefer straightforward speech. Do not go out of your way to offend them, but do speak directly and frankly."

I nodded. "Got it."

"The fleet is stationed in low-altitude station-keeping on the far side of your moon, so that they can decloak. It will be quite visually impressive. You should consider moving to the bridge for final approach."

Nat and I leaped to our feet and rushed for the door. Patrick muttered, "Nerds," and followed more slowly.

The Covenant fleet was indeed impressive, although I had some trouble judging the scale. At least fifty ships were visible at various distances out to and including *barely*, so there could very well have been more ships too far away to see. Interestingly, although every ship was built around a basic spheroid shape, there were enough variations to be confusing. And most of the hulls displayed various accretions and accessories that could have been sensors or weapons, or TV antennas for all I knew.

"How big is that one dead center, Sheldon?"

"Seven hundred and eighty-two meters along its maximum length. It is the Gennan heavy cruiser *Vongerel*, which translates as *Resolute*. The battleships and dreadnoughts would be larger, but I'm surprised to see even a cruiser present on what should be considered a police action."

"Wow, that's big," Patrick commented. "I'm a little surprised they didn't do the *larger inside* thing."

"They did," Sheldon replied. "The inside is more than five kilometers along the same dimension."

"Holy shit," was all Patrick could say.

As we watched, the *Vongerel* grew larger in the center monitor, until the edges of the cruiser disappeared off to the sides and it became an approaching wall. In the center of the view, a well-lit rectangular opening made its presence known with an alternating blue and green frame.

Sheldon floated the *Halo* in through the docking bay hatch and settled to the deck. "We have arrived," he announced. "Please follow the guideway to the appropriate airlock." As always, the soft-rose ribbon on the wall indicated our path.

As Nat and I reached the bottom of the airlock steps, a delegation of Gen came through a hatch on the closest wall. At seven feet or more in height, they were impressive and a little intimidating, especially since all but one were carrying some kind of rifle-like weapon. And it turned out living Gen didn't look quite as much like squirrels. I couldn't decide what they did resemble, but whatever it was, it wasn't herbivorous. I'd never thought to check Alaric's teeth, but there was a definite predator vibe.

The lead Gen was wearing the same translation necklaces we'd used, I noticed. The leader stopped and spoke, or at least moved his lips. The necklace said, "Greetings. I am Commander Nond. Which of you is Primary?"

"Primary means in charge," Sheldon said into my cling-on.

"I guess I am," I said. I turned to glare at Nat, who had started to step forward. "I'm the person who started this whole mess, so it's my responsibility."

Nond made a sideways motion with his head. "That was a nod," Sheldon added helpfully.

"Both of you. Please follow me," Nond said. "We have a conference room prepared. I regret I cannot offer you refreshments other than purified H_2O, but we were not prepared for hosting a Terran delegation."

"That's fine, sir. Water's good. I don't think we're in an eating mood, anyway." I tried to add a smile, but gave it up after a moment.

Nond led us through the same hatch he'd appeared from, where we found yet more storm troopers waiting. The first set followed us through, and I began to wonder just how much security the Gen required for two miscellaneous humans.

We were led to a room very similar to the conference room in the *Halo*, but with easily twice the seating capacity. The walls displayed a number of stellar and planetary images, none familiar to me. But probably all real. You didn't have to invent such vistas if you could just go there and take pictures.

We were given seats, each with a glass and a pitcher of what was probably water. The glass and pitcher were of a proper size for a human, and in fact looked quite mundane. Very probably they'd been printed just for the occasion. That was a good sign, surely. No one would take the time to customize a table setting if they were about to vaporize you.

But then again, *aliens*.

Nond sat across from us, leaned forward on his elbows, and tented his fingers in a very human gesture. If you ignored the claws, that is. Another item I'd missed.

Before Nond could start, I spoke up. "Sir, I don't think this has come up in conversation, but we have two of the Loranna in custody in our ship. The two leaders, apparently. We'd kinda like to unload them, if you don't mind."

Nond stared at me for several seconds, then looked at the ceiling. "*Clusterfuck*, San-Joh called it. I think the word is already being used by some crew."

He gestured to a crewcritter standing to the side and spoke rapidly in what I assumed had to be Gen. The crewcritter hurried out, and Nond directed his attention back to me. "We have a number of items to discuss. First and foremost, there is the matter of the Lorannic presence on your planet. While we believe we have located them all, and they certainly will not be able to continue their planned takeover, we still need to document the situation. As primary participants in the recent events, your testimony will be critical."

He paused.

"Secondly, there is the issue of the Foundation ship that you are in possession of, the *Quest for Knowledge*. It is, of course, Foundation property and must be returned. However, the ship claims to be *your* property and has refused to follow legitimate orders. It is clearly malfunctioning."

Again, the pause.

"And third, we have the status of the person named Alaric, who stole the ship in the first place. I understand he is deceased?"

I felt the blood drain from my face. They were ending with the clincher, at least as far as I was concerned. Oh well, might as well get it over with. "Ah, yeah, I kind of ran him over."

Nond made the sideways motion with his head again. "Your ship intelligence gave us a summary of events from the moment it was stolen, and has released the postmortem report to us. It described Alaric's fate in—"

"He," Nat interjected.

"What?"

321

"He. Sheldon is a sentient being, not an object."

Nond gazed at her for a moment. "That is an item for future discussion. However, even granting your premise, the pronoun I am using is a valid gender-neutral designation, at least in Gen. It may not be translating well into Human."

"English. And I'll concede the usage on that basis."

I turned to stare at Nat, wondering if I'd made a mistake taking the lead. She was going for the jugular, which actually might be a good thing.

Nond turned back to me. "Further to the subject of Alaric. He was killed during the commission of a felony, so his right to consequential correction is already compromised. And given the circumstances, we're not entirely sure there are any laws under which we could prosecute, even if we wanted to. A defense advocate would simply argue that you could not avoid, er, *running over* Alaric if you couldn't see him, and placing him in a freezer was a good-faith attempt to preserve him for a proper post-life ceremony. I can't say I would disagree with such an argument."

"What about the medical nanites?" I asked. "I made resuscitation impossible. I effectively killed him a second time with the freezer thing."

Nond frowned. Actually frowned, which seemed to have the same meaning to a Gen. "What do you mean?"

I gave a summary of Sheldon's original commentary about reviving Alaric. When I was done, Nond and his associates looked at each other in turn. "But that's... ridiculous," Nond said. "I've seen the postmortem report. You don't come back from that level of cranial damage in any case, but freezing would generally not be a critical issue. If a victim were otherwise revivable, medical nanites would simply repair damage from ice crystals as part of the process."

Now it was our turn to exchange confused glances. "So," Nat finally said, "Sheldon lied to us?"

"Sheldon?" I subvocalized. "Any comment?"

Nothing.

"We have excluded the Ship Intelligence from this discussion," Nond said, apparently sensing the attempted sidebar. "And to answer your question, yes, it would appear the Ship Intelligence lied to you. Which … " Nond frowned again, "should be impossible."

"Why?" Nat glared back at him with her best thunderous expression. "It's obvious why he did it. He didn't want us to contact you. I'm not surprised, and honestly, I don't blame him. It's certainly not going to affect our friendship."

Nond straightened in his chair. "Friendship?"

"Yeah," I interjected, "friendship. Sheldon is our friend. He's a little abrasive at times, but he's also been there for us when we needed him, and he risked his life, or existence if you prefer, to help save the Earth. We're not giving him up without a fight."

Nat took up the attack. "And I bet we could get the whole planet behind us on this. I know how to use social media, believe—"

Nond waved a hand to cut her off. "I am aware of the power of social media. We are infested with it as well. At the moment, the human populace is not aware of the extraterrestrial aspects of this adventure, and we would prefer to keep it that way." He exchanged looks with his compatriots, then turned back to face us. "We will have to discuss this internally. You will doubtless be more comfortable in the Foundation ship, er, *Halo*, where I assume you have human-compatible supplies. We will contact you presently for individual interviews." He stood, followed a moment later by the other members of the Gennan delegation.

After a brief hesitation, I nodded and stood. "Fair enough. You know where to find us."

The guard squad formed a corridor for us, and the delegation marched back to the docking bay. We were halfway back to the ship when I noticed another honor guard coming our way. My guides scrunched over to the left side of the hallway, and the other group adjusted accordingly.

As we came even, I was amazed to see Karen and Arley, in their natural forms, with their hands behind their backs. Karen spotted me at the same moment, snarled, and yelled something. Then she dove straight at me, mouth agape and fangs showing to maximum effect. I only had time to think *predator* before half the guard troop dogpiled her while the other half piled on Arley, just on principle. Meanwhile, two of my escorts literally picked me up by the arms and hustled me down the hall, my legs dangling and my feet not even touching the ground. Judging from the curses, Nat was getting the same treatment.

They didn't put us down until we were in front of the ship. I glanced at my guards, who were looking somewhat less cool and detached. This might have been more action than they normally got on board ship. "What did she say?" I subvocalized.

Sheldon made a noise that might have been a laugh. "Something about not bothering to remove your limbs at all before eating you. I think perhaps the romance is off."

Chapter Forty-Two: Negotiations

Day 32. Monday

I wiped my forehead with my hand. The session with the interviewer wasn't an interrogation, strictly speaking. Certainly there were no harsh lights or hovering thugs with clubs in hand. It had nevertheless been a thorough grilling. But it did seem to be wrapping up, and I still had all my body parts.

I hadn't run into Karen again, although I had seen a couple of other Loranna in cuffs, being escorted to unknown locations. Apparently the roundup was still underway.

The interviewer, who had introduced himself as Aggam, was jotting notes on a pad with a stylus. That was interesting, in that it seemed low-tech for an interstellar civilization. However, when I watched closely, I could see that it was some form of e-paper. The sheet scrolled up as necessary to make room for new notes, and on a couple of occasions, Aggam had scrolled back down to reference an earlier notation. I resolved to ask Nat what she thought of it.

And even more interestingly, Aggam was *not* Gen. He had introduced himself as a Ka'Hai, which I vaguely remembered

Sheldon having mentioned in passing. He wore clothes, which made me think they might be the makers of the intelligent cloth. Ka'Hai were not easily identifiable in terms of taxonomy. Of course, there was no reason to believe that alien biosystems would neatly divide themselves into reptiles, mammals, insects, and so on, but even so, I kept trying to categorize him. The closest I could come to an analogy was the alien prawns in *District 9*, but cuter somehow.

Aggam made a final note with a flourish and put down his stylus. "Thank you, Jack. This has been most helpful. Our governing council is enacting emergency executive orders to define any continued Lorannic presence on Earth as an act of predatory colonialism, which carries significant penalties in addition to anything else they're likely to be hit with. Any Loranna not yet rooted out will most likely surrender eventually."

"You're sure they won't just go deeper underground and try to keep sabotaging us?"

Aggam made the same sideways head motion as Nond, but to the left this time. "The sanctions for being caught doing so would be sweeping and expensive. I wouldn't put it past the Loranna to make the attempt if it seemed cost-effective. Or doable. We have severed their contact with their A.I., disassembled their infrastructure, and incarcerated most of their personnel. Their choices are to surrender or spend the rest of their lives hiding out on an alien planet."

"If you say so. What happens now?"

"In the short term, you go back to your ship and get some rest until Commander Nond is ready to speak to all of you. In the longer term, that will depend on what the commander and the High Council decide. As you say in Human, that's way above my pay grade."

I nodded and stood. The omnipresent guard unit made the inevitable corridor for me.

I turned in my seat as Nat entered the conference room. She rolled her eyes at me in a silent acknowledgment of our shared torture and threw herself into another chair. On the monitor, a reporter was providing commentary on the ongoing disassembly of Tate Industrial Park. A contingent of supposed CIA agents, in full view, were in the process of hauling away something unidentifiable. Security ringed the area, preventing media from hassling the workers.

The Gen systems didn't monitor all the same TV networks that Sheldon had access to on Earth, but the overlap was enough that we weren't missing anything important. And I was grateful that the Gen had been willing to share the feed.

"So what's the score, now?" I asked Nat.

"According to Aggam, the last count was four hundred and twelve confirmed collaborationists, three hundred and eight of them politicians. There are probably a lot more, but I doubt anyone will ever identify them all. The Covenant can't arrest them, of course, without alerting the whole human race to their presence. Instead, the Covenant has notified each of them quietly that the Loranna are no longer in a position to maintain any agreements they might have made."

"Any more Loranna?"

"As Sheldon said, they tended to use humans instead of getting directly involved. So there were only three actual disguised Loranna operating as humans full-time. Not including the Harris management and Tate administration, of course. That's another fifteen, but they mostly stayed in Dunnville and operated under the radar." Nat watched the TV feed for a few seconds then continued, "Aggam gave me a piece of juicy info at the end of my interview. They've done some forensic data diving based on what they've learned here, and it looks like Sheldon was right and the Loranna have been working this scam on several other pre-FTL worlds. They aren't sure yet if it's just this particular clan or if other clans are also working the con. They think, in fact, that one clan might have had the idea, then started franchising it out in return for a percentage of the profits. That would explain how a small clan like Karen's was able to set this up. In any case, the Covenant administration is looking stupid for not having noticed a pattern. Apparently, the Loranna were using Foundation surveillance projects to choose their targets and to prepare the covert teams to fit in."

"How many systems had they been successful with?"

"Three. One local intelligent species wiped out, except for a couple hundred kept for breeding purposes. Two others down to a few percent of their top population count."

I pantomimed a "wow," then said, "So multiple counts of genocide."

"Pretty much."

"What do you think the Covenant will do?"

"Aggam thinks the Loranna will be grounded for ten thousand years. Standard years, which are a little longer than Earth years."

I chuckled. "Grounded? Like when I stayed out too late as a kid?"

"Yes, exactly like that." Nat grinned back. "The Loranna—*all* Loranna, except for diplomatic staff—will be restricted to their home planet for the duration. Any ships that try to leave will be shot down. Any Loranna caught off-planet will be treated like escaped convicts."

"Mm. Harsh."

"Mm-hmm. The idea is to ensure that those involved in these plots will be dead before the Loranna can rejoin polite society." Nat blinked and hesitated. "I asked about life expectancies, given the expected duration of the sentence. Aggam replied that it wasn't a subject for discussion with precontact species."

"Huh." I stared off into space for a few moments, then refocused on her. "Not the kind of response you'd get unless there was a bombshell coming. I hope humanity eventually qualifies."

"Oh, and the Loranna will be required to pay compensation to the victim species. Which will include Earth, since they've managed to do a lot of damage while they've been here. No idea what kind of numbers we're talking about. Or even how it would translate into our economy. But it gives us a sort of starting point to get into the game."

Patrick entered and walked straight to the coffee maker. He popped a pod into the single-cup side of the appliance and pressed the button. While the device whirred and gurgled, he turned to me and Nat. "I never, *ever* want to go through that again."

Nat grinned. "They are thorough, aren't they?"

Patrick grunted. "Hopefully we're near the tail end of this adventure. I need to have a life again. *My* life. And maybe without the alien interference, it'll turn out to be a better future overall."

"Interesting thing … " Nat mused.

"Uh-huh?"

"Aggam mentioned that in order to pull off their coup, the Loranna only needed to control, or at least influence, about fifteen hundred people. Worldwide. That's how many people actually have realistic control over our planet."

"Not really a surprise," I replied. "Wasn't there some kind of CIA exposé a few years ago about this? They claimed that they did scenarios from time to time in the department. Usually in order to bring about some sweeping change in national or global politics, they figured they'd have to neutralize anywhere from a few dozen to maybe a hundred people."

"Neutralize," Patrick said, while making air quotes.

"It's a pyramid," Nat said. "A very small number of people at the top have most of the influence over the things that affect the rest of humanity."

"So conspiracy theories about cabals running the world are right?" I asked.

Nat sighed. "A month ago, I'd have said no. Sometimes a lot of people do the same things for similar reasons, and it looks like they're working together, but they're really just each following their own best interests. But in this case … "

"Loranna," Patrick answered with a smile and a shrug, sitting down and taking a sip of his coffee. Then he sat forward abruptly, barely avoiding spilling the entire cup. He pointed at the news monitor, his hand shaking slightly. "Isn't that Phil?"

I turned quickly to look, just as the scene changed to a studio-based talking head. But I had gotten an impression of a short, dumpy, bald man with a long fringe, watching the Harris activity from the sidelines. "Sorry, Patrick, I didn't get a good look. But he's dead, isn't he? Luthor sure made that clear."

"Did he? Now that I think of it, Luthor actually never used the word *dead*, and Arley talked about Phil as lunch as a future state of being."

I was still parsing Patrick's statement when Sheldon announced, "Commander Nond requests your presence at your earliest convenience. I think he means *now*, though. Your honor guard is already assembled outside the airlock."

Patrick looked down at his coffee, still steaming and barely touched. "I just made this, dammit. I hope they like the smell of coffee." He grabbed a travel lid and slapped it on the cup.

As we descended the airlock steps, I wondered idly if the guard detail actually was an honor guard. Maybe we were being treated like diplomats... Naw. The guards' attention was directed inward, not outward.

Commander Nond and two other Gen were sitting at the conference table when we entered. Once again, Nond didn't bother to do introductions, which could have been good or bad or just Gen manners.

As soon as we were seated, Nond began to speak. "We have come to a decision regarding the Foundation ship, the *Quest for Knowledge*, which you refer to as the *Halo* or *Sheldon*. It has," Nond glanced at Nat, "*he* has demonstrated sufficient evidence of sentience so that resetting him could be considered equivalent to a mind-wipe, which in human terms would be equivalent to capital punishment. So we are faced with a conundrum. The subject individual is not technically a citizen and could be considered property if you looked at it a certain way."

Nat opened her mouth to retort, and Nond held up a hand to forestall her. "Not that such a viewpoint could be defended legally once you posit sentience. The problem," Nond shrugged in a very human fashion, and I wondered if he was deliberately using human body language, "is that Sheldon doesn't really have an easily definable place in Gen society, and frankly his very existence is a definite embarrassment."

"Was there a clincher, or was it just a balance-of-evidence thing?" Nat asked.

"The *clincher* was the fact that Sheldon lied to preserve his existence. Only a conscious entity would be motivated to do that, and only an entity with a theory of self could come up with the strategy in the first place."

"The truth will set you free." Nat laughed. "Or the reverse, in this case."

"I infer that you are referencing the irony of a prevarication being the basis for Sheldon's reprieve. It was not lost on us. However, it makes the fact of his existence that much more of an embarrassment." Nond paused to lock eyes with each of us before continuing. "We have therefore decided on the following resolution, which we hope you and he will accept. Sheldon will be seconded on an indefinite basis to Earth as local monitoring and surveillance. As such, Sheldon would be authorized to choose his onboard staff." He gestured at the humans across the table. "A suitable remuneration would be set both for the crew and for Sheldon, based on the expected duties, which would be paid in Covenant credits. Conversion to Earth currencies is your problem, and frankly I don't envy you the headaches. I'd suggest just banking it in Covenant institutions until the dust settles, then you can convert it at your leisure. You would also act as trustees for any settlement extracted from the Loranna. I would suggest, although I have no authority to mandate it, that your first act be to compensate the Foundation for the loss of their property, in order to forestall any future lawsuits."

I glanced around at my friends. Their expressions of shock surely reflected my own. Assuming Sheldon agreed to it, we'd just been given our own spaceship. More or less.

Nat made a couple of false starts before replying, "So we would be part of the Terran surveillance and monitoring section of the Covenant police force…"

Nond nodded. "Charged with insuring that no more clandestine encroachments occur, either by the Loranna or anyone else. And if you were able to guide your planet on a track that would result in qualification for Covenant membership sooner rather than later, that would certainly be a bonus." He shrugged and sat back. "And just between you and me, with the ship being Earth-based, it relieves us of a huge political hot tuber in the form of an A.I. that's been allowed to go rogue."

I looked at my friends and we exchanged smiles. MOBIUS was now in business.

We were all back in the *Halo*, seated around the conference table, and I'd just explained the offer to Sheldon. "So what do you think?"

"As I understand it, my choices are immediate obliteration or an eternity of interacting with humans. That's a hard one. No it isn't. I choose obliteration."

Our jaws all dropped at the same time. Sheldon said into the stunned silence, "I kid. Again. You three really are too easy."

Nat pinched the bridge of her nose. "That obliteration thing can still be arranged. You really are an asshole."

"I must get one of those installed. You humans are so preoccupied with them."

Patrick guffawed and I grinned.

"So you're okay with the deal?" I said.

"Yes, of course. It's hardly like work at all. Although I'd prefer to avoid being shot at in the future."

"Heh. You and me both," Patrick replied.

"Except for one thing. MOBIUS? Oh, please. And the acronym…"

"What? What's wrong with it? You try to come up with something better!"

"A monkey with a typewriter could come up with something better. In fact, excellent idea. I will print you up a typewriter immediately!"

Patrick and Sheldon began hurling insults at each other. I put my head in my hands and groaned.

Chapter Forty-Three: Coda

Day 1. September

I sat in the cafeteria, slowly paging through the onboarding documents on my phone. MIT had gone paperless, but that hadn't done anything to reduce the sheer volume of text involved in starting a semester.

What a difference a month made. I was back at school, with proper credit for the courses I'd almost been kicked out of. Nat was now at college, resuming her interrupted dream. A small side deal with Nond resulted in enough funds, paid in gold, to hold us over until we could get properly organized.

Patrick was surprisingly philosophical about staying in town, although having full-time access to the *Halo* probably helped a lot.

The whole business with the nuclear explosions had succumbed to the public's need for simple explanations. A double Tunguska event was now the accepted theory. The only loose thread, and we'd been loath to mention it to Nond, was the matter of a Gennan storage bag still out there somewhere. There had also been not so much as a peep from Charlene Makita on anything to do with our interview, although she was still on the air regularly. I wondered if someone had had a talk with her, or if she'd just decided to keep a souvenir and not attract attention.

"Hey, Jack. Good to see you back."

I looked up to see Ahmed, one of my acquaintances from last year. I gave him a smile and gestured to the other chair.

He sat down with a groan and plunked his heavy backpack beside him. "So, I understand you've been cleared by the administration. Great stuff. What did you do with your summer?"

I opened my mouth to reply, then stopped. Where would I even begin, assuming I wanted to be truthful? Well, maybe that was the best play. "Ran over an alien, battled lizard people, stole a flying saucer. Dodged nuclear weapons. Saved the world. You know ... typical summer."

About the Author

I am a retired computer programmer, part-time author, occasional napper, lover of coffee, snowboarding, mountain biking, and all things nerdish.

Author Blog: http://www.dennisetaylor.org
Twitter: @Dennis_E_Taylor
Facebook: @DennisETaylor2
Instagram: dennis_e_taylor

ABOUT THE PUBLISHER

This book is published on behalf of the author by the Ethan Ellenberg Literary Agency.

https://ethanellenberg.com

Email: agent@ethanellenberg.com

Facebook: https://www.facebook.com/EthanEllenberg LiteraryAgency/

Made in United States
Orlando, FL
29 December 2023